WATCHING AND WAITING

Looking down into the valley, Graham spotted the rider off in the distance. He moved the Appaloosa back where she would not show above the rim of the cliff and tied the horse to a mesquite. Then he lay on his belly and watched the horseman come up the valley.

Look at him, Graham told himself grimly. *There he is, just below me now. I could pick him off easy. He doesn't even know I'm up here watching. He's got no idea that I'm even on the mountain. No one knows I'm here. If I picked him off, he'd only be getting what he had coming to him. I know, if he was in my boots, he wouldn't hold back. He'd grab his rifle and let me have one in the back . . . the way I should let him have one. And I'm of a good mind to do just that. . . .*

UNDER THE BURNING SUN

H. A. DeRosso

LEISURE BOOKS NEW YORK CITY

A LEISURE BOOK®

April 2000

Published by special arrangement with
Golden West Literary Agency.

Dorchester Publishing Co., Inc.
276 Fifth Avenue
New York, NY 10001

ISBN 0-8439-4712-8

TABLE OF CONTENTS

Foreword

H. A. DeRosso: Under the Burning Sun

Most writers of Western fiction past and present were either born and bred in one of the thirteen western states, or made that part of the country their adopted home. Henry Andrew DeRosso was among the notable exceptions. Like another prolific teller of Western tales, T. V. Olsen, DeRosso spent almost all of his relatively short life in upstate Wisconsin. The area in which he lived, in the northeast corner of the state near the Michigan border, is rich in its own pioneer history: his birthplace, Carey, and its neighboring community of Hurley in which he made his home for many years, were once rough-and-tumble iron-ore mining towns not unlike the gold, silver, and copper camps of the Far West frontier. This rural milieu, with its harsh winters and its proximity to the vast North Woods, may explain DeRosso's early interest in adventure and Western fiction and his lifelong fascination with the southwestern desert country, a wilderness and a climate exactly opposite of the one in which he lived.

Born in 1917, DeRosso aspired to be a fiction writer from a young age. He began producing Western short stories while a high-school student and persevered through a self-professed total of seventy-nine rejections before making his first professional sale to Street &

Smith's *Western Story Magazine* in 1941. (That first story, "Six-Gun Saddlemates," appeared in the magazine's July 19, 1941 issue.) After graduation from Hurley High School in 1935, DeRosso attended a local community college for two years and, briefly, the schools of journalism and agriculture at the University of Wisconsin. Health problems kept him out of military service during World War II. Thus, he was able to continue writing on a daily basis and to begin piling up sales to *Western Story* and other pulps during this period, supplementing his income with farm work and as a mail carrier. By the end of the war he had established himself to the point where he was able to devote his full time to writing. A bachelor with modest needs, he supported himself almost entirely through sales of his fiction for the last fifteen years of his life.

Until the early 1950s his primary market was the Popular Publications chain of pulps. It was in his work for such magazines as *Dime Western*, *.44 Western*, *New Western*, and *10 Story Western* that he developed his own special brand of Western story: an admixture of the traditional and the offbeat literary, the historical and the darkly mythical. Nearly all of his tales are set in the stark, desolate wastes of the southwest. Some make use of real locations, a few of actual historical figures and occurrences. A large percentage are set in imagined, often surreal landscapes — shadowlands of "Twilight Zone" dimensions, where violence is the norm and men (and women) must struggle constantly against malevolent forces within themselves as well as in their surroundings.

DeRosso's objectively realistic style owes far more to the *Black Mask* school of detective fiction developed by

Dashiell Hammett and Joseph T. Shaw than it does to the influences of Zane Grey or the Western pulp writers of the period. His characters — most often gunslicks, bounty hunters, drifters, hardscrabble ranchers, outlaws — are lonely, disillusioned, self-doubting men, often plagued by a lingering sense of alienation and doom and by a desperate yearning for love, stability, peace of mind. Few of his protagonists are all good or all bad; their motives are generally mixed, and their victories, if indeed they do triumph (some do not even survive), are invariably bittersweet. An aura of melancholy pervades even those of his stories which have upbeat resolutions.

In these and other respects DeRosso was a Western fiction pioneer. He shared with Noel M. Loomis the introduction into the genre of an objective portrayal of violence. Along with Les Savage, Jr., he introduced moral ambiguity of character. He was among the first to subordinate plot and to concentrate, sometimes at incisive depths, on the inner complexities and conflicts of his characters. And he was the first to integrate elements of mysticism and the supernatural into his stories — elements normally anathema to hard-bitten Western pulp editors such as Rogers Terrill, Robert O. Erisman, and Jim Hendryx, Jr.

Nevertheless, too much of DeRosso's work was outside the acceptable pulp norm for him to sell his entire output to the better-paying markets. (The preponderance of his sales to topline Western magazines, in fact, were formula stories with obligatory hero-vanquishes-villain-and-wins-girl endings.) Conversely, his fiction was too uneven in quality (a common flaw among nearly all prolific pulp writers), his prose too mannered and sometimes clumsy and overblown, his subject matter too bleak, to find favor with either slick-paper or literary magazine editors. Many of his stories were published in obscure category magazines and small newspaper supplements; others did not sell until years after they were written, usually for tiny sums, and in a few cases not until years after his death; still others did not sell at all. Those nonformulaic tales which were purchased by the better markets often saw print under flagrantly lurid titles so as to mask their anomalous content (e.g., the story, "Vigilante," first published in *New Western* as "Swing Your Pardner High!"). Of his more than 250 published short stories and novelettes, one appeared in a major, general-interest magazine: "Under the Burning Sky," a 20,000-word novelette serialized in two parts in the slick-paper weekly, *Collier's* (5/30/53 - 6/6/53). Significantly, "Under the Burning Sky" has a routine Western plot, involving a stolen gold shipment and a cattle drive and stampede, and is not among DeRosso's stronger efforts.

Over the first ten years of his career all but a handful of his stories were Westerns. The collapsing pulp market, brought about by television and the advent of inexpensive paperback books, led him in the early 1950s to try his hand at other genres more stable than the Western story: science fiction, with minimal success, and crime fiction, with greater success. He published some forty mystery shorts in such magazines as Street & Smith's *Detective Story, Manhunt, Hunted,* and *Alfred Hitchcock's Mystery Magazine.* Most can be classified as Westerns in contemporary dress, inasmuch as they feature outdoor backgrounds and pursuits and have as their protagonists the same sort of disaffected loners who populate DeRosso's frontier fiction.

For the most part H. A. DeRosso's stories in all categories appeared under his own name, though on a limited basis he employed three pseudonyms: David A. Hartman, Clem Yager, and John Cortez. The Hartman and Yager names were used exclusively when two of his tales were published in the same issue of a magazine. Occasionally, for reasons of his own, he submitted a story to his literary agent which carried the Cortez byline; these include some of his best work, like "Fair Game" in this collection.

DeRosso also turned to the writing of novels for the burgeoning paperback market. Four Westerns were published during his lifetime, all as softcover originals; one other western novel, and one young-adult novelization of an episode of the TV series, *The Rebel*, appeared posthumously in hardcover. In addition to these six he submitted to his agent completed manuscripts or portions-and-outlines of five other novels — three Westerns, one mystery, one mainstream. None was accepted for publication, although the mainstream effort, evocatively titled IN THE IMAGE OF DUST — "a long, drab, slow-moving, gloomy yarn about a Wisconsin mining family," in the agent's assessment — came close to being purchased by Doubleday.

DeRosso's first Western novel, TRACKS IN THE SAND, carried the imprint of a short-lived paperback house, Reader's Choice Library, and was released in 1951. His second and third novels, .44 and THE GUN TRAIL, were both published in 1953 by another small and none-too-successful company, Lion Books (the latter title was also reprinted by Lion in 1957 as THE MAN FROM TEXAS); these represent his most accomplished work in the longer form. The novels for Lion Books are unrelentingly grim studies of violent men who find love too late, taste salvation, and then are destroyed by a combination of fate and their own actions — powerful, existential set-pieces reminiscent in their thematic essence of the contemporary crime stories of Jim Thompson that were also being published by Lion Books at the time.

The last two adult novels to appear with DeRosso's byline — END OF THE GUN (Perma Books, 1955) and THE DARK BRAND (Avalon, 1963) — are less violent, less bitterly despairing, and feature men — rancher Steve Britton in the former, ex-rustler Driscoll in the latter — who survive their personal trials and find redemption as well as the love of a strong woman. It is their traditional happy endings, perhaps, that make these works less memorable than either .44 or THE GUN TRAIL. DeRosso was at the apex of his abilities when dealing with demon-haunted personalities whose lives are either destroyed or retain a measure of tragedy.

It should come as no surprise, given the nature of his fiction, that Hank DeRosso had much in common psychologically with the men about whom he wrote. He, too, seems to have been plagued by loneliness, despair, disillusionment, and other personal demons — to have been himself a rider in the shadowlands. On Sunday, October 16, 1960, he was found dead of a gunshot wound in a shed at his Carey home. The county coroner ruled the death accidental, stating that DeRosso was fatally injured when a firearm he was carrying discharged as he slipped on a rug. However, he was in failing health at the time — he had been a patient at a Marquette, Michigan hospital prior to his death — and his agent speculated that this had led him to take his own life.

Early in "Under the Burning Sky" DeRosso wrote of the protagonist, U. S. Marshal Burt Grayson: "Like all lonely men, [he] was a dreamer, and if there was nothing good to dream about, then a man might just as well be dead." The description fits Hank DeRosso as aptly as it does any of his fictional creations. Those words, in fact, could have served as his epitaph.

The ten short stories and two short novels in this volume represent a cross-section of H. A. DeRosso's Western magazine fiction, both chronologically and thematically: examples of the traditional and non-traditional, the historically based and the darkly mythical, stories of hard-boiled realism, raw emotion, sentiment, mysticism, and the supernatural. All the elements of good fiction, not just good category fiction, are here — many more than may be found in many Western stories, past and present. (It should also be noted that with the exception of "The Hired Man," all the selections were carefully — and in most cases lightly — edited. This was deemed necessary to eliminate superfluous and repetitive passages contained in the original magazine versions; pulp writers, after all, were paid by the word and thus were encouraged sometimes to engage in excesses. In no case, however, were any substantive changes made in plot, characterization, or thematic intent or content.)

"The Bounty Hunter" is a feverish shadowlands tale of a bounty man, Spurr, led by enemies to kill an outlaw who may or may not be Spurr's own son, and of his odyssey — in tandem with an outcast Apache woman known as Fuego — in search of the truth about himself and his long-lost family. "Vigilante" is likewise a brooding character study, but the setting — Virginia City, Montana, in the turbulent days of Henry Plummer and the Innocents — is sharply authentic in background, and the protagonist, John Weidler, is a far different personality than Spurr. Weidler may be DeRosso's most remarkable creation — an "average" man whose inflexible nature and unflagging devotion to his duty as he sees it make him an individual of frightening Old Testament proportions.

"Long Lonesome" concerns a pair of lifelong friends on a gold-mining expedition and combines an unusual variation of the theme of B. Traven's THE TREASURE OF THE SIERRA MADRE with profound personal tragedy. An O. Henry-like twist ending adds even greater poignancy to the drama.

"Hold-up" is perhaps the best of DeRosso's early pulp stories. Although it lacks the unconventional plot elements and emotional depth of his later work, it is nonetheless a suspenseful account of a planned train hold-up. In the relationship between the conductor, Mike Conner, and his desperate young son it foreshadows the trenchant interpersonal conflicts of the post-war and especially post-1950 stories.

A recurring theme in DeRosso's fiction is that of a man seeking desperately to overcome a crippling fear: of other men, of mustangs and wild animals, of natural phenomena, of destructive forces within himself. In "Whitewater Challenge" the source of lumberman Joe Clark's dread is a roiling section of river rapids that once nearly claimed his life. The circumstances that lead Clark once again to "shoot the rapids" and the outcome of his struggle make for an entertaining and satisfying tale.

A pair of stories first published in *Alfred Hitchcock's Mystery Magazine*, each quite different in tone and content, demonstrate DeRosso's ability to blend the Western story with the contemporary crime story. "The Hired Man," one of his last stories — and also one of his most mature, stylistically and in terms of development and handling — is a bitter coming-of-age story in which an eleven-year-old boy exacts a terrible vengeance that may or may not be justified. Its time-frame is the Depression of the 1930s, but in all respects it could just as easily have taken place fifty years earlier; its bittersweet flavor, in fact, is distinctly Western. The same is true of "Fair Game" with its wilderness hunting background, stark winter setting, elemental theme, and its own brand of moral ambiguity. An artfully constructed storyline, that carries the reader to an inevitable and yet not quite predictable conclusion, is another of its plusses.

Native Americans are featured in many of DeRosso's stories, most notably Chiricahua and Mimbreño Apaches. His treatment of and attitude toward Indian men (and women, e.g. Fuego in "The Bounty Hunter") were honest and often quite sympathetic. "The Last Sleep," unpublished until ten years after DeRosso's death, is a fictionalized rendering of what actually happened to the Chiricahuas after the tribe's leaders, Whoa and Geronimo, led them off the San Carlos reservation in the summer of 1885. Told entirely from the Apache point of view, it is a mordant condemnation of the duplicity of the "white eyes" on the frontier and in Washington, D. C.

"Man-killer" tells the tense, deceptively simple story of a hardscrabble rancher, Graham, and his hated neighbor, McCready, who set out separately to track and kill a mountain lion that has been feeding on their cattle. As the hunt progresses deep into mountain wilderness and the paths of the two men continue to cross, the quarry shifts from lion to man — and the tale's focal point becomes the effects of hate and fear on the minds of decent, solitary men.

A solid blending of violent action and the genuine, deep-felt sentiment that was a DeRosso trademark recommends "My Brother: Killer." The ultimate gift given by the narrator, at enormous personal cost, to the dying old man who raised him is fitting and compelling without being maudlin.

In "The Mesteños" the fate of a herd of wild mustangs led by a stallion called Ruano is inextricably linked to that of Feliz, an old half-breed rancher. The peculiar, symbiotic relationship between man and beast ends in a grimly appealing mixture of realism and mysticism, as only DeRosso could meld the two.

Another excursion into the shadowlands — "Those Bloody Bells of Hell!" — tells of a vengeance-haunted cowman, Carmody, and of a trek into the badlands of Mexico to retrieve a pair of bells made of solid gold — a trek that involves Carmody with a vicious partner whose favorite weapon is a Bowie knife, revolutionaries and *federalistas* who are also after the golden bells, and a woman named Raquel who alters the pattern of his fate. Bleak and harrowing, this novelette vividly evokes the utter desolation of DeRosso's external landscapes as well as those of his characters' internal perspectives.

These dozen works not only serve to showcase H. A. DeRosso's talents, but also demonstrate why he and his fiction have been compared to suspense writer Cornell

Woolrich and Woolrich's *noir* vision. Both men wrote sometimes crude, not always successful, objectively realistic, and violent stories told in dark, visceral prose. Both were obsessed with what they perceived to be the ultimate futility of human existence, and yet, paradoxically, both depicted the constant striving need for man to maintain and pursue his dreams, to find some sense of meaning and salvation in his own life. Both understood and dealt feelingly with unrequited love, lost innocence, lost hope, loneliness, desperation. And both were demon-plagued private individuals who lived spare lives and met their deaths tragically: Woolrich as a bitter alcoholic in a New York hotel room, DeRosso of a gunshot wound at his Wisconsin home.

Woolrich's biographer, Francis M. Nevins, Jr., once referred to Woolrich as "the Poe of the 20th Century and the poet of its shadows." H. A. DeRosso, with equal justification, can be accorded a similar distinction — a poet of the Western shadowlands.

Bill Pronzini
Petaluma, California

THE BOUNTY HUNTER

I

The bounty hunter emerged from the pass early that morning and started down the lonely, barren western slope of the mountains which were called the Desolados. The country he was sloping into was hardly more appealing. It was desert, as austere and forsaken as the Desolate Ones.

The lonely desert growths seemed to exist more in a stubborn defiance of death than in a joyful acceptance of life. And this was proper, the bounty hunter thought, and fitted in with his mood and purpose; for, if everything worked out right, a wanted killer would be dead by nightfall, and he would be a thousand dollars richer.

High noon found him at the edge of the desert. The tracks he was following were plain in the sand. Silence lurked everywhere, and heat, and desolation. They surrounded him with an aura of comfort, the only comfort he knew, the comfort of misery and aloneness and the ever-presence of death.

He reined in the bay for a breather, dismounted, and loosened the cinches. He gave the bay some water from his canteen, and then drank sparingly himself.

A roadrunner hen, followed by her brood, darted across the trail in the sand and into a growth of mesquite. Something stirred in the ashes of his memory, and he closed his eyes to the ache of it. Then, from long training and the imposition of a stubborn will, it passed. His eyes opened and welcomed the sight of the cruel and bitter land.

He mounted the bay and rode on at a lope. The westering sun made the sands glisten, and the bounty hunter pulled his wide-brimmed hat still lower over his eyes. Grit worked into the growth of whiskers and made them itch.

The sun lowered. The meager shadows of the desert growths grew long and slim, and the awesome hush over the land became even more deep and solemn.

The bounty hunter grew cautious now. The trailing was about over — the stalking was at hand.

He stopped the bay, dismounted, and made his way on foot to a height of ground. There, he watched the sun go down. His eyes squinted as he scanned the land, and in the quick twilight of the desert he spotted it — a thin tendril of smoke curling straight up in the windless air, a beacon that beckoned him.

He returned to the bay and tied it to a greasewood. He removed his spurs and hung them on the saddle horn. Then he drew his rifle from its saddle boot and went up over the rise and down the other side on foot. Nightfall was not yet complete when the red eye of a fire winked at him. Just beyond it, watching the frying pan on the coals, was the quarry.

Somewhere out of the bounty hunter's past something stirred, the remnant of a sense of honor and fair play, the last remaining link with gentleness and compassion.

"Albuquerque," the bounty hunter called.

The quarry tensed for the briefest moment, chin tilting. Then he thought to seek the shelter of the developing night and whirled that way, away from the fire that betrayed him.

The bounty hunter fired.

The quarry cried with pain and hit the sand with violence, spraying dust, and rolled on his side and stretched out an arm holding a Colt, eyes seeking a target they could not see.

The bounty hunter fired again.

The quarry gave another cry. The Colt fell unfired from his hand. His arms convulsed, then he rolled slowly over on his face, his arms fell about his head, and he seemed to be lying there, weeping silently over his frustration and defeat.

The bounty hunter stood and stared down at death. With his own hands he had wrought it, but there was no sense of power or accomplishment in him, not even a sense of loathing or regret. He stood looking down at what he himself sought, though he did not know it.

Out in the darkness that was now complete the quarry's hobbled horse snorted nervously and whinnied, calling — but there was no reply for its master lay still in death. The horse called again, querying, and mocking silence answered.

The bounty hunter bent and rolled the dead man over. The light from the fire played redly on the face, and the bounty hunter saw that he had not made a mistake. He picked up the dead man's Colt and carried it to where the man had laid out his bed, his blankets unrolled and his saddle for a pillow. The bounty hunter set the Colt down on the saddle, and then he took a blanket and spread it over the dead man.

After that, the bounty hunter added wood to the fire, and then he took off in the direction from which he had come. The bay heard him, and nickered. The bounty hunter answered with a low whistle. He untied the bay and stepped up into the saddle and rode at a trot back to the fire.

He picketed the bay in company with the dead man's horse, a blaze-face chestnut. The two horses nuzzled each other and were instant friends with none of the reserve and suspicion and guile of men.

The bounty hunter carried his saddle and bedroll over to the fire that flickered and crackled as though trying to tell him something. He could feel the cold breath of prescience on his spine, and he glanced swiftly at the dead man, but he lay as before, straight and still under the covering blanket. The sense of peril, however, whispered a warning to the bounty hunter.

He had no idea what was amiss until he glanced at the dead man's saddle and saw the Colt gone from where he had put it. Instantly he reached for his own weapon, and it was then that the voice spoke out of the darkness.

"Hold it, Spurr!"

The words were said loud and clear, and the echoes picked them up and tossed them back and forth a couple of times, and then the silence of the desert triumphed again. The bounty hunter froze with his hand on his gun. His grip turned clammy, his flesh cringed once in expectation of the smash of a bullet, but he knew it would not be anything as kind and as merciful as that.

"Raise your hands, Spurr!"

He willed the action, but his arms refused to respond. His hand clung to his Colt butt with all the desperation of fingers clutching a precarious hold on the face of a mile-high cliff.

"Raise your hands, or I'll raise them for you!"

With regretful reluctance the bounty hunter complied. He stood there with hands shoulder-high, listening to the approaching steps behind his back. Now that the instinct of survival had spent itself, he was calm and even indifferent. That was death walking in crunching boots and jingling spurs, and death was a thing he did not fear. If anything about it gave him apprehension, it was not the end but the means.

II

He stood there stripped of his belt and gun, and he had never felt more alone and forsaken in all his life. He could use his hands and his boots, but he could not expect them to avail him anything in the face of their guns.

There were two of the weapons, and they pointed not at his heart but at his belly, where the slugs could rend and tear and burn and sear and make the way to death seem like an agonizing, never-ending journey.

But even that would be too kind and gentle a way, he realized now. The tall one, with the brawny sturdiness of an oak, he had never seen before. But the other, the slight and bearded and one-eyed fellow, he remembered and was hardly able to suppress a shudder.

"Aren't you going to say hello to me, Spurr?" the bearded one asked. "Aren't you going to ask how I've been these past years? You haven't said a word to me." He pouted, and then giggled. The sound teetered on the brink of madness, then caught and steadied. A bit of spume flecked a corner of his mouth. "Don't tell me you've forgotten me?"

"He remembers you, Old Man," the tall one said. "You can see it in his face. No one ever forgets Old Man Hutton. Isn't that right, Spurr?"

The bounty hunter said nothing. He was resigned. This was the play, harmless and teasing at first. In time it would build up in viciousness and ferocity, and the best he could hope for was to deprive them of the satisfaction of hearing him scream and beg. He would save his strength and all his will for that. So he said nothing.

"Answer, Spurr," the tall one shouted.

"He'll talk," the old one said and giggled. "He'll talk because we have lots to talk about. Pick up his belt and gun, Larch."

Larch holstered his Colt, and now there was only the one gun and one eye staring at the bounty hunter's belly, but he derived no comfort from that. Larch scooped up the bounty hunter's belt and gun from the ground, and then Larch slid the holster of the filled shell belt and tossed the scabbard and the gun to one side. He doubled the shell belt, almost every loop of which was filled with brass .44s, and held it with both ends gripped in his right hand. He grinned as he stared at the bounty hunter.

"You shouldn't treat me like this, Spurr," the old one said, shaking his head in mock sadness. "You shouldn't be like this after what you've done to me. It's not nice. Is it, Larch?"

Larch growled, an animal sound, and moved in behind Spurr. The bounty hunter sensed it coming and tried to duck away, but he was too late. The doubled shell belt cracked him on the side of the head, knocking his hat off. He turned and sprang at Larch, but pain shattered his focus, and he missed. Larch, side-stepping, rapped him again with the belt.

Spurr stumbled amid a wave of blackness and through it heard the old one's delighted giggle. With all his will Spurr caught himself and spun and again rushed Larch. This time Larch waited without shifting, belt held high. Spurr looked up in time to catch it against his face. The ground reached for him and folded him to its bosom. . . .

The two men were far away, as far as the distant stars, and Spurr thought it strange that he could hear them so plainly. Their voices traveled through the vast gulf of space with no effort at all.

"He's coming out of it," Larch was saying. "Should I rap him again?"

"No, no, I want to talk with him."

"I wouldn't rap him very hard."

"You heard me, Larch."

Spurr found that he was lying doubled up on his side with the crackling fire winking jeeringly at his face. The brightness of the flames hurt his eyes, and he closed them. Larch's foot smashed him in the small of the back.

"Come out of it! I saw you open your eyes."

Spurr forced himself to sit up. The world tilted sharply once, and he thought he was going down into the abyss again, but he got hold of himself and steadied himself with a hand touching the earth on either side of him. He blinked his eyes in an effort to clear them of the pain that clouded his sight.

Old Man Hutton squatted on his haunches on the other side of the fire. Behind, Larch loomed, large and ominous. Firelight played on Old Man Hutton's features, now concealing then revealing the empty eye socket with the wrinkled lid shut tightly. The other eye glittered brightly. It weighed Spurr and measured him with an evil speculation.

"Do you hear me, Spurr?" Old Man Hutton's voice was deceptively soft and solicitous. "Can you hear me all right?"

Spurr said nothing.

"Answer him," Larch growled from behind Spurr. The brass .44s clicked quietly as Larch raised the shell belt.

"I hear you."

"Good," Old Man Hutton said. "You know, it makes me sad seeing you again, Spurr. It makes me remember." His voice trembled, a tear gathered in the one eye, and another in the empty socket. "I'm a lonely old man, with my two young ones gone. I'm a very lonely old man."

The twin tears trickled down into the soiled gray beard. Two other drops replaced them. "You know why I don't have my two young ones any more, don't you, Spurr? You know why I'm so sad, so lonely?" A sob racked him, and he rose on his feet and came over slowly to stand crouched over the bounty hunter. "Damn your rotten soul, you know why, don't you?"

His boot was as swift as a striking rattler. The point caught Spurr in the stomach, bile rushed up in him, and he toppled over, retching. The .44s in the shell belt clicked softly.

"Sit up, Spurr," Larch growled.

The bounty hunter sat up, holding himself, vision shattered with pain.

Old Man Hutton bent down to look Spurr in the face. A bit of froth bubbled in one corner of the old man's mouth. "I could kill you," he said. "It wouldn't be quick, but still it would be too easy on you. I could stake you out under the sun with your eyelids cut off. I could rip

26

out your tongue and fill your mouth with hot coals. I could. . . . But I want more, lots more, and I'm going to have it. Mark my words, I'm going to have it."

He straightened, turned, walked away to the edge of the firelight, and stood staring into the desert night. He was a while like that, lost in reflection. Once he sobbed, but there was no anguish in the sound, only primal, animal rage.

He stirred finally and went over to the dead man and stood looking down at him. "What have we here?" he asked, his voice controlled and quiet again. "Another bounty for you, Spurr?"

Spurr's eyes had cleared. Pain throbbed in his head and in his back and in his stomach. He said nothing.

Old Man Hutton bent down and threw the blanket back. He dropped to one knee and studied the dead face. "Billy Albuquerque," he murmured. His head swiveled, and the one eye glittered at the bounty hunter. "Am I right? Is this Billy Albuquerque?"

"Answer him," Larch growled, clicking the shell belt.

"That's right," Spurr said.

"How much does he carry on his head? A thousand dollars?"

"That's right," Spurr said.

"A thousand dollars," Old Man Hutton repeated. "A good price. But my two young ones, they carried only five hundred for the two of them."

"I asked them to surrender," Spurr said. "They chose to make a fight of it."

"Yes, they would," Old Man Hutton said, nodding his head in approval and pride. "They were my sons. They would do just that." Then the dark rage mottled his face. "Still you murdered them, Spurr. You murdered them."

He covered his face with his hands and began to weep.

The shell belt clicked loudly and ominously, and Spurr tried to throw himself out of its vicious path, but he was too slow. The familiar pain embraced him, the abyss yawned, and in its dark depths he found sanctuary. . . .

At first he thought that they had bound him or staked him out because he could not move. Then it came to him that it was only the lethargy of pain and weakness. This time he kept his eyes closed and forced himself not to stir. He could hear them speaking.

"I was talking to McKinnon," Larch was saying. "He told me they're paying up to two hundred pesos apiece now."

"I know," Old Man Hutton said.

"That's a good price."

"We can't let them catch us in their territory. You know it's too risky for us right now."

"They wouldn't have to be Comanche or Apache," Larch said. "Any black one would pass."

"Too bad Spurr's isn't black," Old Man Hutton said and tittered.

"I think he's playing 'possum," Larch said.

Pain seared Spurr's eyeballs as Larch's toe found his ribs.

"Come out of it, Spurr."

Spurr knew there was no use pretending. Hurt lashed him when he moved, and he was hardly able to suppress a moan. It took a little while before his eyes steadied and cleared.

The fire had been fed. The flames leaped and danced as though in glee over the spectacle they were watching. A knot cracked once with a sound as loud as a gunshot.

Old Man Hutton squatted beside the dead outlaw. The one eye stared at Spurr without blinking. Light and shadow flitted across the bearded face, heightening its look of ominousness and evil.

"Spurr," the old one said. He purred the word, lingering over the sound as though it gave him a vicarious pleasure. Hate dwelt in the depths of the solitary eye. "Is that your real name?"

A premonition of a great dread settled over the bounty hunter. He could not understand its nature, but something told him that anguish and torture far greater than physical agony lay ahead.

"It is," he said quietly.

"Spurr," the old one said again, dragging out the sound as though reluctant to let go of it. The lone eye shifted to the dead outlaw. "Billy Albuquerque," the old one murmured. The eye swung back, swiftly, and speared the bounty hunter. "You know that's an alias, don't you?"

Spurr nodded.

The old one said: "The kid took that name because he rather fancied the sound of it. Do you know his real name?"

"It was Chisum, wasn't it?"

"Was it?"

Something crawled on clammy feet across Spurr's shoulders. In him a voice was crying, warning him, but he could not quite make out what he was being warned against.

"That was the name of his stepfather," Spurr said. "The kid never liked him which is why he never used it."

"That's right," Old Man Hutton said. "Billy hated Chisum's guts. Talk has it that it was Billy who knifed

Chisum to death. That's how the kid was supposed to have got started on the owl-hoot. But Billy never said anything about the knifing either one way or the other." The lone eye peered hard at Spurr, seeking some inner, hidden secret. "You picked up Billy's trail in La Fugente, didn't you? How come?"

The warning cried louder in Spurr, but he still could not understand it. "I got a tip."

"From an old prospector? The one they call Seldom Seen Saunders?"

It was beginning to make sense now. All the puzzling, scattered bits were falling together, and the pattern they formed left Spurr sick and shaken.

"Yes, it was *me* who told Saunders. I wanted you to kill Billy Albuquerque. Don't you know why?"

Spurr shook his head.

With a sudden vehemence Old Man Hutton grabbed the dead outlaw's hair in one hand and jerked the head up. "Look at him, Spurr," he shouted. "Look at him good."

Death had drained the color out of the youthful face, leaving it waxen under its tan. Death had pinched in the flesh at the base of the nostrils and gaunted the cheeks. Death's everlasting, silent cry issued from the slightly open mouth.

"Look at him," Old Man Hutton raged, trembling with wrath. "Look at the blue eyes, the blond hair. Look at the face. Don't you recognize him, Spurr?"

In the shambles and the ashes of the long ago something stirred that sent a shoot of pain through Spurr's heart. A voice cried *No, no!* within him, but it was a lost cry, a forsaken cry. Horror left him empty — of words, of tears.

Old Man Hutton slammed the dead outlaw's head down so hard it bounced and a small puff of dust rose. The old one jumped to his feet and crossed over swiftly to Spurr. Hutton's chest heaved with the convulsing of emotion.

"I promised myself, when I buried my young ones, that you'd pay a thousandfold for what you did to me. I vowed I would wreak on you the worst vengeance I could. And I have, Spurr, I have. I could have killed you outright. I could have killed you many times but that would not have been enough. I won't kill you with a bullet or with fire or with a club, but you'll die and die a double death, a death of the body and a death of the mind."

He whirled and pointed at the dead outlaw. "Do you know who that is that you've killed, Spurr? That's your son!"

Anguish rushed upward in Spurr, but in his throat he checked it. He had made a pact with himself that he would never cry out, not in their presence, no matter what they did to him. But the torment broke out, in the brightening of his eyes and in the twitching of a corner of his mouth.

"When I buried my young ones," the old man went on, "I swore I'd get back at you in the same way, except that I'd make it worse for you. You'd not only bury your son, you'd kill him as well. So I checked on you, Spurr. It took a long time, but I checked and tracked and found you out. Years ago you lived in Palo Pinto, Texas. You owned a ranch and were known by your real name, Alan Spurlock. Then you had a wife named Jenny and a son named Lance. Your wife! Ho, ho . . . *your* wife! She ran off with a gambler named Flynn, taking your son with her. And you sold your ranch and disappeared . . . and then a bounty hunter came alive, a bounty hunter called Spurr."

What had been imprisoned was now liberated; what had been ashes was now burning coals; what had been forgotten was now searing memory. Spurr marveled that his voice could be so calm: "That's still not my son, Hutton. Billy Albuquerque is all of twenty-one. My son would be no more than eighteen."

"Billy Albuquerque never knew how old he really was."

"That's still not my son."

"All right," Old Man Hutton said. He went over to the dead outlaw's saddle and picked up a pair of saddlebags. "Did you look in these?"

Spurr shook his head.

"I knew Billy," the old one said. "I made it a point to get to know him well. I wanted to make sure. Do you believe that?"

Spurr said nothing. Something clogged his throat. He could not speak.

Old Man Hutton opened the saddlebags and dumped their contents on the ground. He reached down and picked something up and thrust it directly in front of Spurr's eyes.

"Remember, Spurr?" Evil was in the taunting eyes, malevolence in the grinning mouth. "These initials . . . L S . . . your brand, what you changed it to when you honored the birth of your son. This is a toy you made for him. Remember?"

Out on the desert something called to its own, a faint and plaintive cry. The fire flickered and crackled in fiendish glee and played redly on the object in Old Man Hutton's hand. It was a miniature branding iron.

III

Spurr remembered only the flush of pain before he plunged into the abyss for the last time. When he had made the long climb back to consciousness, he was surprised that they had not harmed him beyond that final blow with the cartridge belt. He had expected them to break his legs, or at least his arms, but they had not even bound him.

When he looked about him, he saw why they had been so lenient. The horses were gone and the saddles and the blankets and the guns and the food and the canteens. All they had left him was the dead youth, lying stiff and still with eyes staring up at the stars. As a last mocking reminder they had placed on his chest the tiny branding iron.

Spurr wept then. Years of torment and stubborn denial and stern suppression of memories loosed a torrent of anguish in him. Once he cried out their names, hers as well as the boy's, and the desert heard and answered with several echoes. Then it sought to console him with the only other voice it had, the silent whisper of its ancient loneliness.

And Spurr heard, and his sobs stilled. He knelt there a long time in communion with the spirits of the forsaken and forgotten. Finally, he stirred. He had himself in hand now, and he set about doing what he felt he had to do.

The fire had gone out, but not all of the wood had been consumed. With a stick as his only tool he dug a shallow grave in the fragile sand. He dragged the dead youth into the depression and covered his face with his shirt. He was going to bury the toy branding iron with the boy

33

but changed his mind at the last instant. He would keep it as a memento, an only relic of the days when he had known contentment and pride and tenderness.

He would have liked to have covered the grave with stones as protection against scavengers, but there were no rocks to be found. He tried to remember a prayer, but none would come to him.

He knew he was going to die, and for a while he was tempted to die here beside the grave of his boy. But death for him was going to be a lingering ordeal, and the thought of passively waiting for it was something he could not endure.

So he cast one look at the grave and began to walk, into the night, into the desert, into the cold, black passageway of his tomb.

As the sun rose and beat down on him, he knew thirst. That was the first thing he knew. Yet no matter how bad the thirst became — and he knew it would eventually drive him to madness — it could never begin to equal in intensity the agony in his mind and in his heart. Nothing that could happen to him could be as cruel and as merciless as that.

A strength that had never failed him began to fail him now. It seemed that the sun singled him out above everything else in the vastness of the desert and concentrated the full fury of its heat on him. It sucked moisture out of his already moistureless throat. It thickened his tongue and cracked his lips. It seared his eyes and blurred his vision. It made the whole universe shimmer and dance: It drew the vitality from out of his limbs and made him stagger and stumble and begin to fall.

Yet, if this had been all, he would have accepted it

34

happily and gratefully. It was the anguish in his mind that really pained. It was this anguish that was the greatest torture of all.

Now he no longer moved erect. He was down on all fours, like all other animals, and once in a flash of lucidity he wondered if eventually he would crawl on his belly in the manner of creatures that have no legs.

But that made no difference. The difference that hurt lay in what would happen after he was dead, when he would face his son and watch him turn and walk away and for the rest of eternity show him nothing but his back.

"Lance," he croaked. "My son, my son."

Then he saw them both, her and the boy, and they were smiling and beckoning to him. From out of somewhere a reserve of strength came and he jumped to his feet and went running toward them, so swiftly that his feet hardly seemed to touch the earth. And they still smiled and urged him on, but, as he neared them, they turned and fled into an ebony blackness that swallowed them. He plunged after them, calling, crying their names, but only the echoes came back, lost and bewildered, and no matter where he turned he saw nothing and felt nothing but the enveloping impenetrable black. . . .

Somewhere in the dark nebulosity he found her. He knew it first from the touch of her hands, as soft and gentle as in the old days of their happiness. He tried to talk to her. *Jenny, Jenny*, he called, but she seemed not to hear, for she made no answer. He wanted to ask her about the boy, why wasn't he here with them, but she didn't hear this, either, and he wept.

She spoke then. He heard her words, low and crooning, but they seemed to be in an alien tongue which he could not understand. This made him wonder for he had never known her to speak any language but one. And the words were faint, as though coming for a great distance that wearied them.

Where is the boy? he asked her. *Damn it, Jenny, why don't you speak louder so I can hear you?* She made some answer, but the words were not clear, and then they faded along with everything else, and he roamed the blackness again, searching, searching.

Once he opened his eyes and saw her. He lay on his back in some kind of shelter that served principally to break the full force of the sun. He looked about, trying to make out where he was, and saw only the inevitable sagebrush and greasewood and sand. From somewhere near came the drip of water, drop by drop, soft and muted and soothing. He looked again at her. She had her back to him.

"Why, you're not Jenny," he said.

She whirled, startled by his words, feeble as they were. She watched him a moment out of dark eyes, face barren of expression. Then she came forward, walking on moccasined feet.

She said something in a tongue he did not comprehend.

"Don't you know Spanish?" he asked her. "*¿Habla español?*"

Her reply was a nod.

"Where am I?"

"At a spring only my people know about. Have no fear. No one will find you here."

He remembered now with brutal clarity. To hide the

36

ache he smiled bitterly. "No one wants to find me. No one at all."

She watched him, features revealing nothing.

"Was I here when you found me?"

She shook her head. "I dragged you here."

"You?"

For a moment a tiny amusement softened her lips, then fled as though having intruded there. "I dragged you with my horse."

"Are you alone?"

"Yes."

"What are you doing alone in the desert?"

She watched him without expression. It was as though she had not heard him.

"Are you lost?"

"You should not speak so much. You are too weak."

She turned and walked away. The desert growths cut her off from sight and left him feeling sad and very much alone.

She wore a strange conglomeration, a soiled red blouse and buckskin breeches that had been meant for a brave. When he saw her ride, however, bareback with her legs clasping the barrel of her pinto pony, he realized the practicality of her garb. Still it made him wonder, her being alone, and made him worry, for she was just a girl, until he saw her use the knife.

It was her only weapon. He saw her one day spear a running rabbit and later a roadrunner hen. Though she had saved his life, he still could not suppress a shudder. The path of her thrown knife was as true as the path of a bullet.

She was Apache but there was Spanish blood in her as well. The Spanish blood softened her features, rounded them, made her lips full and rich, and put a blue sheen in her black hair. But her carriage, proud and erect, was Apache and so was the dark, glittering opacity of her eyes.

He had known her three days before he thought to ask her name.

"I am called Fuego," she said.

"Fuego," he murmured. "Fire. Flame." He looked at her with interest. His strength was returning. At times he almost felt ebullient, but always the black and brooding memory was there, to shatter and raze any peace or contentment before they were born. "The name fits you. It fits you very well."

She gave no indication that she understood the compliment or was pleased by it. "And you? How are you called?" she asked.

"Spurr."

"Spurr," she repeated. In her throat it was a guttural sound with rolling r's. "It does not sound good. I do not like it."

He smiled slightly. He was learning to do that again after years of bitterness and disenchantment. He was also beginning to know again some of the old emotions, tenderness and gentleness. But these had been forged anew in the crucible of anguish and torment and a loss that could never be recovered. It made him wonder if they were worth the price.

"Why did you save me, Fuego?" he asked. "Why didn't you let me die?"

The look she placed on him was inscrutable. "I did not care if you died. I had no intention of saving you."

He could not understand. "You did not care if I died? Why did you bother with me then?"

"My horse went lame. I had lost the trail again. So I

came back to you."

"You mean you saw me once and passed me up?"

"Yes."

"And you came back?"

"My horse went lame."

He stared at her, trying to read something in her face or eyes, but nothing was written there. However, he sensed something, something akin to what had rankled in his own heart in the cruel and bitter days.

"What trail did you lose, Fuego?" he asked. His tone was gentle.

She stared out over the desert, into the small wind that wrinkled the sands and whispered of old and forgotten secrets. She made no answer.

"Is it an old man and a younger one?" he asked.

The glance she turned on him blazed with the first fire he had ever seen in her eyes. "Are they your enemies, too?"

Darkness descended on him with the ache of remembrance. In the old days his voice would have been cold and bitter and stern. But he had been tempered in grief and could be bent, like steel, and this made his voice soft.

"I have none greater."

"Good. Then we can kill them together."

He stared at her. She had spoken without fury, and her face betrayed no emotion, but these things made her words all the more terrible.

"Why do you want to kill them?"

She said nothing. She sat and stared over the desert and harked to the voice of the wind.

"Did they hurt your people? Did they hurt you in some way?"

39

She turned her head and gave him a long, examining look. Her lips curved ever so slightly in an expression of disdain and scorn. "Don't you want to kill them?" she asked.

His thoughts turned inward and searched his soul. *I don't think so,* he said to himself. *I don't think I could ever kill again. I have killed too much in my life.*

"Don't you?" she asked.

"We will have to find them first," he said. "That will take time."

"What is time," she said, "as long as we find them? But we must get started. Are you well enough to leave in the morning?"

"Won't you tell me why you want to kill them?"

Her eyes blazed with that angry quickness, then the fire subsided. "Will you tell me why you *don't* want to kill them?"

She had seen through him. He had not thought her capable of that, and it startled him and upset him and made him look at her with a new respect.

"Fuego," he said, pleading, hoping that the saying of her name would explain the torment in him and the futile searching for words.

She jumped to her feet and started off with the haste of wrath.

"Fuego," he called.

She gave no sign that she had heard. She strode through the sage and greasewood until she came to a rise of ground, and there she seated herself on a ledge of rock and stared to the south where the heat hazes danced and the dust devils skirled and the tracks of men and beasts lay obliterated and forgotten in the rippling sands.

With twilight somberness came. The day died, and he knew sadness and mourned all things that died, the men, the beasts, the days, the hopes, the dreams. Some ancestral memory stirred uneasily in him, making him feel lost and forsaken and doubt that the sun would ever rise again.

The girl came back and sat near him in silence.

He remembered many things, things that saddened, things that startled. He recalled the words of Old Man Hutton and Larch when he had been emerging from the abyss of pain.

"Fuego," he said, and there was compassion in his tone, "I have heard of the scalphunters. Is that what the old man and the young were? Is that how they hurt you?"

In the firelight her face looked coppery. The flames reflected themselves eerily in the opaque depths of her eyes. She stared at him without answering.

"I remember them talking," he went on. "They were mentioning prices. Two hundred pesos I think they said. I have heard of the government in Chihuahua and some other state offering bounties for Comanche and Apache scalps. Is that what they did to you? Is that why you want to kill them?"

She stared at him, face blank. Her eyes, however, brightened with the sheen that precedes tears, but he doubted if those would ever come. But she was thinking, and remembering.

She pondered a moment longer. Then she nodded. "Yes. They took scalps. They did not care whose scalps they took as long as they were black."

"Did they take scalps of someone close to you?"

Again that nod without expression but the eyes had

41

brightened still more. "Of my two brothers and of my mother."

"Would it not be more proper for your father to kill them?"

"My father fell fighting under Mangas Coloradas."

"Did they harm you?"

"They took me with them . . . both of them. When I escaped, I went home to my people. My child was taken from me. The elders of the tribe took my child and struck its head against a stone. I did not cry or protest, but still it was my child."

Two tears appeared and quivered on her lashes. They trembled there, threatening to fall, but they never did. He put an arm around her.

"Fuego," he said gently.

She said nothing. She did not stir. It was as though she could not feel his touch.

You and I, he thought. *We've both lost a child, you and I. But I killed mine. That's the difference. That's the big difference.*

The wind had picked up. It cried as it traversed the wastes. The sands stirred and shifted, concealing here, uncovering there. And the desert slept, and paid no heed, for it was an old, familiar pattern, and it always passed, but the desert remained.

IV

They rode into Fort Winston with her trailing him on her pinto in the manner of a squaw following her brave. He was aware of the glances, some knowing, some leering, many disapproving, but it mattered nothing to

42

him what others might think.

He was armed again, with a new Colt in a holster at his side and a new rifle in the saddle boot beneath his leg. The saddle also was new and the horse, a coyote dun. From the desert they had gone to the town called Santa Loma where the name Spurr was known and his credit was good. There he had re-equipped himself, and then, together, they had come here to Fort Winston because this had been the last habitat of the young outlaw who had called himself Billy Albuquerque.

There was emptiness in Spurr now that the moment was at hand. He had come here on the last shred of a hope, the last glimmer of light. If he failed here, then there was only the darkness of despair and regret and remorse.

Fort Winston was built around a square, and in the plaza there was a fountain and shade trees and benches. He dismounted there and watched as Fuego did likewise.

"Wait for me here," he told her.

"You will not be long?" she asked.

He was fingering the tiny branding iron in his pocket. Somehow he had clung to it during his travail in the desert. Fuego had told him it had been clutched in his hand when she had found him. He had seen her eyeing it with childish covetousness, and he would have given it to her to wear as an ornament, but he could not part with it.

"That I cannot tell," he said. "But wait for me. I shall be back."

"If you find them, you will not kill them by yourself, will you? You will not kill them before I have had a chance at them?"

Her tone made his blood run cold. "No, Fuego, I will tell you first."

The hint of a smile, cruel and malevolent, touched her mouth, then was gone, leaving her face inscrutable.

Too much hate, Fuego, he thought sadly. He touched her gently on the arm. *I was like that once, and now I am paying. Do not hate so much.* "Wait here," he said again, and then he started off.

He talked to two men at the livery who could tell him nothing but what he already knew. At the saddle shop the man refused even to discuss the matter and regarded him with hostility and suspicion. The blacksmith spoke readily. "Billy Albuquerque, eh? That no-good little squirt. There's a rumor drifting around he's been done in. You know anything for sure about that, partner?"

Pain caressed the bounty hunter's heart. Pain constricted the walls of his throat and made it difficult to speak. "Not for sure. I only know the rumor. But this question I asked you . . . did he run with a crowd?"

"Yes, he did. But they're not around right now except maybe Chip Rockwell. If he is, you'll probably find him in the Trail Driver. He spends all his time in town there."

"The Trail Driver?"

"Just off the square."

He bought a beer, took a sip of the foam, and asked his question. The bartender glanced down toward the bar and back again and seemed reluctant to speak. Then a voice came from the far end of the bar.

"Were you referring to me, bucko?"

He was young and arrogant and very sure of himself. His curled-brim hat was pushed far back, revealing a damp mass of black curls. The mouth was small, the

44

lips thin. His teeth showed, rodent-like.

The bounty hunter's spurs tinkled, a mournful thren-ody, as he moved down the bar. "Do you know Billy Albuquerque?" he asked quietly.

The rodent teeth showed still more. "What's it to you?"

"I understand you ran around with him. I'd like to ask you a few things about him."

"You the law?"

The bounty hunter shook his head. "Let's sit at a table."

"Who do you think you are, ordering me around?"

"The name is Spurr."

The bounty hunter turned and walked to a table in a far corner. He sat down and waited. After a while the youth came. The arrogance was gone. His eyes flicked here and there as though seeking and memorizing exits.

"I'm clean," he said, almost whining. "There's no bounty on me. Nobody can prove nothing against me."

"Sit down," Spurr said.

The youth sat. His mouth twitched once, in an uncontrollable spasm. "You're just wasting your time. I don't know nothing. Even if I did, I'm no squealer."

"I'm not interested in anything like that," Spurr said with some irritation. "I just want to know certain things about Albuquerque. Where was he from?"

The youth's eyes watched him as though from a distance. They were wary and tinged with fear. "Did you kill Billy?" he asked, voice hardly above a whisper. "There's talk going around that he's dead. They say you followed him out of La Fuente, and he hasn't been seen since. Did you kill him?"

Spurr was thankful for the whiskers that concealed his face and for the years of schooling to reveal no emotion. "If I had, I'd have collected the bounty," he said coldly. "What do you know about Albuquerque's family?"

"I knew Billy good, but that's one thing he never talked about much. He hated his old man but that wasn't his real old man. Not Matt Chisum."

Spurr had to pause and collect himself. When he spoke, his voice was calm. "Who was his real old man?"

"I don't know. He said something once about being a kid in New York and then coming west with his ma. But he was only a kid then and couldn't remember much."

"Did he ever mention his father's name?"

The youth frowned in concentration. "He did mention it once. He told me things he never told no one else. We were real close. But I wasn't in nothing wrong with him, mister. I'm clean."

"What was the name?"

"I don't know. Something like Stockhouse or Stockbridge. I don't know for sure."

Oh, Jenny, Jenny, did you hate me that much? Spurr thought with anguish. *Did you invent a different father for him so he would never know it was me?*

Distress racked him, but his face revealed nothing. He took the tiny branding iron from his pocket and showed it to Chip Rockwell.

"Have you ever seen this before?" Spurr asked.

Rockwell turned the toy over in his fingers, studying it with a crease between his eyes. "No. Why?"

"Didn't you ever see it in Billy Albuquerque's possession?"

"Is that where you got it?" Fear thickened his voice. "You *did* kill him, didn't you? Or you wouldn't have this with you."

Spurr ignored the words. "Then Albuquerque never had this?"

46

"Not that I know of."

Spurr reached over and took the toy from Rockwell's fingers. He leveled a searching look on the youth's face, spearing his eyes, and Rockwell tried but could not hold the stare. His glance shifted.

"I wouldn't try anything if I were you, Chip," the bounty hunter said quietly. "Don't try to square anything for Billy Albuquerque."

Rockwell's head bowed. He stared at the table top, ashamed of his fear, afraid of the gamble that would mean death for at least one of them. Spurr had seen this happen before, to other men, the craven fleeing of courage when faced with the question of dying. In one way he felt a sort of pity.

He left Chip Rockwell like that, bowed and silent in his shame.

Fuego saw what was written on his face. "You did not find them? They are nowhere here?"

Fuego, he thought, *I don't give a damn where they are. I've got other things to do first, other things to find. I don't give a damn if I never find Old Man Hutton and Larch. There's something else I've got to find.* Aloud he said: "Let's ride."

He tightened the cinches on the coyote dun and swung up into the saddle.

"Where are we going now?" she asked.

"I don't know."

She stared at him, on the verge of speaking, but something that she read in his features deterred her. She mounted the pinto.

They rode out of Fort Winston, her in his wake, and he took the road to the southeast where Texas lay. But that was not his destination. He did not know what his destination was. All day he tried to decide on something and could not, and evening found him sullen and irritable.

She sat across the small fire from him, watching him with patient, knowing eyes. He had not spoken half a dozen words to her all day. But her glance said that she had gathered something out of his silence. She had had a glimpse of his soul.

"You are not looking for them," she said, and her voice sounded hurt and disappointed. "You are not looking for the old one and his companion. You have lied to me."

He said nothing. He told himself he did not care what she thought or felt. She could get up and ride away. Good riddance. She was an impediment, not a help. And in a few more minutes he would tell her so.

"But you are looking for something," she went on. "The old one and his companion did something to you, too. I saw a grave in the desert. Is that what they did to you?"

A grave? he thought, and the old hurt came and the sorrow. *If that was all there was to it, but there is more, much more. But you wouldn't understand. You're Apache. You wouldn't understand things like that.*

"Will you not tell me what they did to you?" she went on. "I told you what they did to me. I hate them. I will kill them. But still it was my child."

He stirred and looked at her with a new understanding. Shame came to him for his thoughts of a moment before. She was human, too; the elemental instincts were there. Perhaps her ways were different, and brutal, but they were the only ways she knew.

"Will you not tell me, Spurr?"

The words came with reluctance at first. Then they ran like the running of tears though he did not weep, only inside, in his heart, in the secret intimacy of his pain. The sound of his voice was low and bitter. His eyes stared into the bleak distances of recollection.

"That is what I've got to find," he said. "Whether it was my son that I killed. Once I know that, I will know what to do about Old Man Hutton and Larch."

She rose to her feet and came around the fire and knelt beside him. Her fingers touched his whiskered cheeks. When he glanced at her, she smiled, softly, tenderly, and it came to him that this was the first smile he had ever seen on her lips.

"We will find the truth," she said. "Have no fear. You and I, we will find everything that has to be found. And when everything has been found, then we shall kill."

The quiet assurance with which she spoke comforted him. In the vast domain of his misery and loneliness she was the one bright thing.

The ancient land slept and dreamed its secret dreams. Its restless, troubled creatures found consolation and slept with it in its ample bosom. Hope was born anew, springing from the seeds of longing and despair. Even the wind lost its sadness and sang quietly of bliss and contentment.

V

There had to be a beginning somewhere. That much he knew. He would have to go back, into the past, and pick up the lost and forgotten trail and re-trace it in all its anguish, in all its heartbreak. But not as far back as

Palo Pinto, where the sorrow and the disenchantment had been born. That he could not bring himself to face. He remembered too vividly, and then it really wasn't necessary. He had always known that they had taken a stagecoach westward, for California.

Flynn. A gambler named Flynn.

He found the grave of a Martin Flynn in a little settlement called Doña Ana. But they told him that this Flynn had been a quiet shopkeeper who had looked on cards as the tools of the devil. And he had been short and stout, not tall and tawny handsome.

Progress had brought with it the railroads. The stageline no longer ran across the Territories to the distant ocean. Only remnants of the stageline's greatness remained, short lines that connected tiny hamlets with the railhead. It was at one of these junctions, named Amethyst, that he found a former driver for Butterfield.

The driver, however, had no recollection of a brown-haired woman and a fair-haired boy of three in the company of a tall, tawny gambler. He might have seen them, he said, but that would have been all of fifteen years in the past, and he could not be expected to remember.

Spurr bought the driver several drinks as compensation, and in his cups the driver began to reminisce. He told of the hardships of those days, of road agents and, still worse, of marauding Indians. A thought recurred to him, and he told of a coach ambushed by Comanches in a gorge. He remembered because he had passed through the gorge an hour before, traveling in the opposite direction, eastward, and had always considered himself lucky to have missed the ambush. All the occupants of the coach had perished, either killed or taken captive by the Indians.

Captives?

Yes, the driver recalled, it was assumed that there had been captives because not all the bodies had been found in the gorge. As far as he could remember, two bodies had been missing but he had no idea of their age or sex. Still he considered the dead passengers as having been more fortunate than those who had survived. There was no telling to what indignities and tortures the living had been subjected. . . .

Spurr found that gorge. It had high, steep walls that cut off the sun except for the zenith hours when it stood directly overhead. The road still ran through the gorge, and its ruts were worn deep into the earth. Spurr dismounted and strode about, in communion with memories of death and pain and disillusionment. He searched the ground, but there was nothing to be found. This was not unexpected, however; for fifteen years had passed, and then the corpses had been removed so that there was not a single bone in the whole gorge or even the most innocuous trinket. All that remained was an aura of mourning and a hope that flickered among dying embers.

Fuego watched him without saying a word or dismounting from the pinto. She seemed to sense that this was something holy to him, and she respected it with silence. Even when he mounted the dun and started off, she did not speak. She kicked the pinto with her heels and followed, at the proper distance behind him.

The nearest town was called Solitaire. It was a new village, built after the massacre in the gorge, and no one there could tell him anything beyond what he already knew. Someone mentioned the Diamond Bar ranch whose owner, Buck Greenwood, had pioneered in this part of the territory. Greenwood was supposed to have pursued the Comanches after the ambush with some of his riders. There had been a battle and some of the Comanches had died as well as two of Greenwood's men.

They reached Diamond Bar at sunset. The white-washed buildings gleamed in the rays of the setting sun. There was an air of quiet prosperity and serenity and contentment about the place, the feeling of belonging and mattering and home. It filled Spurr with a great yearning and nostalgia.

He told Fuego to wait for him in the yard. A couple of dogs had heralded their arrival, and the yelping brought the man out on the gallery. He shaded his eyes with a hand and watched Spurr stride up to him.

"Are you Greenwood?" Spurr asked.

The man nodded.

"My name is Spurr," the bounty hunter said. "I understand you were around here when the Comanches ambushed that Butterfield stage fifteen years ago. I'd like to talk about it with you."

Quiet brown eyes weighed the bounty hunter. A hand rose and lightly brushed a brown mustache. There was a pause as though Greenwood were running something over in his mind.

The door opened, and a youth came out on the gallery. He nodded politely and impersonally to Spurr, and then said to Greenwood: "I'll go take another look at the colt. He's all right now, but I want to make sure."

Greenwood nodded and watched fondly as the boy

crossed the yard. "That's my son," Greenwood said with pride.

Your son, Spurr thought. *I have a son, too, but my son is sleeping in a lonely, unmarked grave. My son has no colt to look after. My son has nothing at all to do but sleep in his grave. And I put him there. With my own hands I killed him and put him there.*

In the house they sat and stared at each other. Greenwood offered tobacco to Spurr, but he shook his head. Greenwood watched him with a quiet, examining stare.

"What is it you want to know?" Greenwood asked.

"Were there any survivors?"

Greenwood had filled a pipe, but now he put it aside without lighting it. "Would you mind telling me first the reason for your interest in this?"

"Why do you want to know?" There was a growl in the bounty hunter's voice. He had waited so long, he had known so much frustration and defeat, that impatience gnawed at him like a canker. "Is there something you don't want to tell me?"

Greenwood's brows lifted. "What makes you say that?"

"I know there were two survivors. I'm trying to find out what happened to them."

"Why?"

Hot words rushed to the tip of Spurr's tongue, but then, with an effort, he contained himself. He was in no position to antagonize anyone.

"I'm just trying to find out who they were. Why don't you want to tell me?"

Greenwood picked up his pipe and tamped the tobacco again with a thumb. This was an automatic thing, done without thinking, for his eyes said that his mind was far away, contending with deep and somber matters. After a while he put the pipe aside, still unlit, and his eyes came back to the present.

"There are two reasons why I'm reluctant to tell you." Greenwood's voice was quiet, calm, but there was the taste of steel in it. "First of all, you're Spurr. I've heard of you. You come riding up here with. . . ." He broke off an instant, thinking it best to leave this unsaid, then continued: "You only do things for money, blood money." His glance held Spurr's. There was no fear in Greenwood's look.

He's right, Spurr told himself, once more swallowing heated words. *That's all I've done for a long time. Everyone hates me, decent men as well as outlaws, but this never meant a damn to me, not until now, not until after I'd killed Billy Albuquerque.*

"There's no bounty in this for me," he told Greenwood. "What's the other reason?"

"Your interest then has to be personal," Greenwood said. "What I can't understand is, if that's the case, why you waited fifteen years."

"Let's just say I waited, that's all. Now will you tell me?"

Greenwood shifted in his chair as though seeking a more comfortable spot. "Indians, Comanches or others, do certain things that aren't pretty to talk about. You know that. If your interest is personal, then I hesitate to tell you anything that might cause you hurt. After all, it was a long time ago. Most everyone has forgotten all about it, and the few that still remember don't talk about it."

"You can tell me."

There was sorrow in Greenwood's eyes and a little pity. "Yes, there were two survivors. Me and my boys trailed that war party. It wasn't a big one, and we caught up with them and had it out. They got two of us, and we got seven of them. The rest got away."

"The two captives . . . did you see them?" Spurr's throat was tight. His voice had thickened.

"Yes. We got a look at them, but we couldn't get to them. The Comanches took them with them when they fled."

"Who were the two?"

"I wouldn't know their names. All I know is that one was a woman and the other was a child, whether a boy or a girl I couldn't tell."

Spurr sat and listened to the crying of despair that began anew in his heart. They had not perished in the gorge, but that was small comfort. Fifteen years. Sand drifted and trees grew and other trees died; men were born while others grew old and many passed on; hopes and dreams grew weathered and sere and were forgotten; only the ancient land remained hardly unchanged, for against the stretch of eons fifteen years is but an infinitesimal fraction of a second.

"I'm sorry, Spurr," Greenwood said. There was genuine regret in his tone.

"That's all right," Spurr said. He rose to his feet. "Thanks, anyway."

He went outside. Fuego sat on her pony just like he had left her. She looked at him with those eyes that now could read him well, even when he concealed everything skillfully so that no one else knew what was written in the scars on his heart. Her eyes told him — *Patience, Spurr, patience* — but he had by now used up all his patience. And all his hope.

He mounted the dun and rode away with Fuego, riding behind him. The land reached out and called to him, with its age-old voice of promise, but he rejected it and cursed it, viciously and silently.

VI

He sat and stared into the fire and thought. *Is this where it ended for Hutton, too? Is this the box-end of the cañon that stopped him? Is this where he turned back and then picked Billy Albuquerque because there was enough mystery about him so that he could be passed off as my son? Does my true son still live then, perhaps as a savage not knowing he is white? For Indians have done that with white boys before, and maybe these Comanches did that with my son. And Jenny. Poor Jenny. Are you still alive? After fifteen years?*

He derived some comfort from the knowledge that his son might still be alive instead of sleeping in an unmarked desert grave, but the thought was without cheer. He reached over to throw another stick on the fire, and in so doing the toy branding iron in his pocket pressed against his flesh.

The toy. Where had Old Man Hutton found it? If it had been planted in Billy Albuquerque's saddlebags, then where had Hutton found it? The toy had belonged to his son. If Hutton had not found it, and it had been in Albuquerque's possession all the while, then Albuquerque was his son, and he was back where he started from.

He heard the whisper of movement as Fuego came and

sat beside him. All at once, out of the darkness of his despair, a thought rose, surging. His head lifted. His eyes glimpsed a flicker of hope, faint and all but extinct, yet it was there to be seized in a last desperation.

"Fuego, did your people ever do any trading with the Comanches?"

She watched him with that somber opacity in her glance. "The Comanches? Yes."

"What did they trade in?"

"Horses and blankets and things made of silver."

"Did they ever trade in slaves?"

"Slaves? Yes."

"Slaves who were white?"

She stared at him with a look that could not be deciphered. "Yes. I remember slaves who were white."

Emotion filled his throat, the trembling of hope, the dark fluttering of dread. "Women slaves?" he asked.

"All such slaves were women. We did not keep any white men. We killed them all. But the women were kept and sometimes the children."

"How well do you remember those slaves?"

She frowned slightly in recollection. "I was but a little girl. Our tribe had one for a while. But she was not very strong. We used to beat her and poke her with pointed sticks, and she would scream, and we would laugh because we Apaches never cry out, no matter what the pain. She was not much good, and one day our chief became angered with her and struck her over the head with a club and killed her. We were all sorry for that because we would have liked to have used the torture stake."

It was the matter-of-fact way she said it that chilled him. She might have been describing an innocent pastime for all the feeling in her voice.

She sensed what he was thinking. "I do not think it was your woman, Spurr," she said gently. "When our braves got her from the wagon train, she was very fat, but she was afraid of the dogs and would not fight them for her share of the food. She was not much good, and she cried all the time. I do not blame Nano for getting angry with her. She was not your woman. You told me your woman was thin and very pretty, did you not?"

"That I did."

"Then this was not your woman."

He almost did not ask it for he was afraid of the answer. "Did any of the slaves live very long?"

She stared at him with a tender understanding. "A few. Not many but a few. Those who did not cry too much and who were not too afraid. Some of these our warriors even took for wives."

"Do you think . . . my woman . . . could still be alive?"

She reached up and touched him lightly on the whiskers. "Perhaps . . . if she was brave enough. Was she brave?"

"I don't know, Fuego." Torment tore at him. "I don't know."

"It was long ago, but, if she was brave enough, then she is still alive."

He turned toward her, no longer ashamed of begging, no longer ashamed of any abject act. "Will you help me look for her? Your people will tell you things they would never tell me."

"I will help you."

He bowed his head. Out in the night a coyote cried, a shrill and sad and lonesome sound. The echoes caught the cry and fondled it as though reluctant to let it go,

58

but they could not keep it, and it died and was instantly forgotten.

They crossed the border, that ephemeral line, into Mexico. On the eastern flank of the Sierra Madre Occidental, in a cañon, they found the camp of Oso, which is Spanish for Bear. He was chieftain now, and he was angry and bitter after a foray that had cost him several warriors. Had it not been for the girl, Oso would have had Spurr staked out on an anthill.

Oso, however, was fond of the girl whom he regarded almost as a daughter. "He is your mate?" he asked sternly. "You are not lying when you tell me this?"

The girl shook her head.

"We shall see," Oso said.

They were given a *jacal* and spent the night there. By morning the choler had abated in Oso. The girl asked Oso the question.

He pondered it a while. Then he said: "I do not know of many such slaves. Aguila had one, an old one that he purchased somewhere. Whether from the Comanches I do not remember. You might also try Maguey and Caballo Rojo. But such slaves are scarce. I do not want them. White people are all weaklings." He spat. "I would keep them only for the torture stake."

The warriors of Aguila ringed themselves about Spurr and jostled him and jeered him and hurled insults at him. When the girl sought to intervene, they cast her aside. Spurr stood his ground, evincing no fear, though his heart hammered like mad. When knives pierced his shirt and pricked his skin to draw blood, he swallowed any cry of pain.

The girl pleaded with Aguila, named after the eagle,

who was watching with amusement. He knew the girl; for he visited now and then with Oso and had banded with him under the great Victorio. When he had his fill of the fun, Aguila called the warriors off.

"I had such a one," Aguila said, "but she is no longer with me. She was stolen by that renegade and thief, Oreja Mutilada. You remember him, do you not?"

The girl nodded.

"He is not one of us any more. He has committed the greatest crime, the murder of one of his own tribe. He has fled northward, but we shall be going that way again in the spring, and we shall find Oreja Mutilada and make him wish he had never been born."

"He has the slave with him?" the girl asked.

"He took her for his wife." Aguila's laugh was ugly with contempt. "No one else would have him."

Spurr and the girl rode on. Maguey they could not find, and Caballo Rojo had been killed and his band scattered in an encounter with Mexican troops. So they turned northward and crossed the border again, seeking the renegade Oreja Mutilada, or Mangled Ear.

The mutilated ear helped. A Pima buck gave them the first assurance that they were on the right track. Yes, he had seen an Apache brave with such an ear and a woman had been with him. But she had kept her distance, and he could remember only the light-brown hair.

An Indian agent gave them their next clue. An Apache with a badly mangled ear had shown up at the agency and had been issued some blankets and beef. But he had been alone. Then he had disappeared. Someone had told the agent that the Apache with the mutilated ear had been seen going into the mountain range called the Capitans.

The girl took over now. She saw sign where Spurr with all his skill could see nothing. After a while he would not have doubted that she could track men and animals across the tenuous surface of the sky. And she had the Apache intuition for finding water. She found it where there was only sterile rock and barren sand. And at one of these secret, secluded springs they found the Apache called Oreja Mutilada.

Fuego approached him first, alone. She was young and pretty. Oreja Mutilada, seeing that she was without company, forgot all suspicion and knew only eagerness. Spurr circled and came in from the opposite direction. The click as he cocked his Colt was the first warning Oreja Mutilada had.

Mutilada whirled, and a knife flashed in his hand. Then he saw the gun and the look on Spurr's face, and Oreja Mutilada froze. He stood there all tensed, poised like something wild and untamed on the verge of flight. The only thing that moved about him was the winking of the sun off the blade of his knife.

Fuego took the knife from his reluctant fingers. He also had an old musket and bow and arrows. The girl gathered these and piled them to one side and then stood watch over them. Only then did Spurr look around.

When he first saw her, Spurr's heart stopped. A voice began to cry in him with more anguish than he had ever known. On an impulse he could have shot Oreja Mutilada on the spot, but then it occurred to him that this Apache alone was not responsible nor were the many really responsible. *She* was the product of a way of life which Spurr and his kind could not understand but which was the normal pattern for a savage.

61

She squatted on the ground, Indian fashion, and watched him with alien, hostile eyes. She, who had always been so neat and prim and clean, was so covered with filth and dirt that the true color of her skin could not be told. Only the color of her eyes betrayed her ancestry. They were blue.

"Jenny," he said, and tears stained his voice. He walked up to her and fell on his knees in front of her. "Jenny. Don't you remember me?"

She spat in his face.

"It's Alan. Don't you remember? Palo Pinto and our home? Don't you remember at all?"

She spat again and made a sound of animal rage and resentment. Nothing showed in the depths of her eyes. It dawned on him that somewhere in her dreadful world she had forgotten how to speak.

"Jenny," he said gently, tenderly, "everything's going to be all right. Everything's going to be like it once was. You're going home, Jenny. Home."

She spat once more in his face.

VII

Now that Oreja Mutilada saw that they were not going to kill him, his arrogance returned — and his cunning. He became the bargainer.

"It is not right for you to take her from me," he said. "Not without paying me for her."

"You have no right to her," Fuego told him. "Aguila said you stole her."

"I did not steal her," he said haughtily. "She is my woman, and she goes wherever I go. I took her with me because she is mine."

"She is not yours," Fuego said. "She was first of all the woman of the white man. The Comanches stole her from him."

"I know nothing about that," Oreja Mutilada said with a disdainful shrug. "I know only that she is my woman." His eyes glittered slyly. "However, if the white man desires her, I shall listen to any offer he is prepared to make."

"He does not have to make any offer," Fuego said. "We can take her from you. How will you stop us?"

The Apache's eyes glittered craftily and cruelly. "I shall trail you. Some dark night I shall kill, if not you and him, then surely her."

"Not if we kill you first."

Oreja Mutilada permitted himself the smallest smile. "That you will not do. Or you would have killed me already."

"Tell him I have no gold," Spurr said.

"Gold is of no use to me," the Apache said. "But you have guns and horses."

"We need our horses," Spurr said.

"You have guns," Oreja Mutilada said.

"We need our guns also."

"But you have two guns. Surely you can spare one. The long one."

"No."

"You will be getting not only the woman but also a horse which she has to ride."

"No."

"She will not go without my permission. You know that. She spits at you. If she can get her hands on a knife, she will kill you. I have already told her to do that.

If you do not believe me, ask the girl."

Spurr glanced at Fuego. She nodded.

"You do not dare kill me," Oreja Mutilada said slyly. "That will only make her hate you all the more."

Oh, Jenny, Jenny, something cried in Spurr. *What hell did you go through to become like this? I want to make it up to you. No matter what happened in the past, I want to make this up to you. I hated you once, for what you did to me, but no more, Jenny, no more.* Aloud he said: "All right. But only the rifle."

He unloaded the weapon and handed it to Oreja Mutilada. The Apache weighed it and fondled it, and his eyes glittered with pleasure. He made a small, crooning sound. Then his glance lifted and peered slyly at Spurr.

"I must have bullets," Oreja Mutilada said.

"No bullets."

"What good is the gun without bullets?"

"You'll get no bullets from me. If you want some, you'll have to steal them."

"You are a man without honor," the Apache said. "All white men are without honor." He spat at the ground.

"Tell her to come with me." It hurt Spurr to say the words, but he had no choice. "Be sure you tell her that and nothing more. The girl understands your tongue, and, if you try to trick me, it will go bad with you."

While the Apache obeyed, Spurr gathered up the musket and the bow and arrows and the knife. Anger twisted Oreja Mutilada's features when he saw this.

"You are taking my weapons," he cried. "That was not a part of the bargain."

Hate and loathing clashed in Spurr as he stared at the Apache. "I will give you no chance to kill me."

"Those are my weapons. You have no right to them."

The musket was loaded. Spurr cocked it and pointed it at the ground and fired it. Then he tossed it at Oreja Mutilada's feet.

"I am keeping the powder and balls and also the bow and arrows."

"At least leave me my knife. How will I skin game that I kill without a knife?"

Spurr hesitated. Then he tossed the knife beside the musket. Fuego had gotten Jenny to mount her pony, a shaggy-haired Grullo. Jenny looked at Oreja Mutilada and made whispering sounds that tore at Spurr's heart.

"Don't try to follow us," Spurr told Oreja Mutilada. "If I so much as see you anywhere behind us, I shall kill you on the spot."

That evening he tried again. Jenny had cried several times that day, lamenting sounds of lonesomeness and bewilderment. He knew that whatever mind and memory she had were still with Oreja Mutilada. He could have cried with her, so helpless and wretched did he feel. She was only a living shell, bereft of understanding and true remembrance.

She sat huddled by the fire, staring blankly into the flames. Fuego had wrapped a blanket about her shoulders. Still she shuddered every now and then. Whether from cold or from some dark reaction he did not know.

He got down on one knee beside her. "Jenny," he said. She did not look at him. She went on staring at the flames. "Jenny. Don't you hear me?"

She gave no response.

He took her by an arm. She started, with a sharpness that stunned and pained him, and shrank from him.

"It's me, Alan. Don't you remember yet?"

She watched him with wide, distrustful eyes. She tried to inch away. Only his harsh grip prevented her.

"You've got to remember, Jenny! Our son, Lance. What happened to him? Don't you even remember him? You might have hated me, but you couldn't have hated him."

The wide eyes watched him with not even animal intelligence. All they held was the liquid glow of confusion and fright. She whimpered once, a low and pitiful sound, then was silent once again.

"I've searched," said Spurr. "You don't know how I've searched. I've found you. But him . . . I don't know. I did find one who could have been him, but he's dead and sleeping in his grave. Tell me if it wasn't him. Tell me he died years ago, tell me the Apaches butchered him. Tell me anything just so I'll know."

The eyes watched without comprehension.

"Jenny," he said, and then had to cease. Anguish rose in him, filling his throat, and he knew, if he stayed here a moment longer, he would begin to cry like a baby. So he rose to his feet and walked past the edge of the firelight and stood in communion with the darkness and its secrets, as deep and as somber and as unfathomable as his own. . . .

Something woke him, and he sat up in this blankets, all alert and tense with intuition and dread. The sound repeated itself, an eerie ululation of an owl's hoot, but an inner sense told him the sound emanated from a human throat.

The fire was almost out; only a few embers glowed. A whisper came, of Fuego rousing and sitting up beside him. And another whisper — of stealthy, secret movement, stealing away. He realized what it was and on the instant experienced a great anxiety.

"Jenny," he cried, and the echoes took up his shout and caromed it all about. "Jenny! Come back."

The owl called again. He threw off the blankets and drew his Colt and went after the fleeing figure in the dark. Behind him he was aware that Fuego was coming, too.

The owl called anew, and the dim shadow that was Jenny veered that way, and he veered with her. Behind he was conscious of Fuego, shifting direction also, but it was not to follow him.

The owl called once again, and Spurr stopped his headlong pursuit. That was Oreja Mutilada out there, calling to Jenny. If he pursued her rashly, Spurr knew that he would find the Apache concealed and waiting. Oreja Mutilada had a knife, and in the darkness it sufficed. But if he stopped now, Spurr knew he would lose Jenny.

The owl called once again. Then, from another direction, another owl called — filling the night with confusion. At first Spurr thought Oreja Mutilada had a companion. Then it dawned on Spurr that the second owl was Fuego, baffling the night and possibly Jenny with her mocking echoes of Oreja Mutilada's hooting.

Fuego! Spurr almost wept. *What would I do without you, Fuego?*

He moved on again, very cautiously now, and placed himself between the calling of the two owls. In the lee of a mesquite bush he waited, Colt gripped in a sweating palm. Every time one owl called, the other answered instantly, and with the echoes tossing the sounds about indiscriminately the whole night seemed filled with hooting. It came from one side and another and from all about and seemed even to come from above. And Spurr crouched there, waiting.

He heard a whimper, a lost and bewildered sound, and then he saw her. She moved a few steps at a time, first one way then another, whimpering her fear and confusion. He wanted to call to her or go to her, but that would only startle her, and she would flee from him.

So he stayed where he was, because he wanted Oreja Mutilada. The owl that Spurr thought was Fuego called again, and Jenny started toward it, running. She tripped once and fell but was up instantly and off anew, and then the night had swallowed her.

With all his will Spurr forced himself to stay where he was. The other owl hooted again, urgent calls with a touch of the frantic. The hoots drew closer, toward Spurr, and suddenly he saw the figure, moving along almost doubled over, moccasined feet silent in the sand. Spurr shifted ever so silently. Oreja Mutilada heard something and came hurtling at Spurr. Spurr fired, but the Apache had moved so swiftly that he missed. Before he could fire again, Oreja Mutilada was on him.

He sensed more than saw the thrust of the knife, and he ducked under it and came up under the Apache's legs and with a burst of effort upset Oreja Mutilada and sent him sprawling. Even so the point of the knife pricked Spurr in the dark.

The Apache was instantly on his feet. He whirled and came storming at Spurr once more. This time, when Spurr fired, he knew his bullet had gone true. An involuntary groan tore out of the throat of Oreja Mutilada. Both his arms flung up as if beseeching the sky, and in the moment that he hung suspended there Spurr fired again. This slug dropped Oreja Mutilada. He thrashed about a little on the ground and then was still.

The muscles in Spurr's thighs were quivering with reaction when he rose to his feet. "Fuego," he called. "Where are you? Everything's all right."

The sounds of struggling led him to her, and he found that she had hold of Jenny. Jenny resisted with a silent, savage fury, kicking and scratching, and it took the two of them to subdue her. Back at the fire he bound her arms and legs.

VIII

The next night, when they camped, he was aware of Fuego, watching him intently. All that day she had stared at him as though seeking to read the secrets written on his soul. She had not spoken much, and he had welcomed that.

Jenny had been docile all the while. They had not told her about Oreja Mutilada, and, whether she suspected that something had happened to him or did not recall the events of the night before, Spurr did not know. He found consolation in the fact that she was passive and did not weep or resist any more. But the dullness was still in her eyes and anything that he said to her brought no response.

After they had eaten, Fuego said: "What are you going to do now?" Her tone was cold, distant.

"I've still got to find my son."

"What about the old one and his companion?"

She spoke with a sharpness he had never heard from her. Anger lay in the tight set of her mouth and in her smoldering eyes.

"After we have found my son," he said quietly.

"Your son is dead."

The words pierced his heart like a knife. He stared at her. She who had never hurt him and who had shown him understanding and tenderness in his hours of misery and distress had now hurt him.

"Fuego . . . ," he said, beseechingly, and then could say no more.

"Your son could not have lived," she went on brutally. "It is a wonder that she has lived. You can search the rest of your life, and you will never find your son. Forget him."

"Why?" he asked. "Why are you talking to me like this?"

"I have been patient. I have helped you. Now it is time that you helped me."

"What do you want me to do?"

"Help me find the old one and his companion. They have lived too long. It is time they died."

"After we have found my son," he said.

Her eyes glowed with contempt and wrath. "You have no intention of finding them. You have no intention of killing them."

"After we find my son, Fuego."

"You lie." She spat at his feet, and she was all savage now. "You have lied to me from the very beginning. You cared only for finding your woman and your son. You care nothing at all about killing the old one and his companion."

"My promise, Fuego. After we find my son." He went over to her and put a hand on her arm. She jerked away from him.

"Don't touch me. Don't ever touch me again."

Spurr walked away from her and stood looking down

at his wife. Jenny did not look at him; she had eyes only for the fluttering flames. He glanced again at Fuego, but she had her back to him. She did not look at him any more that night.

When he awoke in the morning, he found Fuego gone.

Spurr was furious. She'd get herself killed, trying to tackle Old Man Hutton and Larch. Spurr cussed her impatience. He'd given her his word, and he had meant to keep it.

"Come, Jenny," he said, taking her by the hand. "We're going home. Once you see Palo Pinto maybe you'll remember what happened to our son."

She uttered not a sound. She was docile and compliant. For him this was almost worse than her displays of hatred; for those at least showed her capable of some elemental emotions. Her present state reminded him of the living dead, who breathed and moved without knowledge or volition.

They rode away together, and she rode the proper distance behind him, as Fuego had, in the custom of the Indians. He had not minded this from Fuego but from Jenny it rent his heart.

The sun was directly overhead when he stopped to rest the horses. He held the canteen at Jenny's lips, and she drank with the helpless, automatic instincts of an infant. He tried to catch her eyes to see if there was any glimmer of recognition or awareness there, and, when he saw the vacuity, he was sorry he had looked.

He had a drink, and then he put the canteen away and stared about. They were on high ground, and he could see a long way. The first glimpse he had was of a tiny curl of dust, and then the two outlaws intruded upon the emptiness of the horizon; for even at this distance Spurr had recognized them.

He grabbed the Grullo and led it and Jenny behind the cover of some jackpine. He sat there on his coyote dun, watching the two passing in the distance. Hate lashed him. He knew the brutal, killing impulse in all its fury. He would have succumbed to it except that he had Jenny.

He did not know what to do with her. If he left her with instructions to wait for him, he would probably find her gone when he returned. He could bind her, like an animal, and he was prepared to do that when the thought occurred to him that he might not return. If things went wrong and he should die, who would there be to free Jenny? She would die, too, like an animal helpless in a trap.

Now he yearned for Fuego. When things had been at their darkest, when there had remained nothing but capitulation to despair, her resourcefulness had pulled them through. Now she was gone, hunting the two, and she could not be far off, and, if she saw them, she would stalk them. Despite her self-sufficiency she was but a girl, and they were two, an exceedingly dangerous pair. Anxiety gripped Spurr.

It came to him that he was not far from Diamond Bar. It had been his intention to take Jenny to the gorge, where the coach had been ambushed and she had been taken captive, in the hope that this might jar her into remembering. Now he forgot about this and thought of Greenwood. He would leave Jenny at Diamond Bar while he sought Fuego and Old Man Hutton and Larch. If he failed to return, Jenny at least would be among her own people.

He turned northward, toward Diamond Bar, and lifted

the horses into a run. The land grew more hospitable; there was graze here and there. He spotted a bunch of white-faces in the distance grouped around a water hole. He was about to pass them up when he spied the two cowboys there, and so he turned in that direction.

The two watched him and Jenny riding in, and, as he neared them, Spurr saw that they were Greenwood and his son. Seeing the boy brought a pang to Spurr's heart. He glanced at Jenny, wondering if anything like that happened to her, but her face and eyes were blank.

Greenwood's features looked drawn and hostile. His eyes peered intently at Jenny. He said no word of welcome, gave no sign of greeting. The boy nodded impersonally and kept shifting his glance from Spurr to Jenny and back again in open curiosity.

"This is my wife, Jenny," Spurr said. "I found her with the Apaches. She was the woman taken captive in that massacre fifteen years ago."

A corner of Greenwood's mouth twitched ever so slightly. "That was a long time back and then it was Comanches, not Apaches. You're mistaken, Spurr."

"I know my wife," Spurr said.

Greenwood shrugged. He said nothing. His patent hostility puzzled Spurr.

"Would you look after her for me?" Spurr asked. "I've got something to do, and she needs looking after. I'm asking it as a favor of you, Greenwood. She's been through hell. You can tell that from looking at her. Just watch her for a few days for me. I'll make it up to you."

"You mean take her in my home?" Greenwood's tone was cold.

"She's a white woman, isn't she?"

"And she's lived fifteen years with Indians. She's just

73

as much Indian as any squaw."

"I'm begging you, Greenwood."

"Why? So you can go back to that Apache girl you had with you the last time I saw you? How will I know you'll ever be back for her?"

Fury flogged Spurr. On the impulse he stepped suddenly forward, hand upraised to smash Greenwood across the mouth. The boy made a sound of anger, drawing Spurr's glance that way, and he saw that the boy had his Colt half way out of its holster. Spurr froze. His hand dropped, and he stepped back.

"All I want you to do is look after her for a little while," Spurr said. "There's something I have to do, and I can't have her with me while I'm doing it. If you don't want to take her in your home, put her in a shed. She's lived in worse places than that. I just want her somewhere so I'll know where to find her when I come back."

"And if you don't come back?" Greenwood asked.

"Should that make any difference? Don't you have a heart?"

"As much of a heart as you've got."

"What do you mean by that?"

"Do you deny that you're going to that Indian girl?" Greenwood demanded.

"She needs me. She is in danger, Greenwood."

Greenwood's scornful smile spoke for him.

"It isn't what you think," Spurr said, fighting wrath and indignation. "She's somewhere out there. . . ." He broke off, realizing that no matter what he said would not be believed. "One last time, Greenwood. Will you take her in, for just a little while?"

"No."

"I'll be back, Greenwood," Spurr said. "I won't forget,

and I'll be back."

He signaled to Jenny and turned the coyote dun, but she did not follow. He whirled the dun, shouted: "Come on!"

He grabbed the Gullo, and she turned pleading eyes on him and began to cry. Something showed in the wetness of her glance, and she made sounds as though trying to tell him something, but he was so caught up in rage that he didn't see it. He wanted to get away, before the check he had imposed on his temper broke, and he killed Greenwood.

He started away with Jenny behind him. He had not gone far when the boy cried out. Something in the tone warned Spurr, and he spun the dun, at the same time drawing his Colt.

They were struggling, father and son. The sun glinted off the gun in Greenwood's hand, and the boy hung onto his father's wrist so that the weapon pointed at the sky instead of at Spurr.

"No, Pa, no," the boy cried. "Not in the back."

All at once it dawned on Spurr. The night vanished; the mists cleared; the truth was bright and stark and aching. He raised the Colt and aimed it at Greenwood's heart, but, even as his fingers tightened about the trigger, something came that calmed and deterred him.

IX

His very being had been shattered and then formed anew in the molds of anguish and deprivation. He was still capable of anger and hate and the will to kill, but he was also capable of other things, greater things, of true

75

understanding and compassion. He had known the torment of irreparable loss and so could commiserate with the unfortunate such as he had once been.

Now that he was disarmed, Greenwood put his face in his hands and wept. He wept openly, brokenly, unashamed of his emotion.

The boy was aghast and bewildered. He kept staring at Spurr and shaking his head, as though that could drive the unwanted truth away. Hurt slashed Spurr's heart.

"Lance," he said, and then had to wait for the cloying to leave his throat. "You're my son. Lance, this is your mother. Don't you remember, either?"

The boy kept shaking his head. His world was crumbling and its pieces rained on him, pelting him, and he looked desperately about, seeking shelter but found none.

"Somehow, when Greenwood chased the Comanches and fought them, he got hold of you. He took you in and raised you as his own. Isn't that right, Greenwood?"

Greenwood wept. He said nothing.

"Answer me, Greenwood," Spurr said. "This is my son, isn't it? That's why you tried to kill me, isn't it? You didn't want to lose him."

Greenwood did not speak.

Spurr turned to the boy. "I know you were little, only three, but don't you remember riding in the stagecoach and the Comanches attacking? Don't you remember anything at all?"

The boy shook his head in confusion. His face twisted in an expression of torment. "I don't know," he said. "It's all mixed up. I remember nightmares, waking up screaming. I still do that, but they're only dreams. I don't remember you or even her."

"She's changed. I can hardly believe myself it's her, but it is. I've changed, too, Lance." Longing and loneliness and desperation all welled up in Spurr. "Greenwood hasn't said a word. He hasn't denied a thing. Doesn't that mean something?"

"I don't remember," the boy said, voice thick with distress. "I don't want to remember. He's the only father I've ever had. He's always been good to me."

Hurt and anguish lashed Spurr. Then a thought struck him. With fingers that trembled he took the toy branding iron from his pocket.

"Do you remember this?" he asked the boy. "I made it for you and gave it to you on your third birthday. You liked it very much and would never part with it."

The boy turned the toy over in his fingers. His eyes misted. After a while he looked at Greenwood who stood there, slumped and suddenly old and very still.

"I'm sorry, Pa," the boy said to Greenwood. "I don't want to, but I can't help remembering now. I'm sorry. . . ."

Spurr felt awkward, and the boy felt awkward, too. They stood ill at ease, father and son yet worlds apart, strangers one to the other. Spurr had dared dream once or twice of this reunion, and in his mind he had pictured it as the most joyful experience he could ever have. In the dream there had been no lack of consolation, no touch of sorrow.

Jenny watched the boy with a small glimmer in her eyes. But, when he made a move toward her and reached a hand out to her, she shrank away. The boy stopped, hurt and puzzled.

"You'll have to give her time," Spurr said. "It was the

77

same with me. She fought me and spat at me at first. She's sick. She went through a lot. I don't know if she can ever come back from where she's gone to."

He touched the boy briefly on the arm. It had been so long since he had touched his own flesh and blood. Then he remembered the urgency that he had almost forgotten in the bittersweetness of this reunion.

"Look after her, Lance. She loved you once. She loved you very much. Look after her while I'm gone, and, if I don't return, remember that she is your mother and look after her."

The boy stared at him with a mixture of disgust and contempt.

"It isn't what you think," Spurr said quietly. "The Apache girl helped me. Without her I never would have found your mother. I would not even be alive."

"But where are you going?" the boy asked.

"I don't know. She's out there somewhere, hunting two enemies that are my enemies, too. She means to kill them, but they are two, and she's just a girl. I wouldn't be able to live with myself if they killed her and I stood around and did nothing about it."

He wanted to embrace his son for there was a chance he might never see him again, but the newness of their relationship reared up between them like a barrier. They were strangers still. So he took the boy's hand and shook it. Then he turned and touched Jenny gently on the cheek. She did not start or jerk away. She did not even flinch. Her eyes, wide and somber, watched him.

He went over and offered his hand to Greenwood. "I can never repay you for saving my son for me. If I don't return, he is still yours. I want it that way. And if I do return, a part of him will always be yours. Will you shake on that, Greenwood?"

The rancher offered his hand in silence.

Spurr did not say good bye to any of them, for he could not trust himself to speak. He mounted the dun and rode away. His eyes sought the horizon and stayed there. The dun broke into a run, lifting a curl of dust that hung a little while in the air and then was gone forever, like the recent moments were gone.

X

It was the second day that he came across the tracks of three horses heading northward. He took off in pursuit. *They've caught you, Fuego,* he thought with anxiety and worry. *You told me about Apache ways, but I'll invent new ones, crueler ones, if they've harmed you.*

He kept glancing back across his shoulder for an intuition told him something pursued him. He did not underestimate Old Man Hutton and Larch. They could have doubled back and picked up his trail and guessed what was up and so taken after him, making him the hunted rather than the hunter.

Once he thought he saw a spume of dust, far in the distance, and he reined in the dun and watched. But nothing more showed against the yellow horizon, and after a while he began to think it had just been the working of his imagination.

He rode on. The land changed. Here in the higher elevations jackpine and stunted cedar grew, but it still was arid country and all the growths were meager and dwarfish, as though reflecting pitifully the lack of proper nourishment. The tracks led him on.

With the westering of the sun he grew more cautious. The feeling still persisted of someone behind him, but the tracks he followed were fresh, and he was positive he was overtaking whoever was laying them down. So he proceeded carefully, like in the old days when he had set himself apart from the world and had hunted its people with mercilessness and ruthlessness.

They camped early that evening. The sun had not yet gone down. It hung carmine and sullen at the edge of the horizon as though reluctant to depart. When he spotted the spiral of smoke from a camp fire, he dismounted and tied the dun to a cedar. He removed his spurs so their jingling would not betray him and with the rifle in his hands moved in on foot.

He was reminded of the last time he had done this. Billy Albuquerque had died that time, and he had known immeasurable torment and anguish. But that was over now and out of it had come something good. Jenny was back among her kind again, and he had reclaimed his son. Yet he had no idea how this would come out.

He moved skillfully, using the scrub growths and boulders and hollows to conceal his approach. When he saw Fuego, cooking at the fire, and Old Man Hutton watching her, an overwhelming rage gripped Spurr, and he had to fight it with all his will. Larch was nowhere in sight, and he could make no play until he knew where Larch had gone.

So he crouched behind a stone and waited, watching the fire and grateful that Fuego was still alive. A coyote cried in the distance and then cried again. Old Man Hutton was quickly on the move. He grabbed Fuego by an arm and, with his drawn pistol cowering her into silence, disappeared into the stunted pines that grew all about.

Spurr crouched and waited, full of dread now. That had been no coyote but a human throat issuing those cries. Larch? If so, had Larch spied him? But the warning calls had come from the south, along the trail Spurr had followed, and he had circled the fire and was facing it from the north. Who was it, then, that Larch had seen?

In a little while Spurr had his answer. The boy was young and new at this sort of thing. And Old Man Hutton and Larch were old and skilled at the game.

The boy, in his innocence and inexperience, had no chance. He rode openly toward the fire — and Old Man Hutton got the drop on him.

Spurr waited. There was nothing else for him to do. He had to wait for the cover of darkness.

Old Man Hutton and Larch, however, did not wait for darkness. Not long after that they openly showed themselves at the fire. Hutton held his cocked pistol at Fuego's temple. Larch held his cocked gun at the boy's.

"Spurr!" Old Man Hutton shouted. "We know you're out there. Larch spotted your tracks. Show yourself and come on in with your hands in the air, or we'll kill them both."

Spurr walked in.

Old Man Hutton's eyes glittered. He was so full of malevolent joy that he could hardly contain himself.

Larch held a pistol in either hand. His grin taunted Spurr.

Spurr had never felt more desolate and hopeless.

They had bound the boy. They had gone through his pockets and found the toy branding iron. Old Man Hutton held it up before his single eye and laughed.

"So you found him, Spurr! So you found your real son. You didn't fall for my story about Billy Albuquerque. It's just as well, though. This way we'll have more fun."

Old Man Hutton held up the tiny branding iron and giggled as he stared at it. "Your son will die, Spurr, but not right away. He will be a long time dying. This toy you made for him. It's a clever piece of work. Did you ever try to stamp a brand with it?"

Spurr could not speak.

"No?" Old Man Hutton said. "Well, we'll try it out. Just for the hell of it." He bent and stuck the lettered end of the toy into the coals. "When it's hot, we'll try it. On your boy. After all, it carries his initials."

Spurr glanced at his son. The boy's eyes were clear, unafraid. *You are my son,* Spurr thought. *But I wish this wasn't how you had to prove it.*

Old Man Hutton tittered. "Aren't you wondering how I got this toy? I took it from a Comanche brave whose scalp I lifted and sold for a hundred and fifty pesos. He was wearing it around his neck along with teeth and bones and beads. He must have been in the war party that captured your wife and son. If so, then I did you a favor in killing him, didn't I, Spurr?"

Hutton bent and took the tiny branding iron from the fire. The small handle was hot, and he used his soiled bandanna to grip it. He held the toy up and showed the glowing stamp to Spurr.

"See it, Spurr? L S. Your brand. With a brand on him he'll be much easier to find if he should ever get lost again. Where should I brand him? On the cheek? On the forehead?"

Spurr took a step ahead.

Larch said: "Hold it, Spurr. I won't shoot to kill. I'll

82

just break your leg. Don't move another step."

Out of desolation and desperation the wild thought occurred to Spurr. He remembered the look in Jenny's eyes, the first faint glimmer of remembrance, and he remembered how his son had trailed him to help him. In this final desperation he turned to Fuego.

"Call her, Fuego," he whispered. "The hooting of an owl. Like that time with Oreja Mutilada. Call her."

Old Man Hutton was bent over the boy, the glowing end of the iron inches from his face. Hutton froze like that as Fuego called. His head turned. The single eye glared at Spurr.

Fuego called once, then again. The echoes answered and then came silence, and after a while Old Man Hutton tittered triumphantly. And then the answer came, soft and crying somewhere in the night.

Larch's head turned, searching for the source of the answer, and that was all the chance Spurr bargained for. Larch was not far away. Spurr charged him with lowered head. Larch was warned by Old Man Hutton's shout and came around. Both his guns blasted, but by then Spurr had hit him with a shoulder, and Larch went barreling back. He tripped over his spurs and went crashing into the fire.

He rent the night with a scream as the flames seared him. The pistols went flying from his hands. Spurr snatched one up and, as Larch, howling, rose up from the sparking fire, Spurr shot him in the heart.

Spurr whirled then, seeking Old Man Hutton. Hutton had dropped the tiny branding iron and had pulled his gun. But Fuego had thrown herself at him. She clutched his wrist so that he could not aim. When he threatened to shake her loose, she sank her teeth into his wrist. He shouted with pain and raised his left fist and clouted her on the back of the neck. Fuego dropped.

Spurr fired with cruel deliberation. His first shot crashed into Old Man Hutton's belly and doubled him up. His second smashed a shoulder and spun Hutton half around. His third broke Hutton's other shoulder. His fourth and last hit Old Man Hutton in his only eye.

Then Spurr was freeing his son and from out of the night came the sounds of running, and Jenny was there. Spurr took them both in his arms and held them tightly. Jenny was crying. She was making sounds, in an alien tongue, and he said to her: "I know, Jenny. I know why you followed me and him. Don't try to tell me. Tell me when you've learned to speak again. We'll teach you, Jenny. Me and the boy, we'll teach you."

He was so engrossed in this second reunion, so much sweeter than anything he had ever known, that he was unaware of Fuego's getting a knife and going over to Old Man Hutton. Only when she was through did he realize.

"How else is Oso to know?" she asked, holding up Old Man Hutton's severed head. "How else are my people to know that the scalphunter is dead?"

It was morning and time for parting. The joy Spurr had known was now dissipated. Sadness was at hand.

"Fuego," he said, "I can never thank you enough. If you ever need anything, come to me. I will never forget you."

She showed him that smile, slow and tender, that he had so rarely seen, and she reached up and touched his cheek. "I will not forget you, Spurr. If things were different, I would not leave you. But you have your woman and your son, and I have what I came after. So

I will go, back to Oso and my people."

She mounted the pinto and started away, her grisly burden wrapped in a blanket, and never once looked back. Spurr watched while she lifted the pinto into a run that sent dust spiraling. He watched until she topped a rise and dropped from sight and watched until the last of the dust had vanished, too.

He mounted the dun. Jenny and the boy were waiting for him. He started the yellow horse and the three of them rode on, eastward, toward Palo Pinto, toward home.

Vigilante

* Bill Leahy brought the word. "The Committee's meeting tonight, John."

John Weidler set down his newspaper and removed his spectacles. "Childress?" he asked.

"Yes."

Weidler carefully placed his spectacles in their case and cast a slight smile at his wife. He was glad that the two children were outside. He could hear their calls and laughter as they played in the back yard. John Weidler placed a hand momentarily on Martha's shoulder, then followed Leahy outside.

The evening air carried a crisp coolness, and Weidler buttoned his jacket. They were silent as they walked along, the rasp of their shoe leather on the hard-packed ground the only sound.

Finally Weidler said: "It's come to a head this time."

Leahy nodded. He was a big man with a wide face and a violent redness to his features. For all his weight his step was light and soft — the tread of a stalking cat. "He has asked for it," said Leahy heavily. "Matt Childress raised hell last night. Shot up half a dozen places, broke the windows of the Mercantile. When the marshal tried to arrest him this morning, Matt tore up the writ and threw it in the marshal's face. Matt sure did go and ask for it."

They walked along in the quickly gathering twilight. Virginia City was unnaturally quiet — such a quiet that it had never known. A far cry from the Virginia City of a year ago — the Virginia City of Henry Plummer and the Innocents. Weidler kept envisioning the old Virginia City that had been a tent city with its gambling houses and saloons and its roughly clothed, roistering miners and thieving, murdering Innocents. Full of wild, primitive laughter and full of sudden death. A year had wrought a lot of changes in Virginia City. The tents were gone, replaced by frame buildings, though the saloons and gambling houses remained. It was a changed Virginia City with its muted laughter and vibrant life. A place where a man could settle down and raise a family. And the Vigilantes had made it so.

"What's the word from Nevada?" Weidler asked.

"Hang him," Leahy said bluntly.

"That will be going kind of far," murmured Weidler, a sudden coldness gripping him. He was a short, stocky man in his early thirties, and there was the appearance of great strength in his arms and shoulders. He had a rather plain face with a blunt jaw, and there was the hint of the bulldog in his features and in his bearing. He looked like a cold man.

"It's up to the Committee," said Leahy.

"This is going to be hard, Bill. Matt was one of us. He's not a bad sort when he's sober. Drunk, he's a wild man. We've warned him time and again, but it hasn't done any good."

"He's been bragging that the Vigilantes are through."

"We'll see about that."

"Matt has friends. They'll put up a fuss. You can bet on Tom Kincaid putting up for Matt."

"Yes, Tom will do that. The hell of it is . . . Tom is our friend, too."

"So is Matt Childress."

They came to Day & Miller's store where the Vigilante meeting was to be held. Miners crowded in front of the store, and they all had rifles, but they were a quiet, somber lot. Weidler and Leahy nodded to a few of them and entered the store.

Two kerosene lamps had been lit and their shadowy, wavering light left heavy patches of black shadow in the corners and on the far walls. About twenty men were waiting. They were all morose and quiet, carrying about them a nervous silence as though wanting everything over with as soon as possible.

One of the men spoke: "I just saw Childress. Warned him to leave town. He laughed and said the Vigilantes are played out. That they won't dare hang a man for shooting up the town."

Every man's glance was on Weidler. He'd been one of the early organizers of the Vigilantes, and he'd placed the noose around George Ives's neck when that first member of the Innocents had been executed. The men were very silent now, only the scraping of their boots when they shifted their weight marring the stillness.

Weidler knew they were awaiting his words. They would put much weight to what he'd say. They had always looked to him for leadership, and he had never failed them. But this time things were different. Matt Childress was a friend, not a thieving, murdering outlaw. His only fault lay in his inability to hold liquor. Weidler felt the cold sweat stand out on the back of his neck. This was not going to be easy.

"There's not much to say," Weidler said tonelessly. "You all know Matt Childress's record. He's not all bad when sober. He has no criminal record. But this is not

88

the first time that he has shot up the town, destroyed property, and endangered the lives of citizens. And it is not the first time he has laughed at and ignored the law. He is a bad example. If he keeps on getting away with it, there will be others to follow his ways. He can't be reformed."

He paused a while, searching his mind for more to say. He could go on and list Matt Childress's good points. In all fairness Matt had that much coming, but the time for loyalty and sentiment was past, Weidler told himself. He had to think of what Childress meant to Virginia City, not what he meant to John Weidler.

At length he went on. "Matt Childress is your friend . . . and my friend. But that should not prejudice our decision. Nevada has sent word that Matt Childress should hang and that is the voice of six hundred miners. Now that decision is up to us . . . the Executive Committee. We all want Virginia City and Montana Territory to be a law-abiding place where honest men can live in peace and security. You will vote aye or nay."

It was Bill Leahy who broke the silence by saying: "Aye." One by one the others echoed Leahy's vote, and the matter was done. Leahy walked behind the counter and took down a rope.

They acted quickly, anxious to get a distasteful thing done and out of the way. John Weidler led them out of Day & Miller's store. The group of armed miners was still there. Silent. Waiting. Some of them had lighted torches. Weidler read their unspoken query, and he bobbed his head in a wordless answer. They fell in behind the Committee.

Matt Childress was in Fielding's saloon, standing at the bar with Tom Kincaid at his side. Childress's face went white, and he seemed to shrink a little when he spied Weidler, but only for a moment. Childress squared his shoulders, and there was a tight smile on his pale lips as he waited for the Vigilantes to speak.

Kincaid had tensed, his face taking on the color of his red hair. Heat came to his eyes. They were friends, these men. They'd ridden through storm and cold to bring summary justice to the cutthroat Innocents. They'd worked side by side — John Weidler, Matt Childress, Bill Leahy, Tom Kincaid.

"We've come for you, Matt," said Weidler.

"This is a hell of a joke to play on a man, John." Childress's voice trembled a little.

"It's no joke, Matt."

Tom Kincaid pushed forward, facing Weidler. "Are you really going through with it, John?"

"Yes."

Kincaid's face worked, and it seemed as though he was going to unloose a torrent of words. But no sounds came, although his eyes distended and a sneer curled his lips. His eyes were flat and ice-cold.

Childress's thick face was very white now. "You can't mean hanging," he said, forcing a quavering laugh. "I know I'm in the wrong, and I'm damned sorry. I swear before God it won't happen again. I got something coming. Banishment, maybe . . . but not hanging."

Slowly, wishing that it could be otherwise, John Weidler shook his head. He was thankful that he was a reticent man who could hide his emotions behind a cold exterior, or he could never have endured watching the life going out of Matt Childress's eyes and the way he leaned against the bar as though he could not stand alone.

"You'll give me a little time, then?" Childress asked dully. "A little time to put my affairs in order and write a few letters? And to see my wife?"

"You have an hour," said Weidler.

"But an hour isn't enough! She can't make it here in that time."

"One hour," said John Weidler, turning away.

They had taken Matt Childress to one of the back rooms of Fielding's saloon where the doomed man had been supplied with pen and paper. Weidler was outside in the cold darkness, leaning against the front of the saloon. There was a cold cigar in Weidler's mouth, but he was drawing on it as if unaware that it had died.

Presently Wayne Dunning came up. He was a young man who clerked in Day & Miller's store. "They've sent a rider for Elizabeth Childress. As soon as the meeting was over and the verdict known, the rider took out for Childress's place. His wife will sure raise hell if she gets here before the execution."

"A woman's tears have a way of moving a man," said Weidler, frowning. "Tears once saved Hayes Lyons and Buck Stinson and Ned Ray from the noose and left them free to murder and rob for almost a year. But she won't get here in time."

"She'll probably use Big Bay. That horse is the fastest thing around here."

"She won't make it. What bothers me is Tom Kincaid. I thought he'd take it much harder than he has. I wonder why he hasn't?"

The hour passed, and Childress's guards came out of Fielding's saloon with the doomed man walking in their midst. In the torchlight Childress's face was pasty gray, and his step was a trifle unsteady. He looked at John Weidler out of wide, haunted eyes, but Weidler would not meet the man's stare.

Weidler led the crowd of men to the corral in back of Day & Miller's store. The corral gate was swung open, and a rope was tossed over the crossbar. A Vigilante came out of the back of the store, carrying an empty packing box which he placed underneath the dangling noose. Bill Leahy and Wayne Dunning lifted Childress up on the box.

Childress's pale face glistened with sweat, and his voice was raspingly harsh. "You can't mean this! You're all just playing a joke on me. You can't really mean to hang me for what I did last night! For getting drunk and having some fun? I'm not complaining. I deserve something for always getting out of hand and causing Virginia City a lot of trouble, but I don't deserve hanging. I ain't never killed but one man in all my life, and he asked for it. I ain't never robbed anyone. I've always been an honest man. Banish me. Cut off my ear or my arm but don't hang me!"

Bill Leahy had climbed up on the packing box beside Childress, and Leahy fitted the noose about the doomed man's neck and then signaled that the other end of the rope be tied to a corral post.

John Weidler stood by watching, the dead cigar still between his lips. For a while he could not believe that all this was real. But the torchlight and the milling men and Matt Childress's gray face were authentic enough, and Weidler suddenly wished that all this were a dream that he might brush aside and forget upon awakening. He hardly heard Wayne Dunning who kept whispering: "We haven't much time. She'll be here soon. We haven't much time."

There was a commotion within the crowd, and Tom Kincaid came bulling his way through the armed miners. His face was very red, and his eyes flashed. He bulled up close to Weidler, so close that the Vigilante leader had to fall back a step.

"Call it off, John!" Kincaid ordered.

Weidler shook his head.

"So you're really going through with it," Kincaid roared. "And I held back. Thinking that you were just trying to put the fear of death in Matt. Let him know the feel of a rope around his neck and that would calm him. That's what I thought you were up to, so I held back. I didn't think you were kill-crazy."

Weidler chewed his cold cigar. "Take it easy, Tom. Take it easy."

"You'll hang Matt only over my dead body," yelled Kincaid, swinging a wild fist at Weidler. The Vigilante had been expecting the blow, and he swayed his head aside and out of Kincaid's reach.

Bill Leahy came in fast, and, before Kincaid could try another blow, Leahy had his pistol against the back of Kincaid's neck.

"Hold on, Tom," Leahy snapped.

Kincaid dropped his arms, and his fists unclenched. He never took his stare off Weidler's face. When Kincaid spoke, his lips curled back from his teeth as though the very words were unclean. "You filthy, kill-crazy murderer! I always felt you had a bad streak in you, John, but I never would own up to it because I called you friend. I felt we needed a cold man like you to put an end to Henry Plummer and the Innocents. I never thought the killing craze would worm into you until you'd hang anyone just to satisfy your filthy craving.

"We need the Vigilantes. I was one of them, and I am not ashamed of what I did. But tonight you're tearing down all the good we ever built. You're blackening the name of the Vigilantes in a way that can never be forgotten. When histories of the Vigilantes are written, you'll be marked down as a kill-crazy murderer, and all those associated with you will have to carry the same black brand."

Weidler took it all in silence. He stood there stolidly, the dead cigar clamped between his teeth, meeting Tom Kincaid's hot stare. Weidler's pulse was pounding, and he could feel the throb of the vein at his temple. He knew a coldness that filled him completely, the identical coldness he'd always felt at moments like these. Kincaid's words fell as from an alien world.

"One word from you and Matt could be saved," Kincaid went on. "Had you stood up for Matt, put in a good word for him, the Committee would never have voted as it did. It's an evil and dark day for Montana Territory when you've taken to hanging men for minor offenses. But Matt Childress will be the first and the last. I can't save him. I know that. But I'll see to it that you'll never hang another. Mind that, John."

Weidler turned his head and his stare away from Kincaid. Matt Childress was mumbling brokenly, incoherently on the packing box. Weidler felt a weakness creeping over his will. The time had come, and he had to make his choice — between Matt Childress and a Virginia City that would be quiet and still and peaceful, where a man could live and be proud of his town.

Suddenly he realized that if he hesitated much longer,

he could not go through with it. So he took the cigar from his mouth and said clearly, coldly: "Men, do your duty!"

Afterward, when Childress's lifeless body was swaying in the night wind, there came the thunderous clopping of a horse's hoofs, and a rider burst into the smoky torchlight. It was a woman, and she flung herself out of the saddle before the horse had halted. She stopped short when she spied the dangling body.

Weidler was up against the corral fence with Bill Leahy and Wayne Dunning on either side of him. They all watched Elizabeth Childress. She was a tall woman with a violently beautiful face. They knew little about her except that she had lived with Matt Childress, and he had called her his wife. She stared at Childress's body a long while, but no tears or cries came. She spoke at last, her voice choking with grief.

"Oh, the shame of it," she cried as she knelt beneath the dead man and clasped her arms around his stiffening legs. "That Matt Childress should be hanged like a common felon. Where were his friends? Why did they let this happen to him who was a far better man than all of them? Better that someone had taken a gun and shot my Matt down. If I had been here, I'd have done that . . . rather than suffer him to hang!"

She seemed to notice Weidler for the first time. The woman rose slowly to her feet, and she walked haltingly, stooped forward a little as if to see better.

As she came closer, Weidler saw the tightness of her features and the way the cords stood out on her neck. He expected her to speak, to burst out in an orgy of denunciations, but she only stared at him, her lips working silently. Then she went back to Childress. Weidler spat the shredded cigar from his teeth and walked away.

He found that Martha had put the children to bed and that she had a pot of boiling coffee on the stove for him. She didn't say anything, but he could feel from her silent presence that she yearned for some comforting words to say to him.

He poured the coffee with fingers that were stiffly untrembling, and, looking up, he caught her eyes and smiled a little. "You'd better go to bed," he told her. "I'm staying up a while longer."

She left the room, and he was instantly sorry she had gone. It felt so empty now — empty as he was himself. All he knew was a hollow feeling within him and a vast restlessness. He went to the kitchen door and threw it open, standing full in the soft sweep of the night wind.

He stood looking off at the sky but not seeing the stars or the moon or the scattered clouds flowing along with the wind. All he saw was Matt Childress's swaying body and the loathing and hatred in Tom Kincaid's eyes.

He was standing there in the chillness of the night when Bill Leahy came again.

"What is it, Bill?"

"Tom Kincaid is after you."

"He'll get over it."

Leahy placed a big hand against the doorjamb. His breathing had calmed. "He's taken on a load of drinks. He's in a bad mind, John. He's coming over here to have it out with you."

"He's drunk. He doesn't know what he's doing."

"But he's doing it just the same."

"Why has he got it in for me?" Weidler asked savagely.

"He blames you for Matt. Says if you'd put in a good word for Matt, he'd never been hanged. There's no telling Tom otherwise. I've tried for half an hour, but Tom won't listen."

"Then I'll have to try," said Weidler.

"He's got a gun, John."

Weidler shrugged. Bill Leahy came in closer and slipped something into Weidler's pocket. He reached down and felt the cold metal of a revolver.

They had turned out into the street when they spied the man coming toward them. He walked with a rolling step much like a sailor's, but Weidler knew that the roll of the walk was due to too many drinks.

Kincaid had stopped, his legs planted wide. His head was thrust forward, and he raised a hand and pushed his hat back from his forehead. Recognition came to him for he laughed and said: "Well, well, if it ain't Bloody John!"

"Hello, Tom," said Weidler easily. "I'm on my way to Fielding's for a drink. Will you join me?"

"Drink, hell!" exploded Kincaid wrathfully. Then he laughed again. "I won't join you in a drink, but you sure will join Matt in hell!"

He had been holding his right hand at his belt, and he suddenly flung up his arm. Weidler saw moonlight flash on the polished metal of Kincaid's pistol.

"Hold it, you damned fool!" Weidler cried, rushing forward. Kincaid laughed, and his cold eyes looked down the sights of his gun, but his bullet was wide.

Before he could fire again, Weidler was on him. Kincaid was bringing his weapon up again, but Weidler grasped the gun, holding it away from him. Kincaid lunged, grunting, and he drove the hard toe of his boot into Weidler's shin. Weidler released his hold, and, as he wavered on the point of unbalance, Kincaid shoved out his leg, sending Weidler sprawling. He rolled over quickly to find himself staring in the bore of Kincaid's weapon.

Weidler hardly realized his actions. Perhaps it was the instinct of self-preservation that prompted him to act so automatically. For the gun in his hand roared, and, as Kincaid staggered, it roared again. Kincaid made a half turn, and it looked as if he wanted to walk away when he said quite clearly: "Oh my God!" and fell.

They came running, the watching men, and they gathered around the fallen Tom Kincaid. Weidler's friends were about him, but he was heedless to their queries about his welfare. Two words stuck in his mind as he walked away. Two words hurled at him by someone looking down at dead Tom Kincaid.

"Bloody killer!"

A strange, cold loneliness settled down over Weidler. He knew that he'd never forget the double tragedy of this night. The memory of it would ever haunt him, but, looking about him, he saw that Virginia City was quiet now, a natural quiet, and that was consolation enough.

Long Lonesome

That spring Jody and I went up into the Pinnacles, looking for gold. We didn't have any luck at all the first month. Then we ran across some likely looking ground, and after our first washing we decided that this was it.

We built a sluice and went to work, shoveling dirt into it, and washing it, and now and then coming up with some fine placer dust. We didn't have anything rich, and we worked hard for what we got. We figured we were making ten to fifteen dollars apiece a day, and, if we could each take a couple of thousand out of these diggings, we would be satisfied. I had a dream of a ranch of my own, and a stake like that would help me get a start on it. Jody hadn't yet decided what to do with his share, and I suppose it was just as well because dreams have a way of seldom coming true.

It was lonely work. In all the time we were in the Pinnacles, we didn't see another living soul. The Pinnacles are isolated mountains with naked crags and peaks and stands of stunted pines and cedars. The land was not much good for anything, which was the reason no one had settled there. The only people who passed through the Pinnacles and maybe tarried a while were men like Jody and me, men looking for gold or silver.

We had been up there two months when Jody began complaining about headaches. At first they didn't seem to bother him much. He would mention them with a look like they annoyed him and nothing more. Jody had been hurt about six months before when a horse he'd been breaking pitched him, and he bumped his head. He was in bed a while, but then the doctor said he was all right, and Jody sure looked it with his broad shoulders and the rich color of happy living in his face.

The third month we were up there Jody dropped his shovel around noon of a bright day. The polished surface of the blade reflected the sun right into my eyes, and I stopped shoveling. His shoulders were slumped, and he was holding his forehead with both hands, and I could tell that he was suffering.

Sweat was running down my naked back and chest. The sun had burned me as dark as an Indian, but Jody, with his lighter complexion, was more pink than brown. The muscles rippled in his arms and shoulders as he rubbed the palms of his hands hard against his forehead.

The sun was hot this day, and I figured it was this and the hard work that had got Jody. I told him to knock off and go and lie down in the shade and rest. He was in more pain than I had thought because he went without a word of protest.

I finished that day all by myself. Jody didn't come back once to see how I was doing, and this worried me a little. At sundown I put aside the tools, shut off the water, and gathered the gold dust that was in the riffles. I put it carefully in a chamois bag and pulled the top tight. Then I started for the camp, hefting the bag and thinking about Jody.

He was lying very still on his blankets under a pine. I thought he was sleeping, but, when I came up and stood over him, his eyes opened. They stared up at me gravely, not winking at all.

"How do you feel?" I asked.

"All right."

"I'll get supper. You just lie there some more."

He didn't say anything. I felt his eyes follow me as I went over and put on a shirt because it was getting chill now with the sun down and shadows filling the hollows and valleys. I felt his eyes until I got the fire started. When I looked at him again, he seemed to be sleeping.

I made coffee and fried some venison Jody had shot the day before and boiled some beans and made sourdough biscuits. It was dark by the time this was done, and I was just going to call Jody when I saw him come over, carrying his blankets. He spread them close to the fire and sat down with his legs crossed under him.

I sat on a stump on the other side of the fire from him while we ate. Several times I caught him watching me, but, when I glanced at him, he always looked away. He seemed all right now. His eyes were clear, and in the light of the fire his face looked redder than usual. He had bronze curls that kept dropping down across his forehead and a wide mouth that was quick to smile. Jody and me had been pals since we were kids.

When he was through eating, he lay down again with his hands clasped behind the back of his head. He was looking up at the stars.

I washed the plates and cups and pans, and then I went down to check the corral where we kept our horses. They had graze and water and were little bother. I made sure the gate was locked, and then I returned to the fire, thinking now of Ruth.

I sat down on the stump and took out the makin's and rolled a smoke. Jody had turned over on his stomach, and he was lying like that, his chin propped on his fists while he stared across the fire at me. I offered him the Bull Durham, but he shook his head.

He went on staring at me without winking. Something in the way he did this made me uncomfortable. I don't know how long he was like that, just staring at me, his face grave and thoughtful.

Finally, he said: "You aren't getting away with it, Slim."

I frowned. The smoke that I blew out drifted up in front of my face and through this I stared at Jody. His eyes had brightened. There was a sly and cunning look on his features.

He shook his head. "You'll never get away with it," he said again.

I shifted my seat on the stump. "I don't get you," I said.

The corners of his mouth stretched out in a smile that said he didn't believe me. "You get me all right," he murmured. The brightness in his eyes grew almost wicked.

"I don't know what you're talking about."

"You'll never take her from me," he said.

On the moment I didn't understand who he meant. "Who?" I asked.

"Ruth," he cried. "Who else would it be? You've never got over the fact that she married me instead of you."

The taste of tobacco went flat in my mouth. I dropped the cigarette, stamped it out with my boot, and went on staring at the ground. At last I saw how it was. He was all mixed up, but could you tell him anything when he was like this? I didn't try.

"Why don't you say something?" he said after a while. "Why don't you deny it, Slim?"

I searched for words and found some, but they wouldn't do. Nothing would do with him like this. So I sat there, staring at the ground and crying in my heart because he was my best friend.

Jody chuckled, happy and unworried, but somehow the sound of it was eerie and unnatural. "You've always loved her," he said, "and you've never given up the hope that some day she might leave me. Isn't that right, Slim?"

I said nothing.

After a while he chuckled again. His voice was calm; he was very sure of himself. "You haven't got a chance," he said. "If she had loved you more, would she have married me? No, you'll never take her from me. You can try, but you'll never do it."

I raised my eyes and looked at him. He still lay on his belly with his chin propped on his hands, and he chuckled once more when he saw me glance at him. He looked happy and unexcited and not at all angry, and I was glad that this was how he was taking it. Because I could not have reasoned with him.

He chuckled again contentedly. "Ruth loves me. She will love me always. You'll never take her from me."

He rolled over on his back. He covered himself with the blankets, and in a little while he was fast asleep.

I sat there a long time, watching him across the fire. I thought of Ruth, and, remembering her, put an ache in my heart, and all at once I was very lonely. *Ruth,* I said to myself. *What am I going to do with him?*

At last I turned in. I lay awake a long time, unable to drop off. Jody slept soundly. He mumbled once in his sleep, but I could not catch the words. Then he was quiet again, his breathing heavy and measured.

The next morning I awoke with fear and dread in my heart, but Jody was all right. I could tell instantly that he did not remember a thing from the night before. I left it like that. I did not mention it because I hoped it would never happen again.

We worked from sunrise to sunset in the long summer days. The placer dust grew in the chamois bags and with it grew my dream. Jody started talking about setting up in business, although he couldn't decide exactly which kind. They were good and happy days, good and happy because Jody never once remembered.

I was beginning to forget. Now that it lay in the past, it began to seem like something unreal, something you remember from a bad dream which grows less and less bright as time wears on. Jody didn't remember it at all, and that was good.

He didn't have to remember it because it was there in him all the while, although he didn't know it. This day he planted the blade of his shovel deep in the dirt, and then he leaned his forearms on the handle and stood like that, crouched over a little, glaring at me. It was the wildness in his eyes that warned me, and I felt myself go sick and sad inside.

"You think you're smart," he said, and there was a growl in his voice. "You think by not talking about it and pretending it isn't so that you can fool me."

I stuck my shovel upright in the gravel and stood there, breathing a little fast. The walls of my throat kept tightening and jerking. I knew a moment of panic, but it passed.

"Well?" he growled, face darkening. "Why don't you say something? Come on. Talk!"

What was there for me to say?

"That's what I like about it," he went on, his tone dry and acid. "Behind my back. That's the part I really like. But you aren't getting away with it. Ruth loves me too much for you to get away with it."

I knew it was no use, but still I tried. "You've got it all wrong, Jody," I said. "Try to think. It's not at all like that, can't you see?"

"I see, all right," he growled. His lips had grown thin and hard. I had never seen as mean a look in his eyes as they held right then. "I see you sneaking behind my back. Maybe you even figure on keeping all the gold. Is that how you're figuring it? A big pile for you to take Ruth away. Not only my wife but my gold, too."

It was all so hopeless I could have cried. But I just stood there, searching desperately for the words that would make him see the thing as it really was and feeling lost and ill when I found none.

"Sure," he said, straightening and stepping in front of me. "That's why you won't say anything. Because it's true." He grinned, and it was like the white, slavering smile of a puma. "She's mine, Slim. You can try, but you'll never take her from me. She loves me, not you."

I was sweating, but it was not all from the heat. Sweat crawled stickily down my cheeks. A few drops fell from my chin onto my boots.

"Try to remember, Jody," I said. "Can't you remember anything at all?"

"Remember?" he cried. "I remember, all right." He lifted a fist and shook it under my nose. "I remember how you always wanted her, but she married me instead. You pretended it was all right, that it didn't mean anything to you, but deep in your heart you started planning to take her from me someday. My wife and my gold. Why don't you be a man and come out and admit it?"

I tried once more, not expecting anything, but still I tried. "But I'm your friend, Jody. Don't you believe that?

105

Would I do a thing like that if I was your friend?"

"You *were* my friend," he said, scowling. "You're not my friend any more. You want Ruth. That's why you've turned against me. But you'll never have her. Do you hear?"

I couldn't bear to stare at him any more. Not with that dark, hating look on his face. I dropped my eyes, and something filled my throat. He was sick, I told myself, he was hurt from that fall off a horse. He wasn't responsible for anything he said or did when he was like this, and I shouldn't mind him. Least of all, I shouldn't try to reason with him because he just couldn't understand. So I said nothing.

"All right," he said after a while, and he didn't sound so mean. "We understand each other, then. You know I'm on to you, so you act accordingly, Slim. If you keep on with it, then we're through. You hear that? Through!"

He turned back to his shovel and started working again. He worked with a vengeance, shoveling dirt into the sluice like he was a machine that never needed any rest. At last he stopped. He straightened and wiped his forehead with his arm, leaving a smear of dirt. He turned to me and grinned.

"Sure is another hot day, isn't it, Slim?" he said cheerily. His eyes were bright and clear.

I knew it was over, then. He was himself again.

I thought many times of telling him about it now that he was all right, but, if he couldn't remember one way, could he remember the other? And if I could make him remember now that he was all right, would he still remember if another spell got him?

He had no idea at all of anything that had passed, and I did not want to bring it up because then it might lie between us all the time. Maybe he would never have another spell. In that case it was better if he never knew what he had said.

One morning I awoke to find him sitting up in his blankets, watching me out of dark, glowering eyes. Instantly I went cold and sick inside. *Here it is again*, I thought. He kept on staring at me like that, but he didn't say a word.

I started the fire and made breakfast, aware all the while of his eyes, ugly and mean, following every move I made. My heart was running fast. Every beat of it was sharp and loud in my ears. I was anxious and scared and full of sorrow.

I brought him his cup and plate, and he took them, lifting his head to give me a look of pure hate. Then his head dropped, and he ate, never once raising his eyes.

The food was tasteless in my mouth. I could hardly swallow anything, and my appetite was gone. I didn't eat half of what I had dished out for myself. Every now and then I would glance at Jody, but he kept his head down as though eating was all he cared about right now. He cleaned his plate and drained the last of his coffee. Then he threw back his head and sighed with pleasure. He looked at me and winked, happy as a kid.

"That steak and coffee sure hit the spot, Slim," he said. He rose to his feet. "Well, shall we start another day?"

He went with long, swinging strides down to the diggings, and I watched him go. He was all right again, but I could not forget the look in his eyes. It had been as though he would have liked to kill me.

After a while I went down to the diggings, too. Jody was already at work. He lifted his head and threw me a grin, the grin that I'd known since we were kids. I bent over and put my back at him as I swung the pick. I didn't want him to see the tears that stung my eyes.

One night I dreamt that I was in a dark pit, and something was choking me. Steel bands were digging into my throat, and, try as I might, I could not free myself from them. They kept squeezing tighter and tighter until I could hardly draw my breath. I came awake then and found that it was not a dream. The fire was still burning, and in its light I saw Jody's face above me. His eyes were wide and burned with an unreasoning glow, and his lips were drawn all the way back from his teeth, and the snarl had put long, deep wrinkles in his cheeks.

It was his hands about my neck that were choking me.

The first thing I did was to grab his wrists. I yanked and pushed with all my strength, but I could not break his hold. He had his thumbs at the base of my neck, and they kept digging in more and more. A great, warm ball was gathering in my chest, pressing so hard against my lungs that the pain of it seemed to reach all the way up until it seared my eyeballs.

I tried to get a knee under him to ram him in the belly, but he just twisted away from that and squeezed harder on my neck. I smashed a fist up into his face, and he moaned with hurt, but his hold did not slacken. I threw another at him, and he jerked his head to the side, and I just grazed him. By this time everything was getting dim and hazy, and my fist found only empty air.

There were glimpses of a terrible darkness in front of my eyes and streaks of pain. The ache in my chest had spread out all over me, even down to my toes. The realization that I was as good as dead hit me with a stunning suddenness. It filled me with panic and a new burst of strength. In desperation I reached up with both hands and grabbed two fistfuls of Jody's hair. I yanked as hard as I could, and the scream that tore out of his throat was as shrill and savage as that of a cougar. I yanked again, harder, and he screamed once more. One hand left my throat to clutch at my wrist. I yanked a third time.

Now he had both hands about my wrists, and the first welcome breath of air entered my lungs. I yanked again and at the same time rammed a knee up into his groin, and he screamed and groaned all together and went rolling off me. I let go his hair and aimed a blow at his face, but he was skittering away, and I missed.

I scrambled to my feet. He was starting to come up, and I jumped at him and smashed a knee against his jaw, and the force of it lifted him, spun him around, and dropped him on his face. He put his rump to me, started to crawl away on his hands and knees.

I went after him. Everything in me cried out against it, but I had no choice. It was a question of my life or his, and I wanted to live. There was Ruth, and I wanted to live desperately. I leaped up alongside him and smashed him on the back of the neck, and he dropped flat with a moan. He rolled over, drawing up his knees and shielding his face with his arms. I thought I heard him sob, but I wasn't sure.

I threw myself down on him, pinning him to the ground with my knees on his chest. I ripped his arms from his face and smashed him on the jaw. He turned his face away and covered it again. I tried to hit him once more, but he blocked my fist with his arms.

"Slim," he started to groan, not fighting back any more. "What're you doing to me, Slim? What're we scrapping about?"

His voice was plaintive and puzzled. He sounded like a little boy who did not understand what was happening to him, and it dawned on me that the madness had left him as suddenly as it always did. I stopped with my fist poised in the air. I stopped, and a sob racked me, and then I got off him and rose to my feet.

"Slim," he said, lying on the ground and staring up at me out of large, unbelieving eyes. "What have I done to you to make you so mad at me?"

What could I say?

He sat up and began feeling his jaw and working it to see if it was all right. I had to turn my back because I could not bear to look at him any more.

"Won't you tell me what we were fighting about?"

I had to wait while the thing that was filling my throat went away. Then I said: "Nothing, Jody. Nothing at all."

After that I didn't sleep so well any more. Night after night I would come awake with the feel of his hands about my neck, my whole body drenched in cold sweat. I would come awake with a shout and sit bolt upright and glance wildly across the fire to where he lay. And always he would be rolled in his blankets, sleeping peacefully.

I began noticing, when I shaved, that my face was growing haggard and drawn. There were deep, dark wrinkles under my eyes and at the corners of my mouth and a strained look in every line of my face. Jody noticed this, too.

One day he said to me: "What's wrong, Slim?"

I pretended I hadn't heard him.

"What's the matter?" he said again. "Something's eating you. What is it?"

I shrugged and said nothing.

He frowned, thinking hard on something. "You've been like this ever since that fight we had. Why won't you tell me what it was all about?"

Yes, why didn't I tell him? I asked myself. But then I thought: *What good would it do if I told him now only to have him get another spell some time?* That was when he had to understand. But when he was like that, he understood nothing but the strange, twisted thing that gnawed at his brain.

So I lied about it. "I guess I had a nightmare," I said. "I must have jumped you without knowing what I was doing." I looked at him closely. "Do you have any other idea?"

"It's all Greek to me," he said, spreading his hands. Then he clapped me on the back and grinned. "I've forgotten all about it, Slim. It didn't mean anything to me. We're still friends. We'll always be friends. Won't we?"

"Sure," I said. "Sure, Jody."

We were almost through at the diggings. The placer dust was playing out, and we began to talk of quitting and returning to town. I had put my dream away. Ruth and the dream would have to wait. Jody came first.

With what both of us had taken out of these diggings, Jody could go and see a good doctor who could maybe fix him up. I never said anything about this to Jody because I didn't want him to know yet and get upset about it. I decided to wait until we were back in town.

Summer was gone, and fall was at hand when we loaded our things on the pack horses and started out of the Pinnacles, Jody riding his roan and me on my Grulla mare. Jody was happy, and now and then he sang or whistled merrily. He had decided to get himself a saddle shop because he knew leather and could work it well. I didn't tell him the shop had to wait. He had to get well first, and, when that was done, we would take another trip into the Pinnacles, and, if we had the same luck as this first time, we could begin dreaming all over again, Jody of his saddle shop and me of my ranch.

We were still high in the Pinnacles when we camped that first night on the way back. As usual I slept very little. I kept awakening, full of dread, only to hear the soft, peaceful sound of Jody's breathing as he slumbered. My nerves were all on edge. There were times when I felt like pounding my fists against the earth and screaming at the top of my voice. But then I would tell myself that soon it would be over. A few more days and we would be back in town, and I would know again the bliss of a whole night's sleep.

The morning of the second day Jody was very quiet. His silence disturbed me, but every time I turned in the saddle to glance back at him, he would grin amiably and nod at me. We stopped around midday and dismounted and chewed on some jerky while the horses rested and grazed. Jody and I chatted a little, and he appeared perfectly all right except that today he did not seem to be much for talking, so I didn't press him.

That afternoon we started working down a high ridge. I rode in the lead, trailing one pack horse behind me while Jody followed with the other one. We came to a rather steep drop, and I rode down this one first with Jody staying behind above. I slid the Grulla most of the way down on her hind legs, for the talus was very loose and came rattling down in miniature slides. I reined in at the bottom, and, when I glanced up at Jody, the breath froze in my throat. The sun glinted off the barrel of the six-shooter in his hand. I could not see his face too well, but still the snarl was plain enough. He leaned forward in the saddle and thrust his arm out as he aimed the gun down at me.

I dropped the lead rope of the pack horse and jabbed the Grulla hard with the spurs. She jumped ahead just as Jody fired. The slug whistled past my ear, and then the Grulla was running swiftly for some trees just ahead. I heard the crack of another shot, and at the same time the Grulla stumbled, and then she went plunging head-long. As I flew out of the kack, I knew that Jody had killed her.

I landed on my left side and slid a little along the ground. Another slug kicked dirt into my face. I saw a manzanita just ahead, and I scrambled behind this as he fired once more. I crouched behind the bush, drew my .44, and looked out and up to see him sliding the roan down the slope.

At the bottom he whipped and spurred it into a dead run straight for the manzanita. He held the gun out ahead of him, and above the thunder of the roan's hoofs I could hear him shouting.

"Steal my wife and my gold, will you? I'd kill you for that. I'll kill you!"

Between the fear and the sorrow there was room for nothing else inside me. I knew now it was a matter of me or him. The choice was as simple and as brutal as that. *Ruth*, I thought, *it's for you, for you and me. I want you too much to let him kill me.*

Still, I tried not to do it. I aimed at the roan and dropped it with my first shot. Jody kicked free of the stirrups as the roan started to go down, and he came out of the saddle with a leap to land on his feet. He didn't hesitate so much as a second. The instant his boots touched the ground, he came at a lunging run for the manzanita.

I wanted to call to him, but would that have helped? When he was like this, would anything help? Nevertheless, I kept from firing as long as I dared. I crouched there with the .44 cocked in my hand, sweat running down my cheeks and dripping off my chin. I crouched there and watched him come with his face all screwed up with madness and rage.

Only when he stopped and aimed his gun at me, did I fire. His gun went off, but the slug from my .44 had already slammed him back, and his bullet missed. The gun dropped from his hand, and he fell, going down slow and gentle.

I didn't know what was tears and what was sweat as I stood over him, the gun still in my hand. He was breathing hard, his face was gray, and the blood was pumping in an awful, sickening way out of his chest. His eyes were closed, but after a while they fluttered and opened. They were clear and empty of hate and madness, and I could have wept aloud. They looked first at the gun in my hand and then up at my face.

"Why, Slim?" he asked, begging with his eyes for an explanation. "Why did you shoot me?"

My mind drew a blank for words. All I could do was stand there, my heart crying, and watch him die.

Ruth was waiting for me when I got back home. She came into my arms, and I held her hungrily and kissed her. I cried a little, and she could not understand this. Although there were tears in her eyes, too, they were tears of happiness.

So I told her about Jody.

Her face grew empty of color, and horror and pain filled her eyes. She looked up at me and whispered: "But why, Slim, why?"

I searched my mind, and these were the only words I found. "When he was like that, he got all confused," I said sadly. "I guess he just couldn't remember that you had married me. . . ."

Hold-up

Murphy's Cafe was down by the Midland Pacific yards, and it was Mike Conner's custom to stop in at Murphy's before taking the 118 west to Sawtooth. The 118 was scheduled to pull out of Wingate at 3:28 in the morning, so it never surprised Mike Conner to find Murphy's all-night cafe empty whenever he walked in. The surprise this night lay in the fact that someone was there, and it was his own son, Dave. Dave was at the counter, staring down into a cup of coffee when Mike entered.

Murphy was behind his counter. He grinned and pulled out his watch. "Three-thirteen," he said. "Always on time just like one-eighteen, hey, Mike?"

Mike nodded. He had no smile and return quip for Murphy this night. One look at Dave's nettled face and all other knowledge left Mike Conner's mind except the thought that here was a desperate man.

Dave picked up his cup of coffee and started toward a booth along the wall. "I want to talk with you, Mike," he said.

Mike Conner watched his son walk with the rolling stride of one who lives much in the saddle. Dave's face was browned by sun and wind, and there were calluses and rope burns on his hands. He wore a faded blue linen shirt and worn Levi's, and his spurs jingled as he moved. He wore the blue of a conductor.

Mike could feel Murphy staring at him. Without taking his eyes off his son, he said: "The usual, Murph."

116

Dave settled himself in the booth. He didn't look up as his father sat down opposite him. Dave didn't say anything until Murphy had brought Mike his coffee and pie and had gone. Then he raised his eyes and read bitterness all over his son's face.

"It's no go, Mike."

"You try them all? You try the First National again?"

Dave laughed bitterly. "Yeah. I tried them all, though I knew what they'd say before I saw them. It's no go. It's pay up or move out. Looks like your son will have to take up railroading, after all."

Mike Conner didn't say anything. That had been a matter of dissension between them several years ago. Mike had railroading in his blood. His son had once said of Mike that, when he married thirty years ago, he'd probably been hitched with a link and pin. When his boy was eighteen, Mike had talked the yardmaster at Wingate into taking on Dave as switchman in the Midland Pacific yards. But Dave had turned the job down cold. He had no mind to be a railroad man, he said. He wanted to be his own boss, to work for himself. He was going to be a cowman, own his ranch and iron, and run whitefaces along the Midland Pacific right-of-way in the Thirty Mile Hills. And he'd sue Mike Conner and the Midland Pacific if train 118 ever ran over one of those whitefaces.

Mike Conner, who had never denied his motherless son a thing, had shrugged and said: "Sure, Dave. If that's what you want."

So Dave Conner had caught on at the L L ranch for a couple of years to learn the why and way of cows. Then he'd borrowed enough to start out on his own — a run-down spread in the Thirty Mile Hills along the

Midland Pacific right-of-way. But the ranch had never worked out well. . . .

"If there was something I could do," Mike offered now.

Shame and anger laid their red flush across Dave's face. "No, no, Dad. You've done too much already. You've sunk your last cent into the D C. That's what makes it tough. Me and Mady and the kid can get along. I can always get a job, I reckon. But I got to pay you back. . . ."

Mike Conner smiled. He hoped that his face would hide the disappointment in him. "That's all right. You don't have to pay me back."

He knew, as he spoke, that he lied. He was getting old. His years all lay behind him, and he could look forward to very few more. He didn't have many years of railroading left in him, and he'd provided against the day that he'd highball his last train. He had set a little aside, but that was all gone in Dave's ranch.

Mike looked at his son and saw the bright flame of desperate hope in Dave's eyes. He was leaning across the table, his chunky body tense, his hands clenched tightly about the edge until the knuckles showed white. He shot a glance at the counter to see if Murphy was out of earshot, then he said swiftly: "How about it, Mike? Tonight?"

Mike had known the question was coming. He had been expecting it and dreading it. Fearing it with all the fear his heart could possess, for he knew what his answer would be.

Still he said, sudden sweat beading his upper lip: "There must be some other way . . . ?"

"There is no other way, and you know it. We've tried everything. You can't raise anything on an outfit that's been mortgaged two times over."

118

"I dunno, Dave, I dunno. . . ."

"All I'd need is time until this fall. My whitefaces are gonna pay off then. That's all I need. Two more months and from then on the D C's gonna be a going proposition. And we'll pay it back, Mike. We won't use it all. Just enough to keep the interest paid up and keep the First National from foreclosing. Then, when fall comes and I've sold my cows, we'll pay off everything and then pay back what we took."

Mike Conner hauled out his watch. He mumbled: "I gotta get moving."

Dave reached out a hand, stopped his father. "I'm through fooling, Mike. Tonight at nine-ten I'm stopping number one-eighteen at Thirty Mile Tank. Whether you're with me or not. Tonight at nine-ten!"

"It would never work, boy!"

"Can't see why not, if you do your part. No one will suspect you. Just hold your crew down at your end of the train. I'll uncouple the express car, then kick the engine crew out, and run the engine and express car down the track a couple of miles. I'll clean out the car and be away in ten minutes. And no one will suspect either you or me. I'm not *asking* you any more, Mike! I'm *telling* you!"

Mike Conner went away from Murphy's with a sour taste in his mouth and the bitter knowledge that he'd consented to something that had destroyed his peace of mind and would make his remaining years an eternity of hell. He had always been an honest man. He had never betrayed a trust. There was a saying all along the Sawtooth Division of the Midland Pacific, an axiom — "as square as Mike Conner." He'd never been caught short in his accounts. Twelve years back, when crookedness ran rife among the conductors and trainmen of the Sawtooth Division, Mike Conner had been the only conductor to come through the investigation with a clean bill. *A thing like that meant a lot to a man*, Mike Conner thought. A man might never admit it, but it always set a warm glow to burning inside him to know that he had other men's trust.

Somehow the hours of the run over the Sawtooth Division seemed to pass. To Mike the events of that run were nothing more than a kaleidoscopic blur. He punched his tickets and collected his fares and reckoned his accounts. But most of the time he spent in the last seat of the rear coach, staring out the window at the changing landscape about him.

He tried running the matter over in his mind again and knew even before he tried that it was useless. There was no other out. Perhaps if the ranch didn't mean so much to Dave. . . .

He recalled the proud light in the boy's eyes the day he'd made his down payment on the D C and said: "Meet Dave Conner, cowman!"

Yet nothing was worth having unless it was worth fighting for, even unjustly. *But I'm old, old*, thought Mike. *My nest egg's gone. I'm a proud man. I've been my own support since I was twelve years old. And I'll be my own support in my old age. And if I can't do that, I'll kill myself first. I won't accept charity, not even from my own son.*

In Sawtooth he made sure that his advance information had been correct — that train 118 east would be carrying a money shipment for the First National Bank in Wingate. The confirmation left him weak and shaken.

Bud Hayes, his brakeman, must have noticed for he said: "You don't look so good, Mike."

They were in the locker room at Sawtooth. Mike Conner finished buttoning his jacket. "I'm all right, Bud," he said.

"You don't look it. I noticed it this morning, too."

"I'll make it."

"Sure," Bud Hayes grinned. "You just take it easy, Mike. I'll handle your end. You ain't missed a run in ten years. No reason why you should start now."

They walked together down to their train. The engine change had just been made. Bud Hayes cast a look at the high-wheeled Atlantic. "Number three-twenty-four," he said. "She's a fast one. We won't lose time with her on the front end."

They rolled out of Sawtooth at the advertised time. Ordinarily this would have been an easy run for Mike Conner. With hogger Pat Roark at the throttle of engine 324, there would have been no worries on Mike's mind. Nothing short of a wreck would keep Roark from pulling 118 into Wingate on time and maybe two or three minutes ahead of schedule. . . .

118 was flagged at Halbert. Bud Hayes, who had pride in 118's record of holding finely to schedule, started cursing. "Now what?" he growled, stepping out on the platform of the middle coach of the five passenger cars. Mike was at Bud Hayes's shoulder.

The dispatcher at Halbert waved a hand. "Couple of customers for you, Mike."

They swung aboard even before the train had stopped. Bud Hayes waved his arm in the highball signal to Pat Roark, and engine 324 started roaring again. The two passengers had passed on into the middle coach.

"Not more than a minute lost," Hayes said.

Mike said nothing. He went into the coach. The two

121

men had seated themselves. One was tall with dark black hair, a hooked nose, and a black growth of whiskers on his face. The other ran more to chunkiness. *Something like my Dave,* Mike found himself thinking, and cursed the thought that had enslaved his mind. Seemed that nothing could happen to let him forget — even for a moment.

The two men wore cowpunchers' clothing. There was the smell of horses about them, just like Dave.

The tall one said: "How much to Wingate?"

"Three twenty-six," Mike said, and saw the man's brows lift. "It's cheaper when you buy a ticket."

"That damn' agent didn't have any."

"No passenger train ever stops at Halbert except when flagged."

The man counted out both fares.

Mike returned to his seat at the rear of the train. There weren't many passengers out of Sawtooth this night. Only those two at Halbert and three who had gotten on at Bender's Crossing. So Mike Conner had a lot of time with his thoughts.

He had nothing to do but sit in his seat and stare out the window. He watched the shuttering of trees and grass and hills and an occasional barbed-wire fence pass his gaze, and the low-hung exhaust of the locomotive that the wind swept back, low to the ground. Vaguely he heard the clacking of the wheels against the rail joints, felt the sway of the coach. His mind was filled with the bright desperation he had seen in Dave's eyes.

It was a crazy scheme. Mike hadn't much faith that it would work, but he could think of nothing better, so he'd said all right. Dave's plan was quite simple. 118 east always stopped in the Thirty Mile Hills at the Thirty

Mile Tank to take on water. It was a forlorn location with only the high red wooden tank and a siding and three loading pens. It was Dave's plan to conceal himself along the embankment. When the locomotive halted at the tank, Dave would break the coupling between the express car and the remaining cars of the train. It would take but a minute to rush into the cab of the engine, force the hogger and fireman out, then run the engine and express car down the track a couple of miles where Dave would have his getaway horse concealed.

He could work in leisure then. The express clerk might provide some opposition, but Dave reckoned he could take care of that. He'd dynamite the car open if necessary. All he'd asked Mike to do was to find some excuse to keep Bud Hayes down at the end of the train long enough for Dave to get away with the engine and express car. It was Bud Hayes's custom to walk along the stopped train toward the engine, inspecting journals and couplings. Dave didn't want to have trouble with hot-headed Bud Hayes. It was up to Mike to keep Hayes occupied until it was too late to intervene.

At Mike's back the sun had set. The air was filled with the first shadows of night, and, when he looked to the east, he saw the first star. He glanced at his watch — 9:04. Another six minutes and they would be at the Thirty Mile Tank. At the rate Pat Roark was rolling the train along, they'd not be late.

Mike Conner went through his kit bag and took out the short-barreled Smith & Wesson .38 he always carried there. He slipped the weapon into his pocket.

Bud Hayes came down the aisle, turning on the lamps. He stood looking down at Mike. The train was beginning to slow down as Pat Roark applied the air.

"I'm gonna have to check the journals on the smoker," Hayes said.

"They're all right," Mike said. "You can let them go. This car doesn't ride so good. We should look at this one first."

Bud Hayes had picked up his lantern. "Don't seem nothing wrong to me," he said. "But we'll look anyhow."

They stepped out on the rear platform as the train slowed to a crawl and then stopped. They could hear the clank of the engine's air pump in the stillness of the night. Bud Hayes skipped down the steps.

Mike Conner followed. He was hardly aware of what he was doing. His brain was all in a whirl, unable to register anything definitely. He knew that he should keep Bud Hayes down here at the end of the train for several minutes. But Mike's throat was dry, and, even if he could have spoken, he wouldn't have known what to say. All he could do was follow Bud Hayes as he walked along the train, holding his lantern up against the trucks — just follow Bud Hayes and hang on tightly to the gun in his pocket.

Hayes had just lifted from examining the front truck of the last coach when he cursed. "What the hell? Hey, Mike! Look . . . up there!"

Mike's eyes raised, and he saw what he'd expected to see. A man dressed in cowpuncher's clothing and with a mask across his features was running toward the engine. Though the night was not yet full, the shadows were nevertheless thick, and Mike knew he recognized that man. His son, Dave! Mike recognized that chunky build and the way Dave always ran with a rolling swing of his shoulders.

But there was something wrong! Dave in his desperate

excitement had got mixed up. He had said that he'd board the engine from the left-hand side. He had asked Mike to make sure that Bud Hayes dismounted on the right-hand side so that he could not spot Dave. He'd made his mistake right at the outset. Bud Hayes was swinging his lantern and yelling: "Hey, you!"

Mike Conner jerked his short-barreled .38 from his pocket. He had the hammer thumbed all the way back, but he could not press the trigger. That masked man up there was Dave!

But Dave wasn't holding his fire. His gun flared twice, and the bullets screamed past Mike's head. Sudden anguished thoughts tortured his mind. *Has my boy gone crazy mad? Doesn't he know it's me? The light is none too good, but I recognize him. Why doesn't he recognize me?*

He held his fire. The next bullet took him — took him in the left leg. Through the fleshy part of his thigh, he reckoned, after the shock passed and the pain began. Dave, his son, had put that bullet there. . . .

"Shoot, man," Bud Hayes was moaning. "What you waiting for, Mike?"

The thought kept running through Mike's mind — *Dave has gone crazy mad. He's not shooting at me just to make it look good. He's trying to kill me! He doesn't know what he's doing any more. He'd be better off dead than turn into a crazy mad outlaw. . . .*

Mike's .38 was still leveled with the hammer at full cock. He looked down the sights now, at the masked man's chunky body. The bandit's gun flamed again, and something tugged at Mike's cap brim. He uttered a brief snatch of prayer. *If only I won't hit a vital spot . . . !*

He pressed the trigger. The gun bucked back against

his palm. Blood had started running down his leg, warm, sticky. He saw the masked man stiffen and rise to tiptoes. He fell stiffly like a man dead on his feet.

Mike had no mind for the pain in his leg. He ran limping, stumbling. Passengers were piling out of the coaches now, and it seemed that somewhere off on the other side of the train there was shooting.

He could see the man at his feet. The way he lay on his face, with his arm flung out and the slackness in his body, told Mike he couldn't have any life left in him. Mike was on his knees. The tears were hot and wet on his cheeks.

"Dave!" he sobbed.

Pat Roark was there. He looked at Mike Conner in amazement and then reached down and turned the dead man over. Roark pulled off the mask.

The world began anew then for Mike Conner. The tears still came, but he was laughing. Someone had an arm around him and was helping him to his feet. Then Dave's voice was saying: "Mike! Mike! What's come over you, Pop?"

And when 118 east was under way again and Mike and Dave were alone in the last coach, Dave told it all: "I couldn't go through with it, Mike. I realized that nothing is worth having, unless it's rightly yours. I didn't want the D C, knowing that stolen money had made it mine . . . I'd rather starve and see Mady and the kid starve than live on stolen money. So I didn't go through with it. But someone else had ideas. I saw him jump off the smoker. He ran to uncouple the express car, just as I'd planned it. I called him, and he started shooting. I got him, Pop . . . just like you got his pal on the other side."

Mike nodded. "They got on at Halbert. That chunky

126

one looked a lot like you . . . in the dark."

"I know, Mike," Dave said, squeezing his father's hand. "I know. And, say! There was a U. S. Marshal on the train. He says those two are wanted for a couple of train robberies. There's a reward on them . . . enough to pay off the notes on the D C with my share. And your share gives you your nest egg again, Dad."

Mike Conner hauled out his watch.

"We'll be a couple minutes late into Wingate," he said gruffly.

127

Whitewater Challenge

Out here the river was quiet, moving along with a placid languidness, but fear was beginning to stir inside Joe Clark. He could feel it first in the cold, small trembling in his thighs. He looked across the water to the pond of the Clark Lumber Company, his company, and he kept the prow of the green boat pointed so that he would not have to see the rapids. But the noise of them was there in his ears, and his arms wanted to speed the boat toward the shore. He closed his eyes to it a moment, forcing his arms to keep the oars still. He could feel the boat drifting slowly and gently along. Finally some of the fear died. He opened his eyes again, keeping them lifted high on the green, timbered slopes, rearing toward the sky. Trying not to think about it, he turned the prow of the boat downriver again.

The craft moved whisperingly through the water. Clark listened to the beating of his heart and found it calm and steady. The trembling was gone from his thighs. A moment of wild, reckless hope possessed him. Then the sound of the rapids hit his ears with a roaring, shattering ugliness.

His legs were suddenly weak again. His arms did not want to obey him. The prow of the boat swerved ever so slightly toward the shore, and a strangled sob came out of his throat. He fought against the fear as he'd fought countless times. The rapids hurled their harsh roar at him. His mind was filled with the surging, tossing waters, the rearing, jagged rocks. He was biting down on his lower lip until it bled.

The trembling was in his arms now, an enervating weakness. Panic filled his throat. The rapids roared louder, closer. A strident shout tore out of Clark. He roared back at the rapids. He flung epithets at them. He railed at them. And then, with the hot tears running down his face and that dead limpness all through him, he turned the boat and headed for shore.

Shame hit him quickly, and he threw a wild glance at the mill. Even if no one had seen, they still must know, for he no longer dared to venture out upon a log even in the still waters of the pond. Hopeless despondency descended on him again. It was always like this. No matter how hard or how often he tried, it always turned out like this. He'd always come in off the river like a whipped dog.

He grounded the boat on the shore beyond the water's reach and threw one last look downriver. The whiteness of the dashing water in the rapids gleamed malevolently in the sun, and its sound was a mocking whisper.

How long he stood staring, Clark did not know. The first awareness he had of the other was the crunching of his shoes on gravel. Clark turned guiltily, feeling the warmth come to his face.

"Hello, Joe," the man said, coming to a stop beside Clark. "Lovely day, isn't it?"

"Howdy, Doc."

They were of a size and age, this Dr. McKenzie and Joe Clark. Both were in their early thirties, both stood six feet tall. Even their clothing seemed identical — the bright plaid shirts, the stag trousers tucked into high-topped, cleat-bottomed shoes. They had both been born in this Kicking Horse River country. Somehow McKenzie had never been able to get away from its ways, even though he was a doctor.

Clark's shame was eating away at him. "You saw, Mac?" he asked.

McKenzie sighed, clapped an arm about Clark's shoulders. "Don't give up hope, Joe. It'll straighten itself out. You've got to give it time."

"But it's a year now, Mac," cried Clark. "I don't know how many times I've tried it. I'm all right until I get out there, and I start hearing them. Then I turn to jelly all over, and before I know it I'm running like a scared kid for shore."

McKenzie was looking downriver. His lean, rather dour face seemed pinched with gentle understanding. "Those rapids are a terrifying thing. Not many men have been able to shoot them. No one ever did it alone. You shouldn't have tried it. You clung to those boulders for almost twenty-four hours before you were rescued, Joe. A thing like that can take the nerve out of any man. You've got to give a memory like that time to die."

The old buckboard came clattering across the wooden bridge and into town. Clark and McKenzie paused in the doorway of the doctor's office to watch the wagon's almost frenzied progress down the street.

McKenzie sighed. "Here I go again."

A cold reserve had hit Clark as he recognized the wagon. It was always like this when he saw Rob Giles. Not that Clark had anything against the man, but Giles was married to Jane Ainsworth, and Clark had had ideas along those lines once. He had stopped brooding about it. It was just one of those things. Still, whenever he saw Rob Giles or Jane the old, faint regret came back to

Clark. He could not help that.

He couldn't help thinking, too, that it was this thing that had prompted his mad try at shooting the rapids. For several months after Jane's marriage, Clark had not cared for much. He lived constantly with a wild reck-lessness, and it was in just such a rash mood that he had tried to shoot the rapids.

Clark stood there, watching as Giles got out of his wagon. Giles was a thick-shouldered fellow of medium height. He was bare-headed, and his thick, black curls spilled down over his forehead. His face was pinched and strained.

He didn't seem to see Clark. He said: "You've got to come, Doc. It's Jane."

Clark felt a sudden, cold tightening about his heart. Just the brief words and the pain was back again.

McKenzie laid a hand on Giles's shoulder. "Come inside, Rob. You can tell me while I get my bag."

Then they were gone, and Clark was outside alone, feeling the warmth of the sun on his bared arms and the flicking of the cool breeze against his face. He wanted to go inside, but he didn't. Jane Ainsworth was Rob Giles's wife now.

He could hear the hum of their voices inside the office. Giles's tones urgently insistent, McKenzie's soothingly calm. Finally the two of them came out the door again.

Giles ran instantly to the buckboard, but McKenzie stopped beside Clark, staring pensively down the street to where the broad blue band of the river showed. Giles's voice was urgent: "Come on, Doc. We haven't all day. It's a five-hour drive."

"I know, Rob," McKenzie murmured, his eyes still on the river. "If only there was a faster way. . . ."

"Faster?" cried Giles. He flung out an arm, indicating the jagged, mountainous crests all about. "You know there's no other way through the mountains. I pounded this buckboard to get here, and I'll pound it to get back. Faster? How else are you going to get there? Shoot the rapids?"

The coldness gathered about Clark's heart. He could feel McKenzie's eyes on him. Then the doctor's voice came, soft and worried: "I don't like the symptoms, Joe. They can develop into something pretty serious if there is too great a delay. Rob lives right on the river. I could make it in about an hour that way."

"You can't do it alone," Clark said.

"I've got to chance it," said McKenzie. "If it saves her life, it will be worth it."

Giles had left the wagon. He came up to McKenzie. "Aren't you comin, Doc?" he asked, eyes wild. "She's awfully sick, I tell you. She's there alone. We've got to get back."

"Your way is no way, Rob," said McKenzie with a sudden determination. "I'm shooting the rapids."

"Shooting the rapids!" exclaimed Giles incredulously. His fingers reached out, clawed at McKenzie's arm. "I know it's the shortest and quickest way through the gorge. But are you sure you'll make it? Jane's life depends on you, Doc. What if you don't get through?"

"That'll be my hard luck. As for Jane, I'll give you medicine and instructions. If I don't get through, you'll have to do the best you can. You take the road around, and, if I'm not there, you can go ahead on your own. Come inside, and I'll fix you up."

When they were gone, Clark stood with a dull fear flowing sickeningly through him. He felt the old hurt, the worry for Jane. He could not get that out of his head. The loss of her was very real to him now, filling him with a poignancy that he'd never experienced before in his rough-and-tumble life.

As McKenzie and Giles came out again, Clark knew what he had to do. He had known it all along.

Giles rushed to the wagon and hurried off up the street. McKenzie said: "How about giving me a hand, Joe? I want to pack my stuff good so it won't get wet in case the boat capsizes. We can pack it in waterproof canvas."

Clark reached out a hand, deterring McKenzie. There was a harshness in Clark's voice, and he could feel the blood pounding in his temple.

"You can't make it alone, Mac. I'm coming with you."

A slow smile crossed McKenzie's face. "I knew you would," he said.

Clark kept telling himself that it was all in his head. There was nothing tangible to his fear. He had just let his mind run away with him, conjuring up all that cold, unreasoning terror. He had only to confirm his mind determinedly against it, and he would be all right. He told himself that he had gone about it in the wrong way. He shouldn't have ventured out on the water alone. He should have got McKenzie to go out on the river with him before.

There was no trembling in Clark's legs, none of that queasy weakness in his wrists and fingers as they got in the green boat and pushed away from the shore. Perhaps it was the cool competence of McKenzie in the rear of the boat that made it like this. Clark felt suddenly he could almost smile.

In the prow of the boat he dipped his paddle in the

water with a new, refreshing confidence. Throwing up his head, he glanced off at the shore, seeing the outlines of his mill beyond the pond and the russet gleam of the logs riding the waters close to the shore. Perched on those logs were the figures of three men, watching. *Let them watch*, Clark said to himself. *This is one time I'm not coming back like a whipped pup.*

Now the river quickened. The boat was caught up in the current, sweeping along effortlessly. It no longer was a matter of using the paddles to propel the boat but only to guide it. The roar of the rapids became thunderously loud. Whitecaps rode the waters, and vicious swirls roiled the river. The harsh slapping of the tossed waters against the jutting jags of rock beat at his mind. Spray whipped back against his face, leaving glistening drops on his cheeks.

There, the trembling was in his thighs. He tried denying it. It just wouldn't be so, not after the way he'd felt moments ago, not after that confidence he'd had. The trembling was in his mind. There was nothing wrong with his legs. He gritted his teeth and stared straight ahead, challenging with his eyes the white, foaming river. The black hulk of a huge boulder loomed suddenly ahead, and Clark dug in his paddle, swerving the boat around it.

Behind him he could feel the sure hand of McKenzie. McKenzie was doing most of the work, and sudden shame struck Clark. The truth was searingly evident to him now. That weakness in his legs was no fear-filled conjuring of his mind. The weakness lay now, too, in his arms, in his shoulders, in his whole body. The paddle was practically useless in his hands. It was all up to McKenzie.

Clark tried to swallow, but the effort was too much for his fear-clogged throat. The roaring of the rapids pervaded all his consciousness. It brought back all the old terrifying recollections — the mad, helpless tossing on the raging waters, the sudden looming of the rocky crag, the frantic paddling, the crashing impact that smashed the boat to shards. Then the hellish struggle with the hungry waters until he'd dragged his battered, exhausted body atop a rock in the middle of the river.

He'd crouched there, waiting, through the long hours of the night, listening to the voice of the rapids, the clothes sticking wetly to his chilled body. Finally the next day they had found him. From the high walls of the gorge they had thrown ropes down to him until he had caught one, and with that they had lifted him to safety.

Clark realized that his eyes were closed. Shamed, he opened them to the cold, stinging spray of the rapids. He tried getting the paddle going again, but his weakness wouldn't let him.

The walls of the gorge hulked ahead. Here the crashing of the rapids was its loudest, the rushing of the river its swiftest. Except at its zenith the sun never touched the river here. A dismal gloom prevailed the rest of the time. Clark saw that shadowy nebulousness reaching out to him above the white, angry tossing of the river, and the fear hit him. He cowered in the boat. He covered his eyes with his arms. The trembling possessed all his body like an ague. Fear was so great as to rise above all shame.

He threw a wild glance back at McKenzie. "All right," Clark shouted hoarsely above the roaring of the waters. "So I'm yellow! You knew it was going to be like this.

135

Why did you take me with you? What's going to happen to Jane when we don't get through? Damn you, Mac, why didn't you leave me behind?"

If McKenzie heard above the roar of the river, he gave no indication. The tight lines of his face remained unshaken. He paddled grimly with swift, skilled strokes.

"Answer me, Mac," Clark screamed in frenzy. "What's going to happen to Jane?"

McKenzie remained silent. His eyes kept darting about, sizing up each new menace that presented itself. His sure, firm hands guided the boat.

Clark covered his face again.

The gloom of the gorge had settled down over them. Clark felt the boat shudder, turn violently around. McKenzie had lost control. Frantically, Clark threw up his head. The boat rode up a high swell and down, turning around once more, almost capsizing.

"Jane," said Clark through his teeth. A sudden anger possessed him. He raised a fist and shook it at the raging waters. "I'll get through to her," he snarled. "Do your damnedest. I'll get through to her!"

It was like a fantastic dream. For a few frantic minutes he knew only the wild surging of his anger, the strength in his arms. He screamed at the rapids while he dug furiously with his paddle. Behind him he could feel the firmness of McKenzie's hands again. The boat scraped against a boulder. With effort, Clark straightened the boat and kept it like that.

His clothes were soaked with spray and sweat. Sudden sunlight hit him, and the intensity of the rapids began to fade. Some of its anger was gone. They were out of the gorge.

There were more tossing spots, more jagged, reaching

rocks, more thunderous roaring about him. Clark laughed in sudden exhilaration. A disdain entered him, a scathing scorn for the threat of the rapids. The fear was gone. The queasiness had vanished from his legs and arms. His strokes with the paddle were sure and strong.

Turning, he threw a glance back at McKenzie. The doctor flashed a sudden, warm smile, and Clark laughed jubilantly. Facing ahead again, he looked down the river to where the waters quieted, flowing their gentle, placid way.

The convolutions lessened, became nothing. The boat swept quietly through the water. Ahead, to the right, was the clearing and the cabin Rob Giles had built on the shore. . . .

Fever flushed Jane's cheeks and a glaze lay film-like over her brown eyes. But recognition showed in them.

"Joe," she whispered tiredly.

Words choked in Joe Clark's throat. It wasn't so much the old feeling for her. That was well left in the past. It was a new gratefulness that lived in him now.

"Hush, Jane," he said gently.

"Where's Rob?" she asked. "Didn't he come with you?"

McKenzie looked up from reading her pulse. "Rob is on his way, Jane. He took the road back. Joe and I shot the rapids." He laid a quiet glance on Clark. "She mustn't be excited, Joe. Wait outside."

Clark could hear the river calling to him, the faintly harsh crashing of the rapids. His feet took him to the river's edge. A long time he stood there, looking up to where the water surged and boiled and bellowed its angry way.

Finally the door opened, and McKenzie came outside, wiping his brow with the sleeve of his shirt. He spotted Clark and came over to him.

"How is she, Mac?"

McKenzie smiled. "She'll be all right. She's sleeping now."

The thing had just begun gnawing at Clark's mind. "Was she really as sick as you said she was?"

"Why do you ask?"

Clark was sure now. "It really wasn't necessary to shoot the rapids, was it, Mac? You could have gone back with Rob and still have had plenty of time. Isn't that right?"

McKenzie laughed again. "You had to be cured, too, didn't you, Joe?"

The Hired Man

Pa found him one morning, sleeping in the haymow, when he went to milk the cows. It was not the first time someone had taken shelter in our barn overnight. This was during the 'Thirties, the time of the Depression when many men were on the bum throughout the land, and now and then one of them would stop at our farm for a handout or, if it was after dark, go to sleep in the barn, and Pa would find them there in the morning. He would always send them on to the house, and Iris would fix them a meal and some sandwiches to take with them when they left.

And that is how Evans came to us.

I was in the house eating breakfast when he rapped on the door. Iris opened it and then grew red as she stood there, staring at him and him staring back at her with a smile on his mouth. He went on staring at Iris until she stepped back and invited him inside.

He told her his name, and she told him hers. I noticed how his eyes followed her as she moved about the kitchen. A couple of times she caught him watching her, and she got red all over again and real nervous. This didn't seem to bother Evans at all. The smile grew on his mouth until two long dimples showed in his cheeks.

He asked me who I was, but I wouldn't tell him. So Iris said I was her stepson. Evans kind of nodded as if that meant something to him. He tried to get me to talk, but I didn't like him. I didn't know why. Of all the tramps who had ever stopped at our farm, I liked Evans least of all.

I got up to go.

Iris said: "Tommy. You haven't finished breakfast."

"I ain't hungry no more," I said.

"Well, finish your milk at least."

"I'm full."

"You know you should drink more milk. Tommy! Come back here! I'll tell your father."

"Go on and tell him," I sassed back, running out the door.

I heard Evans chuckle and then Iris say something in a mad voice. But I didn't care. I was out of the house by then and that was all that mattered.

It was spring. The snow was all melted except for a few spots in the woods where the sun couldn't get at it. The grass was turning green, and the plowed fields were drying out. Pa had said he might start picking rocks, and I knew he was going to when I saw the horses in the barn.

I never liked picking rocks, but it had to be done before the fields could be cultivated and seeded. So I was happy because, after the rocks had been hauled away, Pa would sometimes let me ride on the drag of the disk with him and teach me how to drive and handle the machines though he said they were still a little too much for an eleven-year-old kid to handle by himself.

I went in the barn to say hello to him. He was busy milking away, the sound of it a steady swishing in the foaming milk pail, and he showed me that special smile he'd had for me since my real ma — not Iris — had died. He squirted a stream of milk that hit me in the face, and he laughed as I hollered in surprise and went running into the horse barn.

I climbed up on the manger and petted King and Queen, our team. They nuzzled me with their soft noses, and Queen nipped playfully at my arm. Pa said she was a mean one, but she was like a pet with me.

After I got tired of playing with the horses, I went outside. There was a crow on a fence post, and I put a rock in my slingshot and let fly at him. He took off, flapping his big black wings, and I tried another shot. Though I was pretty good with a slingshot, I never was able to get close enough to hit a crow.

Pa called me then. He was done milking and was going to let the cows out. It was my job to chase them to the pasture. When I got back from that, he was in the barn, harnessing the team, and he had Evans with him.

"I don't know how good a hand I'll make, Mister Dietrich," Evans was saying. "I've never worked on a dairy farm before. I picked fruit in California and Oregon last fall. All I want is a place to sleep and three meals a day for a while."

"I don't know," Pa said, "if I can afford to keep you on after spring planting, Evans. I just can't afford wages."

"No need to pay me. Just three squares a day and a place to bunk."

"Okay," Pa said.

Evans noticed me then. "Hello, there," he said to me. "Find your tongue yet?"

I turned and ran from the barn. I heard Pa say something about me being shy, and Evans laughed. I went and climbed up on the wagon and sat there, wondering why Pa had to go and hire Evans. Couldn't he have found someone else, anyone else? Just so it wasn't Evans.

Pa led the horses out of the barn and then showed Evans how to team them and hitch them to the stone-boat. They were all set to take off for the fields when Pa noticed me.

"Aren't you coming, Tom?" he called.

I didn't answer.

"Tom," Pa's voice had changed. When he spoke like that, he meant what he said. "You come here this minute. Mind me, now."

I climbed down real slow from the wagon, walked over, and got on the stoneboat. When it started with a jerk, Evans was caught by surprise and went stumbling off. But he just laughed and jumped back on.

"First time I ever rode one of these," he said, and Pa laughed with him and explained how to brace himself when the horses started.

Evans dropped a hand on my shoulder, but I shrugged it off. Pa handed me the lines then and let me drive, and, though this was what I liked best of all, it didn't thrill me this time. . . .

That evening, after supper, Pa took me for a walk over the farm. This was the time he liked best, when the air was soft and warm, and there was the rich smell of growing grass and stirred-up soil.

He put an arm around my shoulders as we walked along. "What's wrong, Tom?"

I didn't answer.

His grip tightened a bit. "How come you acted the way you did today?"

"I don't like Evans," I blurted out.

He chuckled. "Why?"

"I don't know. I just don't like him."

He sighed. "Your ma told me you sassed her this

142

morning. And in front of Evans."

"She ain't my ma."

His grip tightened hard for a moment, then eased. "She's my wife, Tom. I know she'll never replace my Laura, and I don't expect her to. That's something you've got to accept, too. She's young and not too bright and kind of foolish at times, not the steady woman your ma was."

"What did you marry her for then?"

He sighed again. "A man sometimes has to have a woman with him. His life isn't complete if he hasn't. There's a loneliness, a. . . ." He ruffled my hair. "When you're older, you'll understand. And . . . you need a woman to look after you."

"I don't," I said fiercely. "Me and you were doing all right after ma died. Iris didn't have to come."

He laughed a little sadly. "Don't you remember all the pork and beans we ate, the meat I burned? Iris isn't much of a cook, but she's better than I am."

"I never complained about what you fixed to eat."

"I know you didn't, but it wasn't good for you." His hand dropped and squeezed my shoulder. "You've got to learn to like Iris because she's going to be around a long time."

"Well, I'm not going to learn to like Evans."

He laughed.

"Will he be around long, too?" I asked.

"I don't think so. His kind have itchy feet. He'll move on as soon as spring planting's over."

But Evans didn't move on. And no matter how hard I tried, I could not make up to Evans. Not that he did anything to me. He tried to get me to play games with him. He made a dandy kite for me, but it was no use.

There were too many outsiders around now. First Iris, then Evans. I longed for the old days when there had been just my pa and my ma and me.

I heard Pa and Iris talking about Evans once. Pa said Evans was green, that he had a lot to learn about farming, but he was a willing worker. For that reason Pa let him stay on. Evans didn't want any money. With haying season coming on Pa would need a hired hand worse than ever.

Iris liked Evans. When they were in the house together, and Pa was gone doing something, and they thought I wasn't around to hear, they'd talk and whisper and laugh. Iris especially would laugh in a way she never did when talking with Pa. Since Evans had come, she'd taken to wearing nice clothes all the time and to fixing her hair and sometimes putting on rouge and powder even if she wasn't going in to town.

Pa liked Evans, too, and that always made me mad. I heard Pa say once that Evans was a smart man, that, if it wasn't for the Depression, Evans would be sitting pretty. Pa began to take Evans fishing with him in the evenings on the small lake that bordered our south forty. I went along a couple of times, but, because Evans was there, I didn't enjoy myself, though I loved to fish.

I thought that summer would never come. I wanted the grass to grow real fast so it would be ready for mowing and drying and storing in the barn because maybe then, when haying was over, Evans would move on.

It was the middle of June when it happened. The timothy was up to my waist, and the clover had the rich, thick smell, but Pa never started to cut hay until the first of July. Spring came late to northern Wisconsin

GET YOUR 4 FREE* BOOKS NOW— A VALUE BETWEEN $16 AND $20

Mail the Free* Book Certificate Today!

FREE* BOOKS CERTIFICATE!

YES! I want to subscribe to the Leisure Western Book Club. Please send me my 4 FREE* BOOKS. Then, each month, I'll receive the four newest Leisure Western Selections to preview FREE* for 10 days. If I decide to keep them, I will pay the Special Member's Only discounted price of just $3.36 each, a total of $13.44 ($14.50 US in Canada). This saves me between $3 and $6 off the bookstore price. There are no shipping, handling or other charges.* There is no minimum number of books I must buy and I may cancel the program at any time. In any case, the 4 FREE* BOOKS are mine to keep—at a value of between $17 and $20!

*In Canada, add $5.00 Canadian shipping and handling per order for first shipment. For all subsequent shipments to Canada the cost of membership in the Book Club is $14.50 US, which includes $7.50 shipping and handling per month. All payments must be made in US currency.

Name _____

Address _____

City _____ State _____ Country _____

Zip _____ Telephone _____

Tear here and mail your FREE* book card today!

Get Four Books Totally FREE* – A Value between $16 and $20

Tear here and mail your FREE* book card today!

PLEASE RUSH
MY FOUR FREE*
BOOKS TO ME
RIGHT AWAY!

LeisureWestern Book Club
P.O. Box 6613
Edison, NJ 08818-6613

where we lived and so did summer. Though haying was a couple of weeks away, Pa started getting the machinery in shape, replacing the nicked and broken knives on the sickle and seeing that the rake and hay loader were in good shape.

I'll never forget that day. It was hot and muggy, and the sun seemed to burn wherever it touched your skin, and you had to sweat even when you were sitting still. Pa and Evans were repairing the hayrack, and I snuck away and went through the pasture and on down to the lake where I stripped off my clothes and went swimming.

The water was nice and warm, and it sure was much more comfortable in the lake than sweating in the sun. Thunderclouds began to pile up to the south, and I figured by nightfall we would have a storm. Time went by real fast, and all at once I heard voices and recognized one of them was Pa's.

I just barely made it out of the water, grabbed my clothes, and ducked behind some bushes before Pa and Evans came into sight. I thought that Pa might be looking for me because I had snuck away and so I crouched there naked behind the bushes with my teeth chattering from the sudden change out of the warm water into the cool shade of the bushes. But Pa wasn't looking for me. Him and Evans were going fishing.

They got into the boat and rowed out on the lake. I remember that my real ma had never liked the idea of Pa going fishing in a boat because he couldn't swim. I watched them a while, waiting to dry, and then pulled on my clothes even though I was still damp. I was ready to steal back to the farm when I heard a cry, faint and frightened, out on the lake.

When I looked, the boat was upside down with Evans

145

hanging on to it. He just seemed to be waiting. There was no sign of my Pa. No sign at all. . . .

I ran all the way back and hid up in the hay barn. At times I cried, the tears running hot and stinging down my cheeks. Then all at once I would grow cold and start to shiver and think that now I was all alone. Even my pa was gone. Only Iris remained — and Evans.

I heard him when he returned from the lake, breathing hard as he passed close to the barn like he'd been running. I crawled down the ladder and snuck around to see what he would tell Iris. I knew he had told her when she screamed.

Evans tried calming her. He raised his voice and shouted at her, and then there was a sound like a slap, and Iris quit howling. After a while she came out the door and started calling me. My legs didn't want to move. I wished I could run, but I didn't know where. Evans was standing there, watching me, and I knew, if I tried to run, his long legs would catch me sure. So all I could do was go to Iris.

She put her arms around me. "Oh, you poor little lamb," she sobbed. "Oh, Tommy, Tommy, how am I going to tell you? Oh, my little lamb."

I looked up into Evans's eyes, and it was like looking into those of the devil. If he knew I'd seen what had happened out on the lake, if he guessed — I shuddered. Iris held me tighter.

"Do you know? Did you hear when we were talking?"
I nodded.

Evans was watching me real close. "Why doesn't he cry?" he asked Iris. Then to me: "Don't you know your pa is dead?"

I nodded again.

Iris said: "Hush, now, Lloyd. Don't you see the poor lamb's in shock? He'll cry later on. You better go and report this to the sheriff."

I could hardly wait for the sheriff to get there. He would look after me; he would see that no harm came to me. He would take Evans and lock him up in a deep, dark hole and never let him out. But all the sheriff did was listen to Evans.

Evans told how the boat got upset when Pa stood up to change seats and Evans went flying out into the water, and, when he came up and looked around, he couldn't see Pa anywhere. So he kept diving and swimming around, looking for Pa, but couldn't find him and swam to shore and ran to report the accident.

I opened my mouth to say it wasn't so, that Evans hadn't dived or swam or looked for Pa at all, but had hung onto the boat all the while. But the sheriff was nodding like he had believed Evans, and then I caught Evans watching me with that hard, cruel look I'd seen in his eyes earlier. So I shut my mouth, but the sheriff had seen I'd wanted to talk.

"Yes, son?" he asked in a soft, gentle voice so much like Pa's I could have cried. "Did you want to say something?"

I looked at Evans. He was watching me, but he was smiling now, though not with his eyes. "Go ahead, Tommy. If you want to ask the sheriff something, go right ahead. He won't bite you." Then, chuckling, to the sheriff: "He's very shy. You can't get a word out of him when there's strangers around."

I'd never seen a sheriff before. I thought he'd be a big man, even bigger than Evans, but this sheriff was small and old with a little, round belly, and he didn't even have a gun. Evans could squash him with one blow of his big fists.

"Go on, Tommy," Evans said, smiling but watching me with those devil's eyes, "speak up. You were going to say something, weren't you?"

I knew the sheriff wouldn't believe me. Iris wouldn't, either. She believed only what Evans told her. Evans never took his eyes off me. I knew I had to say something to keep him from guessing that I had seen what happened out on the lake.

"Is . . . is my Pa really dead?"

The sheriff looked at Evans and at Iris, and then cleared his throat. "I'm afraid so, son." Then to Iris: "Are you caring for the lad?"

"I should say so. After all, Sam Dietrich was my husband. I've always been like another mother to you, haven't I, Tommy?"

She put her arms around me and started to cry again. The sheriff cleared his throat once more and looked uncomfortable.

Evans said: "He'll be in good hands, sheriff. I've never seen a finer foster mother than Missus Dietrich. Now, don't you think we'd better go see about the dragging operations?"

The days turned lost and empty for me after they recovered the body of my dead father. There was no place for me to go because I had no kin. I had to stay on the farm where everything I saw, everywhere I went, reminded me of Pa. A few people came to say they were sorry. The men patted me on the head or shook my hand and told me I was a little man. The women sighed and twittered over me while their eyes turned wet.

Iris was nicer to me than she'd ever been, and I began

to think that maybe she had loved Pa, after all. But then I'd hear her whispering and laughing with Evans, and a couple of times I saw how he touched her, and I knew even then, as young as I was, that she hadn't cared too much for Pa who had been quite a bit older than her.

I begun to catch Evans watching me. No matter where I went, what I did, I'd look up or around and find him there, looking at me with a strange, measuring light in his eyes. He would smile and say something nice and kind, but I knew he was the Devil himself and nothing he could say or do would ever fool me.

I could hardly wait for haying to begin, because of what I was going to do to Evans. That was all I lived for, the day that the bloom came out on the timothy, and it was time to oil the mowing machine and hitch the horses to it, and then go around the fields, dropping the tall grass in long, fragrant swaths.

I was happy when Iris said to me: "Tomorrow Lloyd is going to start cutting hay, and you've got to show him how to operate the mowing machine. You used to follow your pa around all the time, so you should know how it runs. You've got to start cooperating and helping around here, young man. Lloyd needs you, and we need him. I don't know what I'd do if Lloyd wasn't around."

That morning I had to help him harness the horses. Queen was real mean and laid her ears back every time Evans came closer to her. He was afraid she'd bite him, so I had to slip the bit in her mouth and the bridle over her head. Then we led the horses outside and hitched them to the mowing machine.

I showed Evans how to drop the sickle, use the foot lever to raise it when he came to a rock, and how to put the machine in gear. He gave me a big grin.

"You're real helpful this morning, Tom," he said. "I like that. I've got a hunch we're going to get along real good from now on. How about it?"

"Sure," I said. "We're going to get along fine."

He asked me where to start, and I told him the section by the spring. The land was low and wet, and Pa had always had trouble with the mower there. The grass was thick and tough and always choked the sickle, and Pa had to back up the mower and raise the sickle half way while I cleared it. I was hoping the sickle would get clogged up today.

Evans dropped the sickle, kicked the mower in gear, and started off. I followed in the lane made by the sickle as it dropped the tall, scented timothy. I had always liked this walking behind the mower, listening to the chatter of the Pittman shaft as it drove the sickle, hearing the snorting and coughing of the horses as some of the bloom on the timothy got in their nostrils. But today there was no pleasure in me, only sadness, because it wasn't Pa up there riding the mower.

Sure enough, when he got to the low spot by the spring, where the reedy swamp grass mingled with the timothy, the sickle choked. Evans backed up the team, and then, with racing heart, I walked around in front of the sickle and pulled out the grass where it was clogged between the knives and the guards. I told Evans that was how it was done.

I followed him around the field a couple of times, and each time the mower clogged up at the spring, and I walked around in front of the sickle to clean it. The third round I said I was tired and would rest until he came around again. Evans just shrugged that off and clucked the horses into motion.

I waited, hidden in the brush around the spring with my slingshot in my hands and a pocket full of rocks. When Evans had completed another round, the mower choked again. He started to call me, but I stayed hidden, hoping he wouldn't come looking for me. I heard him mutter something as if he was sore at me, and then he got off the mower and stood in front of the sickle like I'd stood and started to clean it.

I had a sharp rock in my slingshot. I took careful aim at Queen's rump and let her have the rock as hard as I could. Then, quickly, I let King have one on the rump, too, and the team burst into a run.

Evans let out one startled yell, then began to scream as the sickle hooked him in the middle, doubled him, and carried him along with the horses' stampeding rush. He screamed quite a long time and that was the sweetest sound I've ever heard.

When the sheriff came to look into the accident and asked me questions, I pretended to be scared and shocked. All I ever said was: "The horses ran away. They just ran away. . . ."

The Last Sleep

A voice said: "Wake, Yanosha. Geronimo comes."

Yanosha rose from his blanket and looked at Gato. His eyes told Yanosha nothing, but then an Apache's eyes seldom tell anything, and they were Chiricahuas, hated and feared even by all the other Apaches.

"Geronimo?" Yanosha said. "And Whoa?"

"I saw only Geronimo," Gato said. "Whoa is not with them."

All at once Yanosha felt strange inside, tight and excited, like that day in the spring when he had found the butterfly in his blanket and something told him that Kootanahay had put it there. Every Apache knows that a butterfly is the most powerful of love charms, and so, when Whoa and Geronimo took their families and left the San Carlos reservation, Yanosha stayed behind and in time took Kootanahay as his wife.

Gato, his best friend, was looking hard at Yanosha, and he knew what Gato was thinking. If something had happened to Whoa, then another chief of the Chiricahuas would be chosen. Cochise had had two sons, but Tahza, the eldest, was dead, and Naitche was too young and did not want to be chief. That was why the Chiricahuas chose Whoa as chief when Cochise died. Whoa was a Nedni Apache whose place was in the Sierra Madre in northern Mexico. He ranged far over the Mexican states of Sonora and Chihuahua. Whoa had great power and had taught Geronimo. They were both medicine men. They could see into the future and heal sickness with herbs and songs. They knew every trail, every water hole, every hiding place. They could outwit the white-eye soldiers. But not everyone trusted Geronimo.

Yanosha went outside, and Gato followed him. Kootanahay was baking bread in a *horno*. She gave Yanosha a look, and he went over and put a hand on her shoulder. He thought she shivered, and it made him wonder, for women can sense things that men cannot. Kootanahay was still very pretty. Her hair was like the wings of a crow, shining blue-black in the sun, and she smelled of wind and smoke and earth, good smells to an Apache. Yanosha smiled at her, and she smiled back. The butterfly love charm still held them in its power. But there was a darkness in Kootanahay's eyes, and Yanosha knew that somehow she had learned of Geronimo's coming.

Whoa and Geronimo always came and went, taking their families with them. In the fall they came to the San Carlos reservation and got their rations and blankets and stayed over the winter. In the spring they left for the mountains where there was water and grass and deer. Yanosha had always gone with them except this last time, when the love charm had held him back, because there was nothing good here on the San Carlos reservation. It was hot and dry in the summer, cold and miserable in the winter.

He could see the dust of Geronimo's coming, a great cloud of it. Geronimo must be bringing horses or cattle with him, and that was good. They would feast and fill their bellies. The winter had been long and hard. The agent kept telling them the government was not sending very many supplies. The children were small and thin.

There was not a fat Apache at San Carlos in the summer of 1885.

Geronimo rode up to Yanosha's *jacal* and got off his pony. The horse was breathing hard and was all but done for. So they would slit its throat, drink its blood, and eat it. The Apaches never wasted anything.

Geronimo's eagle eyes were very bright. He did not try to hide the contempt in them as he looked at Yanosha.

"How goes it, Yanosha?" he asked.

Yanosha looked to where the women were putting up Geronimo's *jacales*. The warriors came and stood behind Geronimo. They looked well as if they had full bellies.

"You have eyes," Yanosha told Geronimo.

Geronimo laughed. "You still think it is good to stay on the San Carlos? You still think Cochise was right?"

Yanosha did not answer that. "Where is Whoa?" he asked.

Kootanahay began to mourn, singing the song of the dead, and the other women who had come up to watch Geronimo joined with her. Yanosha had a feeling, like a cold wind on his neck, a feeling like the old people get when the gods call to them, and they take a blanket, go out into the desert by themselves, lie down, and die.

"How did Whoa die?" Yanosha asked.

"He drowned," Geronimo said. "At Casas Grandes. We pulled him out of the river, but it was too late." He gazed at Yanosha with the eagle look.

"We have no chief. . . ."

They sat in a circle in Yanosha's *jacal*, the leaders and the old men of the Chiricahuas. They passed the pipe around, and in all their minds and hearts there was the one thought — who will be our next chief? Gato's eyes were on Yanosha. He was proud of Yanosha. He would follow Yanosha wherever he led and so would some of the others, but Yanosha had no medicine, none as great and powerful as Geronimo's.

"There is Naitche," Yanosha said, "the son of Cochise."

"Where is Tahza?" Geronimo asked. "He is the eldest."

"Tahza is dead."

There was a long silence. Geronimo sat with his thoughts. His eyes and face did not reveal what they were.

After a long time Naitche spoke. "They took my brother away."

"The white eyes?" Geronimo asked.

Naitche nodded. "Mister Clum. He picked Tahza first of all. Then several other warriors. He told them to take their ceremonial robes and bows and arrows and shields and spears and all their jewelry. They were going to a great meeting, Mister Clum said, many sleeps away, to show their ways and customs to the white man. They were not to fight but only to sing and dance."

Naitche paused. The others were silent, many of them remembering. After a while Naitche spoke again. "We did not expect to see any of them again. Others have been taken from us and never returned. But after a long time they came back. I watched as they stepped down from the wagon. They had all returned, all but Tahza.

"I went to see the agent. For three days I stood outside his door before he would see me. He told me my brother had died of pneumonia in Washington. He said Tahza died in a good hospital with the best doctors and nurses to care for him. He is buried in Arlington Cemetery. That is what the agent told me, but I do not believe him. Until the day I die, I will always believe that the white eyes

155

poisoned Tahza."

They were silent again. It seemed to Yanosha that all the gods came into the *jacal* and mourned for Tahza. The wind wept outside.

After a while Geronimo said: "Whoa is dead. We are without a chief."

Gato's eyes were on Yanosha again and the eyes of several others. "Naitche is the son of Cochise," Yanosha said.

"I am too young," Naitche said, and hung his head. "I do not have any medicine. I do not want to be chief."

"There is Yanosha," Gato said.

Geronimo laughed. "How much medicine has he? Can he outwit the white-eye soldiers? Does he know all the water holes, the hiding places? How well can he lead you in battle?"

Yanosha looked Geronimo in the eyes and said: "There is no need for war. The white eyes are too many. Cochise knew that. He would not have advised us to come to San Carlos and stay if he thought we had a chance."

"Cochise is dead," Geronimo said, "and the Chihuahuas starve and freeze in the winter on the San Carlos and thirst and roast in the summer. I can lead you to green grass and cold water and fat deer. I know where there are many cows and horses to be had for the taking. I have talked with the gods, and they have told me Geronimo will never be captured by the white eyes. Geronimo will never surrender. His medicine is great and powerful, the most powerful of any Apache's. Whose medicine will you follow?"

"Geronimo!" one of them cried. "Geronimo!" another cried. And: "Geronimo, Geronimo, Geronimo!"

Geronimo rose to his feet and folded his arms across

his chest. He looked down at Yanosha with the contempt shining in his eyes. "Very well," he said. "It is done. We leave the San Carlos at dusk."

They left the *jacal,* all but Gato. He looked at Yanosha with a question in his eyes. Yanosha thought of the San Carlos, of the bitter, hungry winters, the dry, hungry summers. He thought of how he had been born as free as the wind, how he yearned when he looked at a mountain far away. He thought of how he was a Chiricahua and a brother to all the other Chiricahuas. Among Apaches blood ties are very strong. Yanosha rose and put an arm on Gato's shoulders.

"We go," he said. "We ride with Geronimo."

They stole away in the dusk. Their loose horses followed them. The horses were used to traveling together in a remuda, and so there was no need to drive them. The Chiricahuas rode hard all night, and it is said they traveled ninety miles that night. They had to get as far away from the San Carlos as they could, so they might hide safely.

Geronimo showed no surprise when he saw Yanosha and Gato. Geronimo showed no feeling at all. He spoke not a word to them. Kootanahay was with Yanosha, and he worried about her because she carried their child in her.

At dawn they stopped on a high ridge from where they could see a long way, and there they stayed all day, hiding, not moving, giving no sign of their presence. No one spoke unless it was necessary and then only in whispers. Mothers held fingers on their babies' noses so they could not cry. Guards were posted. They could not risk fires and ate meat raw.

They rested all day and then in the dusk moved on. That is how it was, resting by day, riding by night. They picked up cattle and horses from ranches on their way to Mexico. They ate well. Their bellies began to lose their wrinkles. The men joked, the women smiled, and the children laughed and played games.

It was good there in Mexico. They raided ranches, ambushed some of the Mexican soldiers, and tortured the captives they took. Geronimo hated the Mexican soldiers most of all because they had killed his mother and wife and three children when he was young. Now he had several wives, but he still remembered his first and killed all the Mexican soldiers he could find.

On one raid the warriors brought back a large herd of cattle, enough to feed all the Chiricahuas over the winter. They remembered their brothers and cousins on the San Carlos, and so they headed north again. They had not yet reached the border when their scouts brought in Lieutenant Britton Davis.

The lieutenant was a good man. He was not like most white eyes. Had he been, the Chiricahuas would have tortured him to death. Instead, Geronimo listened to him.

"I have come to take you back," the lieutenant told the Apaches. "You cannot last forever. General Crook is preparing to march against you. The Mexicans have an army moving against you. It would be wise to return to the San Carlos before you are destroyed."

They all knew that the lieutenant always spoke the truth. Geronimo looked at him with his eagle's eyes.

"We will not be separated from our families," Geronimo told Davis. "If we are sent east, we want our families to go with us, and we will stay away for no more than two years. These are my terms."

"I know General Crook will agree," the lieutenant said.

So the Chiricahuas went north with him, across the border into Arizona, taking the cattle with them. The cattle needed water, grass, and rest. So, when they came to a ranch, Geronimo told the lieutenant they would stay there three days to rest the cattle and then go on to the San Carlos. The lieutenant agreed.

One day two men came. They talked to the lieutenant a while, and then all three came over to Geronimo. Yanosha could tell that the lieutenant was bothered by something he did not like.

"These are tax men," the lieutenant said to Geronimo. "One is from the Customs. They say you have to pay taxes on these cattle."

"Taxes?" Geronimo said. "I know nothing of taxes."

"You have crossed the border," the lieutenant said. "You are now in the United States. When you bring goods from Mexico into the United States, you have to pay tax money. That is what these men want."

Geronimo fixed the lieutenant with that eagle's look. "This is our nation, the Apache nation. I know of no other. Our country runs from the Colorado River to the west all the way east to the plains of Texas. That has always been our nation. For many, many years the Mexicans and you white eyes have used our land without paying us for it or for using our grass and water and killing our deer. So we take horses and cattle to feed ourselves. Why should we pay money for what is ours?"

"These men can make trouble for you," the lieutenant said.

An angry murmur rose from the warriors. Yanosha fingered his knife and saw that Gato beside him was doing the same. Yanosha could tell that Geronimo was

159

laughing inside. He was very dangerous when he was like that.

"Make trouble?" Geronimo said. "The two of them make trouble for all of us?"

The lieutenant's face grew tight. He knew Geronimo well. "Sleep on it," he said. "Tell your people to sleep. Tomorrow things will be different. Trust me."

The Apaches trusted Lieutenant Davis. If all the white eyes had been like him, there would have been no trouble. They trusted him, and so they did not kill the tax men. They went to their *jacales*, and the only ones who did not sleep were the guards. And Geronimo.

Yanosha saw the other officer come. He talked a while with Lieutenant Davis, and then this officer got a bottle. He and Lieutenant Davis got the tax men drunk. When the tax men were drunk and asleep, the lieutenant came to Geronimo.

"Get your people and your cattle and horses," the lieutenant said, "and head for San Carlos. Be very quiet so you will not wake up those who sleep."

Apaches can be very quiet. No one heard them as they left. But it was hard for them to keep from laughing when they thought of the trick Lieutenant Davis had played on the tax men. They were very tired, but they traveled all night. They tied the children's feet under the horses so they would not fall off. The cattle moved slowly, but by morning the Chiricahuas were twenty miles away. They laughed aloud then about what the lieutenant had done. They liked him. He was their friend.

But, when they reached the San Carlos, the white eyes took the cattle away from them. They learned from Lieutenant Davis that General Crook was very angry because they took the cattle and would not honor the terms Geronimo had demanded. So General Crook resigned his command, and another general named Miles came. This was in April of 1886.

The Apaches could not understand the strange ways of the white eyes. They were not sure what would happen to them. So once again they took their families and horses and headed south.

Now it became a matter of running and hiding, feasting and starving. Geronimo found water where no one would think there was any. He knew hiding places that the white eyes and Mexicans never came close to. The Chiricahuas lived like animals, stealing from the mountains, raiding ranches and towns, burning, looting, killing. It was a hard life and told on them and on their women and children, but they had freedom.

One night the Mexican soldiers fell upon them. They caught the Apaches through a trick. They sent some traders in among the Chiricahuas with the strong drink they call mescal. Only the Apaches did not know that the traders had been sent by the soldiers. They drank the mescal and got drunk.

Yanosha did not remember too well. Certain things stood out in his mind, blazing like bright torches in a dark night. He remembered feeling the demons inside him, the shouting and laughing and shrieking inside him, the strange and happy and miserable crazy man who had taken over inside him. He remembered the falling down and the rising again, and the feeling that he was the most powerful man in the world. Even the gods quailed before him.

Then the Mexican soldiers came. Yanosha did not remember them coming. All at once they were there, shooting, knifing, killing. Yanosha seemed to awake in a world running with screams and blood. He saw his friend, Gato, fall. A soldier with a knife grabbed Gato by the hair and started to cut off his head. Yanosha went at the soldier with a knife and slit his belly open, and, as the soldier screamed and fell away, Yanosha slashed his throat. He turned on another and plunged his knife to the hilt in the soldier's back. He had to pull with all his strength to get out the knife.

Then, somehow, Geronimo was there beside Yanosha, saying something to him, making him understand how hopeless it was, how the need was to run away and hide before the soldiers killed them all.

"Kootanahay," Yanosha cried. "My son."

But Geronimo grabbed Yanosha's arm and made him go away. They slipped into the darkness, and soon the screams and shouts and then the shooting were all gone. From far away they could see the fires still burning.

The Apaches always agreed on a rendezvous in case something went wrong. It was there that Yanosha and Geronimo waited. Their people straggled in. The warriors were few, very few. Even the woman and children were not many. To each of them Yanosha asked his question.

"Kootanahay? My son?"

It was Massai who told Yanosha. He was the one who had teased Yanosha more than anyone else because Yanosha was so gentle with his wife. Massai hung his head as he spoke. "Dead," he said.

"Both of them?"

"Yes, Yanosha."

Yanosha went off by himself and looked at the sky beyond the mountains. He listened hard to see if he could hear the voices of the gods, but the wind told of other things, strange things which he could not understand, none of the things he wanted to hear. Geronimo came and stood beside Yanosha without speaking.

After a long time Geronimo said: "Yanosha, you will be avenged. All of us will be avenged."

"You speak empty words," Yanosha told him in anger. "There is no such thing as vengeance for Apaches any more."

"Do you despair? Are you so small an Apache that you despair?"

"I know only the truth," Yanosha said. "The gods have turned their backs upon us. When we pray to them, they block their ears and look the other way. We keep getting fewer, but the gods no longer care. They have found other people to look after. They no longer see or hear the Chiricahuas."

"You are the best warrior I have left, Yanosha," Geronimo said. "I need you. We are not many now, but we are not yet all dead. We are almost without horses, almost without guns. We need weapons and ammunition and blankets and food. We are small, but we shall grow big again. Mangus and Chihuahua have gone their separate ways. We are alone, cousin, but we are not through. Will you deny your blood, Yanosha?"

Yanosha looked at Geronimo. The eagle glint was bright and strong in his eyes. His face was proud and harsh. Yanosha knew the hate and thirst that ran inside Geronimo because they were running inside him, too.

"Lead," Yanosha said. "I will follow."

The ranch was off by itself at the foot of a mountain. The Apaches stole in at the break of dawn. They made no noise. The first people they roused, they killed silently with their knives. Then, as the others awakened and the

163

Apaches now had guns taken from the slain, there was no more need for silence. They shot some and took the rest captive.

The women they tortured along with the men. Some they bound in strips of rawhide with sharp, pointed sticks between the hide and their flesh. As the hide dried and shrank in the sun, it tightened and drove the sticks into their bodies. Others were staked out beside ant hills, their mouths pried open with sharp sticks so the ants could enter. Some were burned alive.

Now the Apaches had horses and cattle and weapons and blankets again. They took them and headed up into the Sierra Madre, to the stronghold that had been Whoa's.

A feeling came over Yanosha that the last days of the Apache nation were at hand. He did not know how the feeling came. Perhaps the gods had whispered it to him while he was asleep.

It was beautiful here in the Sierra Madre. Water and grass and food were plentiful. There was peace. Yanosha was weary of fighting. Most of them were weary of running and fighting. Only Geronimo never tired of killing. That was his only thought. He was always planning another raid, another war, but he let the warriors alone now because he knew they were tired and wanted to rest. Yanosha began to be sorry that he had left the San Carlos that time to ride with Geronimo.

They were few, very few. They were only thirty-seven. Only fourteen warriors. There was Naitche and Perico and Massai and Kanseah and Fun and Eye-Lash and Chappo and some others. The rest were women and children.

They waited for Mangus and Chihuahua to come with

their bands, but they did not appear, and, as each day passed, they knew more and more that they were the last. Even Geronimo knew, though he did not speak of it. He would stand on the edge of the rimrock and look out into the distance, and Yanosha knew he was thinking what Yanosha was thinking, that their days were numbered, that their nation was dead.

One day Kanseah, who was their youngest warrior, was on guard on the rimrock. They took turns there, watching the valley far below with field glasses. Kanseah called out in excitement, and the warriors went running there. Kanseah was pointing down at the valley.

Yanosha saw them, two specks there below. Now and then they merged into one as they drew close together, then they would separate again. They moved slowly, but they came on, and the Apaches watched from high on the rimrock, watched until they saw that the specks were two men, one riding, the other walking ahead carrying a stick with a white rag tied to it.

The day Yanosha had first heard that the white eyes had put Apache scouts on their trail he knew it would not be long. The white eyes they could fool. It took an Apache to trail another Apache. Now they were here, two Apache scouts, and Yanosha knew them. They were close relatives of his.

"It's Kayitah and Martine," Kanseah said.

"Shoot them," Geronimo said. "Wait until they come in range and then shoot them."

"They carry a white flag," Massai said. "They come to talk with us."

"Shoot them," Geronimo said.

"They are our own people," Yanosha said.

Geronimo looked at Yanosha with his eyes hating

165

Yanosha and everybody and everything. "They have betrayed us. They have betrayed the Apache nation. They take pay from the white eyes. I say kill them."

Yanosha put his hand on his knife. "I say spare them. There has been enough killing, enough fighting. We are weary of that, Geronimo. If any fighting is done, it will be between you and I."

Geronimo looked at Yanosha a long time. The warriors stood silently, watching them. Yanosha knew that Geronimo had begun to notice the change in them, the way the warriors listened more and more to Yanosha. They knew that, if Yanosha's wishes had been heeded, there would not be so few of them now. They would not have left the San Carlos but would have stayed and done what Cochise had wanted them to do — learn to live in peace with the white man.

After a long time Geronimo spoke: "Let them come."

Kayitah and Martine climbed the last cliff and stood before the warriors. Kayitah was holding the stick with a white flour sack tied to it. Kayitah spoke to Geronimo.

"Surrender, Geronimo. That is what Lieutenant Gatewood told me to tell you. There is no more hope for you. There are no more places for you to hide. The white soldiers are waiting for you. The Mexican soldiers are hunting you. You have few guns, little ammunition. There is nothing you can do but surrender."

"I will never surrender," Geronimo said. "An Apache does not surrender."

"Mangus has surrendered," Kayitah said. "Chihuahua has surrendered. You are the last."

His words struck sadness in them all.

"The soldiers will kill us," Geronimo said.

"No," Kayitah said. "Lieutenant Gatewood has given

his word that you will not be harmed. He will take you to General Miles. You will be safe. You will be taken back to San Carlos. I know San Carlos is not good, but it is better than nothing, better than what you have here. Here you have only death."

Geronimo was silent, thinking.

"You have women and children with you," Kayitah went on. "Your warriors are few. When they are dead, the Mexican soldiers will get your women and children. You know what they will do to them."

After a long time Geronimo spoke. "I will surrender, but only on my terms. I do not care what they do to me. They can kill me if they want to, but I want my people spared. If they send the men away to Florida, then I want them to send their women and children with them. I will not have the men separated from their families. That is what I demand."

"General Miles is a good man," Kayitah said. "He will agree. He wants to end the war. He will keep his word. Not all white men are liars, Geronimo. Some of them are good men. Come with me and Martine. We will take you to Lieutenant Gatewood, and he will take you to the white soldiers."

They talked it over, a day and a night. They were all tired of running and fighting. If there had been hope, it would have been different. But they were the last. For them there was nothing but death.

They did not give up their arms. It was well that they kept them and that the white troops were there. The Mexican soldiers wanted to fall upon the Apaches and massacre them. The white soldiers would not let them.

In Skeleton Cañon in Arizona the Apaches surrendered to General Miles. It was the third of September, 1886.

But the white eyes on the San Carlos were different from General Miles and Lieutenant Gatewood. They took the men and put them on a train and sent them to Florida. The women and children were left behind. To these white eyes an Apache was an Apache. They saw no difference. They even took some of the Apache scouts who had helped their soldiers track down and capture Geronimo and sent them with the others into exile. The Chiricahuas made fun of these unfortunate scouts, but it was sad fun. Still it was the only fun they had.

They lived in Florida a while, and then they were sent to Oklahoma. Geronimo grew old. He always thought he would be allowed to return home and see his deserts and mountains once more before he died. He changed as he grew old. He was still proud. He still hated the white eyes. But he began to see things the way Yanosha had always seen them.

One day, at Fort Sill, Geronimo pointed to the west and said to Yanosha: "The sun rises and shines for a time, and then it goes down, sinks, and is lost. So it will be with the Indian. When I was a boy, my father told me that the Indians were as many as the leaves on the trees, and that in the north they had many horses and furs. I never saw them, but I know, if they were once there, they have gone. The white man has taken all they had. It will be only a few years when the Indians will be heard of only in the books which the white man writes."

When Geronimo died, the others were released. After twenty-seven years they finally returned home.

Now Yanosha, too, had grown old. He had a long way to look back and only a short way to look ahead. Some day, when the gods called to him, he would take up his blanket and walk up into the mountains, all alone. In the custom of his people he would lay his blanket on the ground, and there, with his gods to welcome him, he would lie down and sleep the last sleep.

Man-killer!

That morning Graham saddled his Appaloosa mare and started up the mountain. For some time now a mountain lion had been coming down out of the Jabez and killing Graham's Bar G cows, and he finally had his fill of it. So he started up toward the rugged heights of the Jabez with but one purpose in his mind — to track down and kill that mountain cat.

Graham did not have any delusions that this was going to be an easy job, nor was he too optimistic about his chances for success. There would be more than one cat up here in the Jabez, and he had no way of knowing which was the one preying on his cows. So Graham was going to shoot each and every cat he happened to encounter, and if the right one was among them so much the better.

All Graham knew about this particular cat was that it was a big one. That much he had deduced from the size of its tracks. Not much to go on, he realized, but he couldn't put up with the cat's depredations any longer, and so here he was, riding up the Jabez to try to kill any cat he might see.

Graham's Bar G ranch lay in the lower half of a small valley. The upper half belonged to a man named McCready with whom Graham had never gotten along. Going up the mountain, Graham skirted the rim of McCready's place, hoping he would not run into the man. The land looked deserted. Though Graham was climbing here, a hill in between shut off sight of McCready's buildings and for this Graham was thankful. The mare threaded her way through a stand of nut pines and came out on a small meadow. It was in the middle of this that Graham spotted the dead cow.

He rode the Appaloosa over to the dead animal and dismounted. The cow had been killed by a mountain lion which had already begun to devour a hind quarter. The cow carried the M A C brand, McCready's iron.

A feeling of ugly pleasure stirred in Graham. So he wasn't the only one losing stock. McCready was a victim of the cat, too. *Good*, Graham thought. He didn't like thinking this way, but he supposed that McCready gloated over Graham's losses, so why shouldn't he gloat over McCready's misfortunes?

He began examining the ground for tracks and quickly picked them up. The cow was freshly killed. The raw flesh of its hind quarter gave off a small swirl of steam in the chill morning air. Evidently the cat had just made its kill and had begun to feed when it had been warned of Graham's approach and had fled. Its tracks pointed a path across the meadow and into the pines and thus, perhaps, back up the Jabez where it had its lair.

His heart quickening a little with excitement, Graham mounted the Appaloosa and started following the tracks. This was a break he hadn't dared to hope for. With just a bit more luck he might sight the cat, draw a bead on it — and the job would be done.

The grove of pines was not very large. The grayish soil showed distinctly the passage of the mountain lion. Graham rode warily, his Winchester out of its saddle scabbard and held in his right hand, his eyes carefully scanning the green pattern of the trees. But the tracks kept right on, as if the cat were aware of pursuit and was in a big hurry.

Still following the tracks, the mare emerged from the pines into open country. Here the land rose sharply. Great slabs of rock dotted the steep slopes. There was not much vegetation. A lonely pine tree grew here and there. A forlorn, empty silence seemed to hang suspended over the land. The tracks of the cat abruptly vanished at the edge of an immense slab of bare rock. Graham began to curse bitterly. He studied the slopes above and beyond him, but nothing alive or moving showed, only the somber, inanimate indifference of the age-old hills.

Grimly he realized that this wasn't going to be an easy job, after all. He had allowed himself to be fooled back there in the meadow. Now it was as he had at first suspected it was going to be. A long, hard hunt. . . .

In the middle of the afternoon Graham paused a while to allow the mare to rest. He took a piece of jerky from his pack and chewed on the dried meat. He was hungry, but he decided to forego building a fire and cooking a meal until that evening.

Graham had halted on the lip of a high ledge. From here he could look far down the mountainside. He could see the barren slant of the slopes beneath him, the harsh, weird rock formations, the green line of the timber below. Graham lay on his stomach as he scanned all the country below, hoping to catch some sight of the cat.

Up to this moment Graham had felt that he was alone up here in the Jabez. Now, as he watched, he saw the horseman far below. The rider had come out of the timber, and he seemed to be coming up the mountain.

172

Graham watched idly, rather welcoming the sight of another human being after more than half a day of desolate barrenness.

The rider came ahead, sending his horse up the steep pitch of a slope, and for a while it appeared as if he were heading for the ledge on which Graham was resting. But when the rider reached the top of the slope, he veered off to the left, following the winding crest of the hill. It was then that Graham recognized him. The man was McCready.

Obviously, he was up in the Jabez on the same mission as Graham. McCready, too, was undoubtedly tired of having his stock killed by the cat, and so he was up here to ferret out the lion and kill him.

Then a thought occurred to Graham. *If I was a mean, rotten sort of a man, I could kill McCready now. All I'd have to do is pick up my Winchester, draw a bead, and let him have it. There's only the two of us up here on the mountain. No one saw us come up here. There would be no witnesses. I'd get away with it easy. I could kill McCready as easy as eating pie . . . if I was that kind of a lowdown man.* All this, Graham thought idly, not meaning any of it, he told himself, just something to pass the time. He watched McCready ride on out of sight. Graham heaved a sigh of relief. It looked as if McCready had not noticed Graham, and for this Graham was grateful.

Graham rode off in a direction opposite from the one McCready had taken. The Jabez was big enough, Graham figured, that he could do his hunting without ever coming across McCready. Besides, if he kept on the way he had been headed, he would cover the mountain north of this point. Graham, therefore, could cover the south.

Since they both had the same purpose in mind, it made little difference which one of them got the cat. Both would profit equally from the death of the lion.

A thought struck Graham, and he smiled a little wryly at it. *Should either he or McCready get the cat, it would be the first time one of them had done a favor for the other.*

A couple of times Graham came across cat tracks, but they quickly petered out on the hard, blind surface of the rocks. Then, too, these tracks were smaller than those of the huge beast Graham was after, so he did not try to pick them up again, since apparently they weren't the tracks of his quarry.

That night Graham camped down in a small draw. There was a trickle of a creek wriggling down the center of the draw and some graze for the Appaloosa. Graham spread his blanket under the overhanging lip of the draw where he would be out of the way of the chill breeze that was moving down from the heights of the Jabez. He built a fire, cooked himself a meal of bacon and beans and coffee, and then lay down on his blanket.

From somewhere on the mountain came the faint, barely audible scream of a prowling cat, sounding weird and full of a primal savagery. Graham tensed and listened for it to come again, but it wasn't repeated. Perhaps it was the cat he was after, he thought, but it was dark now, and it was futile to try to go after it. There would be time tomorrow.

He was very tired, and it did not take him long to fall asleep. Just as he dropped off, he was wondering what McCready might be doing at this particular moment. . . .

Early the next morning Graham came across the track of another cat. He examined the size of the tracks carefully, and his heart quickened. This should be the cat he was after. There might be two of the immense beasts up here, but this Graham doubted, as it wasn't often that lions ran to this size — the size of a jaguar almost, he'd guess.

Graham set the mare in pursuit of the tracks. For a while they moved down the mountain, then the tracks doubled back, and finally turned northward. Graham paused, thinking of McCready, then a sullen fit of anger passed through him. He had as much right up here in the Jabez as McCready did. Besides, if this were really the cat he was after, why should he hold back? Just because of McCready? Damn McCready anyhow!

Graham urged the mare on.

Once he lost the tracks among the rocks, but he scouted around and finally picked them up again. The tracks seemed to be laid in an idle, meandering pattern as if the lion had just been wandering aimlessly about. The trail now began to climb up the face of a steep slope, and Graham had to dismount and lead the mare. Even so, the Appaloosa made it up the hill only with the greatest difficulty.

On the other side of the crest the hill dropped away in a precipitous bluff that looked down on a long, narrow, barren valley. The tracks of the cat disappeared abruptly on the smooth surface of the rock. Graham cursed. Anger swirled in him. All this work had gone for nothing. Just when he had begun to hope that maybe he'd accomplish what he had set out to do, the sign of the cat had to vanish into thin air.

Looking down into the valley, Graham spotted the rider off in the distance. McCready again. He moved the Appaloosa back where she would not show above the rim of the cliff and tied the horse to a mesquite. Then he lay on his belly and watched the horseman come up the valley.

Graham felt mean and ugly inside. The futility of his hunt had begun to nag at him. He scratched irritably at the bristle of whiskers covering his chin and cheeks. Wrath mounted in him. Balefully he watched McCready come on, remembering all the things that had passed between them. There had been several disputes: over the matter of trespassing cows, over the line between M A C and Bar G, over a half section of timber which Graham had wanted but which McCready had purchased. There was also the matter of a spring on Bar G land, just inside the line, which M A C cows had been using and which Graham had fenced off.

Graham grinned with satisfaction as he remembered that one. That was one time McCready hadn't come off on top. That was one time he'd taken it instead of dishing it out.

Now could very well be a second time, Graham told himself grimly. *Look at him. There he is, just below me now. I could pick him off easy. He doesn't even know I'm up here watching. He's got no idea that I'm even on the mountain. No one knows I'm here. If I picked him off, he'd only be getting what he had coming to him. I know, if he was in my boots, he wouldn't hold back. He'd grab his rifle and let me have one in the back . . . the way I should let him have one. And I'm of a good mind to do just that. . . .*

But Graham only watched McCready ride on. Sweat had come out on Graham's face; sweat dampened his beard stubble; sweat made wet splotches under his armpits. He watched McCready move on, diminishing with distance, and then drew a shirt sleeve over his eyes, wiping the wetness away, and went over to his mare. Graham's whole body was trembling.

As the day wore on, he ran across more cat signs, but none of the tracks was as large as those of his quarry. Once, looking down a slope, he thought he saw a flash of movement, something like the swift, lithe passing of a tawny form among some boulders. He sent the Appaloosa at a swift run down the slope, but by the time he reached the boulders, the cat had fled. Graham picked up its track in a small patch of sand, but these paw marks, too, were too small.

Late that afternoon Graham was riding up a cañon. He was worn out from two days of futile hunting, and he had begun to think of pitching camp early this night. He promised himself that the first likely spot he ran across, there he'd stop and rest for the night.

Weariness lay so heavily on him that the sharpness had passed from his mind. The feeling kept angling into him, but he was too tired and disgusted to pay any heed to it. Finally, however, he lifted his head and glanced up the high sloping wall of the cañon.

Silhouetted against the yellow sky was a horseman. He was up on the rim of the cañon, watching Graham. McCready! Graham whirled the mare around with a sudden, cruel wrench on the reins. Then he froze in his saddle, staring up at McCready while McCready stared down at him.

Graham's throat slowly constricted. An ominous chill laced the back of his neck. Now McCready knew he was in the Jabez. McCready, who hated Graham's guts. . . .

I can't kid myself about the kind of man McCready is, Graham said to himself. *If I've thought about killing him, then I'm sure he will think the same about me, only he won't be thinking about it for fun. He'll be dead serious about it. That's the kind of man McCready is. Look at him. Look how he's watching me. He knows we're alone up here in the Jabez. He hates me, and right this minute he's thinking how easy it would be to kill me and get away with it. Damn you, McCready. Damn you, you dirty son. . . .* For a long time the two men stared at each other. They sat motionless in their saddles, neither one making any attempt to call a greeting to the other or to make a friendly gesture.

Finally McCready whirled his horse away from the rim and jumped the animal out of sight. Graham began to breathe again. He started the Appaloosa up the cañon. All the way Graham kept looking apprehensively up at the cañon rim, but nothing showed. Sweat stayed out on his face. . . .

That night, Graham did not build a fire. The air was thin and cold, and there was nothing he desired more than some boiling coffee, hot pan bread, and sizzling bacon and beans, but he did not dare build a fire. If McCready had intentions of killing him, and Graham was positive of that, then a fire would be a beacon light to guide McCready while he crept up under cover of the night and put a slug in Graham. No, Graham decided, no fire. He'd as soon freeze to death as build a fire.

In case McCready had been watching, Graham, at dusk, had pitched camp at the foot of a jutting rock that poked out at the base of the cañon wall. But all the while he had his eyes on a small hummock in the middle of the cañon floor. As soon as it was dark enough, Graham moved his camp to the hummock. The ground was bare all about. It would be difficult for a man to sneak up undetected to the top of the hummock, even under cover of darkness.

Graham began to wait out the slow passing of the night. Drawing his blanket tight about him, he tried to warm himself, but the air was too chill. Still, he would not consider building a fire. He kept his Winchester close at hand, and he placed his six-shooter next to the saddle on which his head rested.

Graham found that he could not sleep. His joints ached; every muscle was tired and sore; everything in him cried out for sleep; but just as he'd start to drop off, an insistent feeling of alarm would jerk him abruptly awake again. Then he would lie there, wide-eyed, his heart hammering in his chest, listening to the silence of the night.

At first there was nothing to hear, only the awesome, brooding stillness of the mountains. Now and then the Appaloosa stirred fretfully, moving about a little on its picket rope. The time passed, interminably slow, dragging more and more as the night wore on. Somewhere off in the darkness something sounded. Graham tensed in his blanket. His fingers tightened about the Winchester. *Was that the mare?* Sweat trickled down over Graham's upper lip.

There, the sound came again. This time he was sure it wasn't the Appaloosa. The horse was to the right of Graham; the sound had come from the left. Carefully Graham brushed the blanket from him. He twisted it around as quietly as he could until he faced the direction from which the sound had emanated. He could feel his heart beating against the sand.

The noise came again, just a tantalizing whisper, just enough of it to make itself real beyond a doubt but not enough of it to be definitely recognizable. Graham gritted his teeth. The palms of his hands were wet where they gripped the rifle.

Graham strained as he listened. There. There it was again — or was it? With his sleeve he brushed the sweat out of his eyes and tried to pierce the darkness. A prowling animal? His imagination? His nerves were taut enough, but he was sure it wasn't a fabrication of his mind. The sounds had been real. McCready?

That could be it. McCready! That would be just like the man, sneaking up under cover of the night. McCready didn't have the guts to come out in the open and fight like a man. *McCready, you dirty, sneaking son of a bitch!*

The sound came again, faint but definite. Something moving out there, all right. Graham aimed the Winchester. He thumbed back the hammer, drew a deep breath, and pulled the trigger. The crash of the shot went slamming up against the cañon walls, starting an eerie series of echoes. Out of the night came a startled, feline scream, a savage, feral spitting, and then a rush of movement going away.

As he pulled the trigger, Graham had rolled violently over, in case it was McCready out there and he answered Graham's shot. Now Graham was on his belly, listening to the noise fading. He wanted to throw another shot but figured it would do no good.

He found that the tension had eased a little in him as he crawled back to his blanket. The Appaloosa was snorting and pawing the ground, but she soon quieted. Then the silence filled in again.

Graham began to feel a little pleased about it. If McCready was out there with ideas, he knew now that Graham wasn't asleep. He knew now that Graham wasn't an easy mark. That shot would have told McCready enough.

McCready. Graham began to swear under his breath. He'd have to tend to McCready. In the morning he'd have to do something about McCready. . . .

Before dawn broke, Graham saddled the mare and started back down the cañon. An apprehensive feeling prickled the back of his neck. He sent anxious glances up at the cañon rim. Though nothing showed, the uneasiness grew more and more in Graham. To him the lack of any sign was not reassuring but ominous. If McCready were up there and he had it in his mind to kill Graham, the man would not show himself. He would remain concealed and let Graham have it when he was least expecting it.

Panic rose and lodged in Graham's throat. He tried not to yield to its terrifying insistence, but he could not control himself. *I've got to hurry,* he told himself. *I'm in a trap here in the cañon. It isn't that I'm afraid to die. It's just that I haven't got a chance here. If he's up there, he can pick me off without me knowing it . . . until it's too late. If only I had a chance to fight back. That's all I ask. Just a chance to fight back. . . .*

He spurred the mare, breaking it into a run. The mouth of the cañon shouldn't be far off, and, once he had gained that, Graham felt he could begin to breathe again. He turned and threw another look up the cañon wall, and there far behind him, racing along the rim in pursuit of him, was McCready mounted on his buckskin.

I was right all along, Graham thought. *There's the dirty son now, but I fooled him. He thought I'd camp in the cañon and wait there for him so he could take his own sweet time about putting a slug in me, but I got an early start on him. Now I'm ahead of him, so let him try to catch me. . . .*

He urged the mare on faster, prodding her flanks with his spurs, quirting her with the loose ends of the reins, sending her along at a breakneck gallop, raising a great cloud of dust behind him. Through this he glanced back and saw McCready had increased the speed of his buckskin.

All right, McCready, all right, Graham said to himself. *Just let me make it out of the cañon. I won't run forever. Just let me go where I've got a chance, and I'll stop running and show you a thing or two, you lowdown, rotten bushwhacker!*

He drove the mare without mercy. The Appaloosa's flanks were lathered with sweat by the time she reached the cañon's mouth, and through all this McCready's buckskin had been unable to gain on her. A triumphant grimace broke the tight, thin line of Graham's mouth.

The cañon debouched on a small plain, and then the land lifted again, rising in serrated humps into the immense height of a barren, jagged peak. Here, at the base, there was a smattering of trees — pines and balsams. Graham paused long enough to ascertain that McCready was following him across the plain, then rode up into the trees.

He did not ride far. The spot he selected appealed to him instantly, and he gave it only a brief, peremptory study. A rock jutted out in front of the hill, and behind the rock, lying across the slope, was a giant, rotting cedar windfall. Graham saw that the rock formed a natural parapet and that from behind the rock he held a commanding view across the plain.

He tethered the mare to a pine. Then, carrying his

Winchester, Graham went behind the rock. Below, on the hill, the trees fell away in a long, open lane down which he could look across the plain. No one could cross that plain if he was of a mind to stop them.

McCready must have gathered the portent of this for he had reined in his buckskin half way across the plain, and now he was sitting motionless in his saddle, warily studying the lay of the land ahead of him. Graham grinned mirthlessly. *Come on, McCready. Come right ahead. Don't be bashful, McCready. Come ahead another hundred feet. Just another hundred feet. Who's top man now, McCready? Who's got the upper hand now? You can turn and run, but I'll get my mare and take after you. You're the one that's being hunted now, McCready. Come on, damn you, do something!*

Graham never quite knew what it was that warned him. He was so preoccupied with McCready that he had nothing else in mind. With that one big urgency in him he hadn't bothered to look too closely at what lay behind him. Now, with an ugly, chilling premonition tickling the back of his neck, he turned, hands gripping the Winchester tightly, to face the windfall — and there Graham saw it. He saw into the huge trunk of the tree and inside its rotting, hollow interior, heard the savage, feral spitting, the beginning of a ferine scream that abruptly changed into a throaty snarl of rage. He threw up the Winchester and fired as the cat leaped from its lair. The great tawny body rushed through the air at him. He had a brief, horrible glimpse of razor-sharp claws, of glaring white teeth, of a crimson, snarling mouth. Then he was rolling frantically, twisting violently to get away from beneath the plummeting body of the cat.

The slug took the lion in the chest, and the beast

screamed with hurt. It convulsed even before it hit the ground, and it was this that caused it to miss Graham. He had come up with his back against the windfall, and he swiftly levered another cartridge in place. The cat was far from done for. Its baleful, glowering glance fixed on Graham, and the huge body tensed, ready for another spring at him.

Graham fired. The cat was just beginning to come ahead when the bullet struck it. A scream of mortal agony ripped out of the throat of the cat. He fired again. The beast moaned in pain-racked, frustrated fury and gave a leap up on the windfall. Graham fired once more. The tawny body quivered, then tensed, claws ripping into the surface of the windfall. For an instant the dying cat hung on, then the great body began to sag, the claws began to slip with a harsh, scratching sound, and abruptly the cat dropped off the windfall to the ground — dead.

Just to make sure Graham put one more slug into the lion. The impact of the bullet shuddered the massive head a little, but that was the only movement. Breathing heavily, sweat coursing down his whiskered face, he stared dully at the cat. Reaction set in, and for a brief while he felt weak in his stomach, and the muscles of his thighs quivered, and there was a sick feeling in his throat.

Then he remembered McCready. Graham's head flung up. He lifted to his feet, rising above the parapet, and there below him, coming up the slope on the buckskin, was McCready. Graham kept the Winchester on McCready all the way up.

McCready reined in the buckskin and stared at the dead lion. Finally he shifted his stare to Graham. The man's face was drawn; his mouth was a tight line; a haunted, hunted look glimmered in his eyes; and it came to Graham that McCready had gone through the same thing he had.

"So you got him," said McCready. "Big son, isn't he?"

Graham nodded. He still had his Winchester on McCready, but now he lowered the rifle. McCready gave no indication that he had noticed. Graham realized suddenly that for now the war between them had been put aside.

"What are you aiming to do with him?" asked McCready.

"I guess I'll skin him and save the hide," said Graham.

"You want a hand?"

"I can manage."

McCready shrugged. "Suit yourself." He reined the buckskin around and started down the slope. Graham watched him go, all the way across the plain and then over a rise. McCready never once looked back.

Graham rolled up his sleeves, got his knife, and fell to work.

My Brother: Killer

He was sitting under the shaded front of my house with the sadness in his eyes. I knew it was there even before I could see it. I cradled the shotgun under my arm as I went up the steps.

"How'd it go today, Dad?" I asked.

He smiled, but only with his mouth. "Just fine, Lew," he said. "And you?"

"The desert is as dry as it ever was," I said, brushing dust from my shirt and pants. "I'll bet I've got half of it in my throat."

I looked at him, and he was staring off over the scorched hills and beyond the purple-misted mountain range. It was like he didn't know I was there any more. He was like this all the time, just staring into the distance while he waited to die.

A blanket covered his legs as he sat in his wheelchair, and his hands rested in his lap. The fingers of his left hand drummed slowly and silently; those of his right hand were curled and useless. He hadn't walked in a year.

"Smells like Rita's got a good supper," I said, taking a deep breath.

He said nothing. He never took his glance off the distance. The sadness seemed to go a little deeper in his eyes.

I went inside. I put the shotgun in the rack, and then I walked into the kitchen and kissed Rita. She was flushed from tending the warm stove. I thought she was prettier now than two years ago when I'd married her.

"What happened today?" I asked her.

She frowned. "You mean Dad?"

"Yes."

"Missus Quinn was here to visit him. She should have known better, but she told him about Rory and that fracas he got into at the Mother Lode Saturday night. She even had to go and tell him it was over one of the girls there. I wish I could have stopped it, Lew, but I didn't know how."

"It was bound to come out," I said. "You can't keep things like that from him forever."

"But it hurts him so much. He never says anything, but you can see it hurts him. Rory's all he's got . . . besides you."

I rolled up my sleeves, poured water in the basin, and washed up. I felt Rita's eyes on me all the while. Something started to burn, and that snapped her out of it with a gasp. I heard a pan rattle as I hung up the towel.

When I turned, she was looking at me again. "Are you sure there's nothing between you and Dad?" she asked.

"I've already told you. We're no kin. My folks died in an epidemic when I was little, and Dad took me in and raised me. I grew up with Rory like he was my father, but we're no kin at all."

"That would have helped," she said wistfully. I guess she liked Dad Standish as much as I did. "If you'd been his flesh and blood, he wouldn't take it so to heart about Rory. Do you think Rory will ever change?"

"Rory's no good. He never will be any good."

187

"What're we going to do, Lew?" she whispered.

"I don't know. . . ."

Rita fed him because he couldn't even do that. I know he was ashamed, but there was nothing else to do. He worshipped Rita for the way she had taken him in and tended him after he'd got sick, but he was still ashamed of having to be waited on all the time.

When it got dark, I wheeled him into his room and put him to bed. "I'm such a bother, Lew," he said.

I looked at him, hard and mad, but there was something thick in my throat. "I was a bother, too, when I was little."

"But you had no one," he said, blinking his eyes and dabbing at the corner of his mouth with the tip of his tongue. He didn't say any more, but I knew what he meant.

"Rory's not married," I told him gently. "He has no one to cook for him and keep house. I've got Rita. It would be pretty hard for Rory."

"I know," he said, "but he's my son."

"So am I."

He reached out his good hand and caught one of mine. "Thank you, Lew," he whispered.

Rita was sitting in the parlor, mending one of my shirts. I told her I was going out for a couple of beers, and she just nodded and smiled. I went out, thinking how lucky I was to have a wife like Rita, but somehow it didn't make me very happy tonight. I guess it was because I couldn't forget an old man who had nothing to do but wait to die.

I stopped in at the Argyle for a while. I had two beers, and I watched a poker game. I strolled to the edge of town, and then I went down the road a way until I came to the big Joshua tree. I stopped there and built a cigarette. I had just tossed the butt away when I heard the footsteps coming down the road.

I knew who it was instantly because the moonlight glinted off the silver discs of his hatband and down the sides of his batwing chaps. He had no use for chaps because he never rode through the brush, but he wore them because he figured they made him look good. That was his only interest in life — looking good. I remember when he was a kid how he had started admiring himself in a looking glass. He would spend hours in front of it. He still did.

He stopped and peered a moment because I was in the shadow of the Joshua. "Is that you, Lew?" he asked.

"Hello, Rory."

"I was hoping I'd find you alone."

"What do you want?"

"You sound like you're sore," he said. "What've I done now?"

I didn't answer him. He tipped his head to one side and studied me. A hand lifted and caressed the hair-line mustache he wore. He was very proud of his handsome face. He shaved twice a day, although he didn't have to, and his mustache was always trimmed and so was his hair. He liked to use cologne water, and I could smell it now, and it made me a little sick.

"You know I'd like to help you out with the old man," he said when I didn't speak, "but what is there for me to do? I'm always on the go. I don't have a place to keep him. What do you expect me to do?"

Stop helling around and get yourself a job and make him proud of you before he dies, I wanted to tell him, but it would have been a waste of breath. So I said nothing. I just stood there, thinking of the sad look in an old man's eyes.

He coughed like he was embarrassed about something, but it wasn't about what I was thinking. A thing like that never bothered Rory Standish. He could never see farther than his own narrow and mean self.

"I'd like to make a deal with you, Lew," he said.

Something cold touched the back of my neck. "What are you talking about?"

He coughed again, very softly. "You work for Downing and Waddell, don't you? You ride shotgun on the Silver Rock-Amethyst stage, don't you? You and me should get together, Lew."

Again I knew that feeling like a cold palm pressed against my neck. "I don't get you," I growled, but I did. I did in a way that left me sick and mad inside.

He paused, and his eyes studied me hard for a moment. Then he said: "You know when gold is shipped to the railroad at Amethyst. You just tell me in advance."

"I never know until the last minute."

"That's not true."

"Why isn't it?"

"Just say that I know." Again his eyes swept me. I could feel them in the shadows, ugly and mean, just like the inside of his heart. "You won't be doing it for nothing. You'll come in for a share. You don't owe nothing to Downing and Waddell. You get paid for riding shotgun, but is it worth it if you get knocked off some day? Get smart, Lew."

"Smart like you?" I said.

"You'll never be that smart," he said. "The way I got it figured a shipment should be going out in about a week. You let me know for sure. If you're on the stage, all you got to do is forget about your shotgun. How does it sound?"

"Go to hell, Rory."

"Oh?" he said. He paused while his glance searched me. I could see him smiling in the shadows. "Would you do it if it was for the old man?"

I guess my heart skipped a beat. I had no idea what it was about. I just knew Rory and how mean he could be. So my heart missed a beat, and my blood ran a little cold. I stood there without an answer.

"You wouldn't want to hurt him, would you, Lew? He thinks the world of you. You wouldn't want to take that from him, would you?"

"I'd take it from him if I threw in with you. You being rotten is enough for him. What makes you think it would be easier for him if both of us were crooks?"

"That's the point," he said quietly. "We'll keep him from finding out about you."

"I haven't done anything. What is there to find out?"

"Hear me out," he said. "You remember Curt McNally? Of course, you do. He rode shotgun for Downing and Waddell until he was caught dealing seconds in Amethyst and was beat to the draw. You remember the stick-up six months back between here and Amethyst. Curt was riding shotgun that time. He did just what I want you to do."

"No, Rory," I said hoarsely, "was that you?"

He laughed like it was something to be proud about. "See? I didn't get caught. Me and the boys pulled it off real slick. If Curt hadn't got so clumsy with those cards, I wouldn't be bothering you."

"Get out of my sight. If you weren't Dad's son, I'd turn you in. Get out of my sight!"

"You better hear me out," he said as I took a step toward him. Something dark in his tone made me pull up. "Curt is dead, and he can't talk, but I can. I can go to the sheriff and say I pulled the stick-up and that you tipped me off to the shipment. I can say I shared with you. Sure, I'll lose, but so will you. The old man will be the one to lose most of all, though. Think of how he'll feel to have both of us in the pen. It'll kill him. He's gonna die anyway, but this way he'll die of a broken heart. You wouldn't do that to him, would you, Lew?"

I hit him then. I smashed him in the mouth, and he stumbled back. I crowded him. I hit him in the belly. When he started to double up, I slammed him on the jaw, and he went sprawling in his pretty clothes in the dust.

I was crying. I could feel the angry tears on my cheeks. He started to rise, and I smashed him in the face with my knee. He fell back with a moan and lay on the ground, holding his face and panting hard with hurt.

I stood over him. Even with the tears in my eyes I kept seeing an old man who did nothing but wait for death. "Get up," I snarled. "Get up, Rory. I've only begun. Get up, you dirty, stinking son of a bitch!"

He stayed on the ground, huddled in the dust, covering his face with his arms now. "You can hit me again," he said, his voice thick, "but you won't kill me, and you've got to kill me if you want to keep me from talking. You're throwing in with me, Lew. You've got no choice."

I kicked him in the ribs, and he screamed. I tried to kick him again, but he rolled away. "Damn you, Rory," I was sobbing. "Damn you!"

He rolled fast and hard with me going after him. Suddenly he came to a stop, and I saw moonlight glint off the silverwork on his .45. He had the barrel pointed at my heart, and I froze with my boot poised in the air.

"Listen to me, Lew," he said, lying flat on his back with his fancy .45 aimed at my chest. "This is too good of a thing for me to pass up. I've got a hold on you, and I won't let it go. I don't give a damn for the old man. All he ever did was preach to me, and I've had enough of that. But he means something to you. So you're going along with me. If you don't, I'm framing you, and he'll die from hurt and shame. I've got you over a barrel, Lew, and you'd better come through. . . ."

I didn't see Rory for three days. During that time I'd got to thinking that maybe the beating I'd given him had scared him. But that wasn't Rory's way. When he got hold of something, he hung on to it like a bulldog.

I was on my way to work the third morning when he stopped me. He wasn't alone, however. He had two friends named Joe Slade and Tate Wingard. They were no-good loafers like himself. It was out in the middle of the street, but Rory wasn't caring who saw us. After all, everyone accepted us as half-brothers, and there was nothing strange for us to meet and talk. So Rory got in front of me while his two friends fanned out on either side of him. I saw the looks on their faces, and I slipped the shotgun out from under the cradle of my arm into my hand. Rory's face went a little white and tight when he saw this.

I knew now why he'd stayed out of sight for three days. I had marked him good. There was still a scab at the edge of his mouth and another one on his cheek where I had smashed him with my knee. He didn't look very pretty, and I suppose this hurt him more than the pain of the blows. But his face would heal. I wished I could have marked him for life.

"Anything yet, Lew?" he asked, his lips moving stiffly. I shook my head.

He lifted a hand with three fingers raised, marking the days. "I'm not kidding," he said, his voice a little harsh, and it came to me that he was putting out a great effort to keep himself under control. The hate showed bright and sharp in his eyes. "Something's going out before too long. You let it go without telling us, and I'm going to the sheriff. I don't care if it means a stretch in the pen for me. Just so you get a longer one, and you will, because I'll have turned informer. What's the old man gonna think then?"

I couldn't trust myself to speak. I just pushed ahead, walking blind. I brushed against Rory, felt him yield, and then heard his vicious snarl: "No more than another week. Remember that, Lew."

Then I was beyond them. I didn't see anything until I was passing through the archway that was the entrance to the yard of Downing & Waddell. The sun was very bright in my eyes. That wasn't what made them sting. . . .

The night I told Rory I wouldn't stand for any rough stuff. He promised me no one would be hurt. He said all I had to do was throw down my shotgun and raise my hands. There was nothing to worry about, he said, smiling and happy like a kid with a new pair of copper-toed boots.

I went to the Argyle after that. I hardly ever touched whiskey, but tonight I did. I was weaving when I went home. Rita smelled it on my breath, but she said nothing, even though it was late. I didn't tell her anything. I got in bed and put my back to her. I thought I would never drop off that night, but I finally did. And then all I did was dream about an old man's sorrowful eyes. . . .

That morning we left Silver Rock right on time, the gold shipment in the chest under my feet. There were no passengers, just me and the driver sitting side by side up in the box. The thoroughbraces squealed and the wheels rattled, and a bunch of dogs escorted us, barking and yipping, all the way out of Silver Rock.

He was sitting in his wheelchair in front of my house with the sun on him. I waved to him, and he lifted his left arm in return. Then we had passed, but I was still seeing the look in his eyes. I was seeing it all the time now.

The road dipped and rose and twisted as it wound through the sunburned hills. Dust started to settle on my shirt and pants. The hoofs of the six-horse hitch churned up a thick cloud of it that at times gagged me. The coach pitched and rocked, and I swayed with it, the shotgun in my hands. The sun was lifting and growing hotter, and sweat began to make channels down through the dust on my cheeks.

The driver was old Bisbee Johnson. He'd driven for Butterfield when he'd put his line through to the Coast. Bisbee was forever talking. He had a wad of tobacco in his cheek, and the only time he stopped talking was when he spit over the side of the coach.

I don't remember what he was talking about that morning, but I suppose it was the usual thing. He was old and thinking of retiring, and so he had given up drinking and smoking and was saving all the money he could. After all these years in the desert he had a place picked out high in the mountains, where the pines grew tall and green, the air was cool, and the spring water was like ice. He was going to retire there and build himself a cabin and spend his last days sitting in the cool air, listening to the wind in the pines. He had told this to me so many times that I knew it by heart. That's why I say this was what he was probably talking about that morning, because I wasn't listening to him.

We were half way to Amethyst when the riders jumped their horses out from among some large stones into the road. There were three of them, and Bisbee swore and hauled back on the lines, drawing the six-hitch to a sliding halt. Dust boiled up so that for an instant we were lost in it.

I could have lifted the shotgun and used it, but I didn't. Then the dust began to clear, and I could see them good again. One of them was at the head of the six-hitch to keep them from bolting on. The other two rode in, one on either side of the coach. The sun kept winking off the barrels of the six-shooters they aimed at us.

The one on my side was Rory. I knew that because I caught a whiff of cologne water. He was wearing old clothes, and he was using a plain, black-handled six-shooter, but he still had that trace of cologne about him. The mask covered all of his face except his eyes and forehead.

"You," he said to me, wagging his gun a little. "Throw that scatter-gun and your six-shooter down here and be careful about it. We ain't playing games."

I dropped the shotgun over the side and heard the sound it made when it hit the ground. Then I lifted my

.44 from the holster and let it fall, too. Rory wagged his gun again.

"All right," he said, "throw the chest down now."

He backed his horse away a few steps. The chest was heavy, and Bisbee gave me a hand. We got it over the rim of the box, and it made a loud thump when it struck the earth. Rory's horse snorted and shied, but he reined it in.

His eyes glared at me. "This better not be a trick," he said, his voice muffled by the mask. He dismounted.

He aimed his six-shooter at the lock and fired. Then he flipped back the lid and bent over to look into the chest. The gold was there all right, and Rory gave a soft little laugh. He straightened and called to one of the others to give him a hand.

The one at the head of the six-hitch rode over and dismounted beside Rory, and they began transferring the bars of bullion to their saddlebags. The one on the other side of the coach kept his gun on me and Bisbee.

Rory and his pal worked hard and fast. Rory strained so much in his hurry that his mask became loose and started to slip. He had his hands full with a bar of bullion so that he couldn't catch the bandanna before it had dropped enough to let Bisbee know who he was.

"Rory!" Bisbee said, his voice harsh with surprise. "Rory Standish!"

Rory dropped the bar in his saddlebag. "Yes, Bisbee," he said, looking up, "it's me." He smiled and drew his six-shooter. He did it as easy and careless as though he were shooting a tin can off a fence post. He tipped up the barrel and fired.

Bisbee let out a cry that choked in his throat. I turned in time to see him grab his chest and pitch headlong to

197

the ground. He lay there without moving.

There was ice in my belly. Then the anger began. I could feel it start to burn behind my eyes. "Damn you, Rory," I shouted. "You promised there wouldn't be any shooting."

"What the hell did you expect me to do?" he hollered back. "He recognized me, didn't he?"

"I'll get you for this," I said. "I swear I'll get you."

The one beside Rory — it was Joe Slade, I think — said: "Maybe we better get rid of him, too."

A cruel little smile was on Rory's mouth. His six-shooter was pointing at my belly, and he kept caressing the hammer with his thumb. His eyes were very bright as they studied me.

"No," he said after a while. "He won't do anything. We've got him good now. He's in this as much as any one of us. I'd kill him, but he's too valuable to us alive. There'll be other gold shipments. Won't there, Lew?"

I told him what he could do, but he only laughed. He got on his horse and laughed again when he looked at me, standing helpless up in the box.

"I'll have your share for you in about a week," he said. Then he reined his horse around and rode off. The others followed him. I watched them go over a rise and disappear. Then I climbed down to the ground.

Bisbee lay with his face pushed into the dust. I rolled him over, and, even before I felt for his pulse, I knew he was dead. A trickle of blood had come out of his mouth, and his white beard was stained with dirt. He would never hear the wind in the pines that he loved.

I would have cried, but there were no tears in me. Besides, tears wouldn't have helped. I kept thinking of another old man who had a dream. I remembered him

198

telling me once: "If only Rory would do just *one* decent thing before I die." I heard him saying it again. I heard it so clearly that I looked up, but all I saw was the sun-scorched hills and the lonely patches of sage and greasewood. There was nothing else, only this and the burning sun and old Bisbee lying as dead and lonely as his dream.

I walked around the coach and picked up my six-shooter. I wiped the dust and grit from it, checked the action, and saw that it wasn't harmed. I flipped open the loading gate and spun the cylinder to make sure that every chamber was loaded. Then I slipped the .44 in my holster and picked up the shotgun. I broke it and saw the brass heads of the twin shells, loaded with buckshot. I laid the shotgun on the empty chest and unhitched one of the horses.

I rode off on bareback, holding the shotgun in my left hand. I followed their trail over the burning hills and across an alkali flat. The tracks led toward the mountains. As I drew closer, the mist faded from them, and they rose gaunt and clear.

I lost their tracks once on hard, flinty ground, and it was an hour before I picked them up again. I rode on, driving the horse with little rest. Every time I reached high ground, I studied the country all about, but it was sundown before I saw them.

They must have been pretty sure of having made their getaway. I could see their side of it. They hadn't figured on me taking out after them. They must have thought I'd go on to Amethyst to notify the sheriff. By the time he organized a posse and got to the scene of the hold-up, night would have come, making tracking impossible. Then, too, a wind had started coming down off the mountains, sweeping the desert clean of any sign.

They were down in a hollow ringed with large slabs of rock and mesquite which broke the wind a little. I saw them there, and I dismounted and sneaked in on foot. In my right hand I held my six-shooter. In my left I had the shotgun.

The mesquite and the rocks made it easy to work in on them, and then they weren't expecting anybody yet. Tate Wingard was bent over the fire of dried mesquite, poking at the coals with a stick. Joe Slade was standing there, watching him and smoking a cigarette. Rory was off to one side.

He was changing clothes. He had worn those old duds just for the hold-up, and he couldn't wait to get back into his fancy ones. So he was there, his gun and belt laid out on a rock while he stepped into his expensive corduroy pants.

I moved out with the .44 in my hand. Joe Slade saw me first. He started to cry out something and went for his gun. I shot him in the chest, and he fell with the cry choking in his throat.

Tate Wingard whirled and straightened, all in one swift movement. His gun was coming up when I put a slug in him. He dropped his gun and clasped his middle with both hands as he doubled up.

I swung my .44 on Rory. My heart was pounding fast. I could feel the sweat in my palms where I gripped the six-shooter and where I still held the shotgun. I aimed the .44 at Rory, sweat running down my cheeks.

He'd been caught unawares. He had just finished belting his pants and was going for his gun on the rock when I swung the .44 on him, and he froze right there. His face went white, and a corner of his mouth twitched.

He took a deep breath now, and color started coming back to his face. His eyes narrowed as he studied me. He took another breath, and his eyes turned bright.

"Why don't you shoot, Lew?" he said. His voice was mocking.

I said nothing.

He laughed a little. "Is it because of the old man? He'd never get over it if you killed me. He'd die a miserable death. Is that why you won't shoot?"

I didn't speak. Something was crying silently and achingly in me.

He laughed again. He sounded confident and even happy now. "This is just fine, Lew. I'm not mad because you got Joe and Tate. That makes it better. Half for you and half for me. That's how it's going to be in the future. Just you and me. We'll make a fortune, Lew."

I didn't say anything. I was thinking that we had been raised together as brothers; we had played together as kids. I remembered the first times that I began to wonder why my last name was Camden and his was Standish, and Dad had told me I wasn't his real son. I remembered how lonely and forsaken I had felt then, but not for long, because Dad Standish had made me feel that I was his son, after all.

Rory laughed and reached down and picked up his chaps. He belted them on and laughed again as he started for his horse. "Half the bullion is in my saddle-bags," he said. "The other half is in Tate's. You can have that. Fair enough?"

"Rory," I said. My voice sounded thick and harsh.

"Oh, no," he said chuckling, and kept right on going. "You won't shoot. Because of the old man you won't shoot."

"Rory," I said again. "Look at me."

This time he stopped and turned. I saw the smile on his face. I saw it flicker and die, and the alarm and terror widen his eyes. I saw his mouth open to shout. I saw all this down the twin barrels of the shotgun because that was where I aimed.

I fired both barrels together. The recoil slammed hard against my shoulder, and through the black gunpowder smoke I saw that he had no face to be pretty any more. . . .

The wind was still blowing when I started back the next morning with the three of them packed across their saddles. The sun was high, scorching the hills, when I sighted the sheriff and his posse. I reined in and waited for them to ride up.

I told the sheriff that two men had held up the stage and killed Bisbee Johnson. The shooting attracted Rory, and the two of us rode after the bandits. We caught up to them, and in the fight one of them would have had me but for Rory who killed him. But the other had my shotgun, and he killed Rory before I could get him.

The sheriff looked at me a long time like he was weighing something in his mind. Then he looked at the three, but they were dead and beyond talking. He just shrugged and turned his horse, and we all rode on to Silver Rock. The sheriff went to Dad Standish, because they were old friends, and told it to Dad the way I had said.

He was sitting in the shade when I went up the steps with the shotgun under my arm. I stopped and looked at him, and he looked back at me. His eyes were wet and sad.

"I owe him my life," I said. "No man could have done more than Rory did for me."

He reached out with his good hand and grabbed mine fiercely. He opened his mouth to speak, but he couldn't. He began dabbing at the corner of his lips with his tongue while twin tears rolled out of his eyes. They were still sad because he had lost his son, but there was something else in them, something like a fierce and happy pride. I knew that pride would stay there until the day he died.

I went into the house, sat down at the table, and put my face in my hands. My throat felt dry and aching, and I guess I sobbed once. Rita came and put her arm around me. I don't know if she understood, but I could never tell her, not even Rita. I would never tell anyone what really happened back there in those dry and burning hills. . . .

Fair Game

She had kind of a sad face. The gray eyes were set wide apart, and they had a way of taking on a gaze as though she were thinking of something far away and forever lost. Her high cheekbones gave her the hollow look of pining away, and the long, rose-colored lips were almost always grave. She seldom smiled. Still she was beautiful, beautiful in a haunting, unforgettable way. I know.

She was not tall or short for a woman, and she was slim, very slim. You could see the fine bone structure beneath the skin when she closed her hands. She was like a piece of delicate china. Even her voice had a fragile quality, like the last echo of some forgotten whisper.

Every time he took her in his arms, it seemed as if he would crush the breath, maybe even the life, out of her for he was a big brute of a man, but I suppose he could be gentle because she seemed to like it. These were the few times that something like a smile would touch her lips, and she'd hug him in return and then kiss him. I always tried not to watch, but no matter how quickly I averted my eyes the picture was there, sharp and lasting.

She had seen us coming, had stepped outside, and was standing there, bare-headed, in the snow. She waved and that was enough to send him on ahead with long, fast strides. I hung back, looking out over the hard rippling blue of the lake which was still unfrozen after this first light snowfall of November.

I heard them murmur things to each other, sweet,

tender things, I imagine, and I tried to pay no attention to them. *What's eating you, Ludlow?* I asked myself. *Why let it get you like this? There's been nothing, not even a hint of it, between you and her. She scarcely knows you're alive. Besides, she's married, and he's a good joe.*

I circled around them and heard her say: "Please, Elroy," and sensed her pushing away from his embrace. Then I was on the steps, which she had swept clean, stamping snow from my boots. I looked to the south and west, seeing the expanse of leaden sky and the endless stretch of the evergreens, for this was what we call big country up here, miles and miles of wilderness.

Endicott said: "Aren't you coming in, Ludlow?"

I shut the door behind me upon entering.

Endicott had shed his red hunting jacket, and she took it from him and hung it on the rack. His big chest swelled as he inhaled deeply. "That coffee sure smells good, Rosemary," he said. "Get the whiskey, won't you, hon? I feel like a good stiff slug of it."

I stepped into the room where I bunked, unloaded my rifle, and stood it in a corner. I dropped my jacket and cap on the bed, and then sat down on the edge. I don't know how long I sat there like that with my hands clasped between my thighs, staring at the floor.

Endicott's voice brought me out of it. "Coffee, Ludlow?" he called from the next room.

"I'll be right there," I said.

He had a cup half full and the whiskey bottle in his hand. "Hold it," I told him. "I'll take mine plain."

His brows went up. "I've seen you drink coffee royals before. How come?"

"I don't feel like it today."

He shrugged. "Suit yourself."

I could feel her watching me, like she often did, but I pretended to be unaware of it. She went on staring, however, and finally she said: "No luck today either, Sam?"

I shook my head.

"I don't know whether to be sorry or glad," she said. "Those poor little deer aren't hurting anybody. Why must you men be so brutal? Why must you slaughter them?"

"Don't mind her, Ludlow," Endicott said. "Never known anyone as soft-hearted. She'll walk around a bug on the ground rather than step on it." His laugh loomed in the room. "You've got to get more spunk, hon."

"It isn't that, Elroy," she said. "You know it. I just can't stand the thought of anything being killed."

Endicott's laugh boomed again. "You'll get over it. Just come out with me and watch me knock one over. That'll cure you."

She shuddered. "You know I couldn't stand that, Elroy. I'd be sick for a week. I hope you don't even get a shot at one."

He was a big man, and, I suppose, like a lot of big men he was attracted to women who were small or seemingly helpless. If that was all there was to it, then I guess they were a perfect match. But he was much older than her, fifteen or twenty years older, I'd say.

There you go again, Ludlow, I told myself, getting mad. *What business is it of yours their difference in age? Just because she looks at you sometimes . . . ! He's crazy in love with her. Can't you tell?*

He had asked her to get chow ready, but he did most of the cooking. "My only chance, Ludlow," he said, winking and grinning. "At home she won't even let me in the kitchen."

206

After we'd eaten, he washed the dishes while she wiped. I went to my room. I lay down on my blankets with a magazine, but I couldn't read. I could hear them talking, low and soft, and his pleased chuckles and once the sound of scuffling followed by her tone of reproach and his light laugh. I lay there, pretending not to hear, remembering how I'd got into this.

When he'd offered me an even hundred bucks rent plus my wages as a guide during the nine-day deer season, I'd marked him for what he obviously was: a rich guy from the southern part of the state who owned a construction business down there, or was it a small factory? I never bothered to make sure. He paid the rent in advance, and that was enough for me. When he said his wife would be along, I said okay because I figured it would be someone middle-aged like him and probably built like a tank, but then it turned out to be her.

I had put the magazine aside and was lying there, staring, just staring at the ceiling, when she looked and then came in.

"Am I bothering you?" she said in that small, almost timid voice.

"Not at all," I said. I swung my legs over the side of the bunk and sat on the edge.

She stared at my carbine and my rifle, both of which were leaning against a corner. She pointed a long, slim finger. "How come you've got two guns?" she asked.

I cursed the quickened beating of my heart. *She's just bored*, I told myself, *she's just tired of being alone during the day while you and Endicott hunt. She's probably used to shows and night clubs. She's not used to being cooped up way out here in the wilderness miles away from any doings.*

I tried to be flippant about it. "I'm a two-gun man," I said, "like in the Western movies. One for each hand."

She glanced at me sharply and showed me that shadowy smile. "You're making fun of me," she said reproachfully. "I'm serious. Is there any difference between the two?"

I went over and picked one up. "One's a rifle," I told her. "This is a carbine. It's a little shorter and lighter to carry around in the woods all day. I prefer the rifle, though. There's no difference in caliber. They're both Thirty-Thirties."

"Would you show me how it works?"

I stared at her.

For a moment a little color showed under the pallor of her features. "I . . . I'd really like to know. Because of Elroy. He likes so much to hunt, and I . . . I'd like to be a part of that. I like sharing things with him. But he won't take me seriously. He makes fun of me when I ask him certain things, and that gets me rattled. Would you show me how that gun works?"

I went on staring at her. Her glance started to shift, but then she brought those gray eyes back and the moist appeal in them decided me. "When the hammer's back slightly like this, it's on safety," I said. "When you want to shoot, you cock it with your thumb like this. Then you squeeze the trigger. To eject the empty shell and get a fresh one in the breech, you work the lever like this. Then you squeeze the trigger again, or, if you aren't shooting any more, you let the hammer down like this and set it back on safety. See?"

She nodded.

"Here," I said. "Take it and try. It's unloaded."

Her eyes went wide as if I had thrust a poisonous

snake at her. "Oh, no, Sam. I can't make myself touch one."

"Then how are you going to learn to shoot?"

"Give me time. When I'm alone tomorrow, I'll try. You'll leave it unloaded, won't you? I'll try when I'm alone, so no one will make fun of me. I know it's silly to be like this, but that's the way I am. I so much want to learn to shoot a gun . . . for Elroy. You'll teach me, won't you?"

I knew a moment of loneliness and a hopeless yearning. "Okay, Missus Endicott," I said. "I'll teach you."

The deer came out of the thicket and stood still a moment. I caught him in the sights, and then I hesitated, thinking: *if he'll go over that rise, he'll be set up just right for Endicott. After all, that's what he's paying me for. I could drop it for him, but there's no thrill like shooting your own.*

The deer was a big buck with a large rack of antlers, but he was far enough away so that I couldn't count the points. Probably as tough eating as an old inner tube, but he'd make a fine trophy. I tightened my finger around the trigger. If he wasn't going to move soon, I'd shoot.

Just then the buck stirred and started up the slope. He moved without hurry, ambling up the hill. A moment he was silhouetted against the gray sky. Then he was gone.

I waited. The shot cracked out loud and sharp in all that stillness. The echoes rolled past me and beyond me, far into the evergreens and into silence. Then came another shot and on the heels of that a third one. These echoes, too, rolled and faded and died.

A strange reluctance gripped me as I started up the

slope. I could not understand it. All I knew was that it unnerved me. Was it the temper of the day, the low, dismal clouds, the first hush of winter like the deep, eternal silence of the tomb? Then her image crossed my memory, and I knew what it was.

I stopped on the crest of the hill. He was there below, sitting on a stump with his back to me. I stood and watched. And I felt it begin in me, mildly at first, just swirling around, and I didn't know what it was; then something nurtured it, and it grew, and I felt it rise overwhelmingly in me; and at the last moment I caught myself and forced it back to whatever depths had spawned it. I lowered the rifle from my shoulder, aware that I was trembling all over.

When I had myself in hand again, I went down to him. He heard me coming, rose to his feet, and picked up his rifle. His face wore a disgusted look.

"Missed him," he said bitterly. "Three shots and every one a miss. I suppose you heard?"

I said nothing.

"He came over that rise," Endicott went on, "walking slow and easy. I couldn't have asked for a better target. But I missed, and he really took off. I tried two more on the run, but what can you expect when I can't even hit a walking target?" He peered at me. "You listening, Ludlow?"

I hauled myself out of it, out of the black thoughts and the fear of the great evil that I had never known existed in me until a few minutes ago. "I heard you shoot," I said woodenly. "Tough. But you'll get another chance. Better luck, then."

He was still peering at me. "You don't look so good."

I stared off at the green ring the balsams and spruces

and hemlocks made around this clearing. "I'm all right."

"You look all in," he said. "I'm pretty well bushed myself. How about calling it a day?"

I didn't like the thought of going back to the cottage, and seeing her move around, and hearing her voice, and feeling her eyes on me every now and then. I didn't like that at all, but there was no way to run from it. So I said: "Okay, Endicott. Let's start back."

That evening I didn't even try to read. I lay on my blankets with my hands under my head, my eyes closed, and straining everything in me to keep from remembering the incident of that day and trying not to pay attention to their voices beyond the curtain. They were playing cribbage, and she squealed delightedly every time she won, and he grumbled, but you could tell it was good-natured grousing and that he was really glad she had won. Maybe he had even let her win. There wasn't a thing he wouldn't do for her.

I didn't hear her come in. My eyes were closed, and it was the fragrance first of all and then an awareness of her, and I opened my eyes, and there she was, staring at me with that grave, faintly wistful look in her eyes, the lamplight turning the ends of her dark hair to golden brown. Endicott was moving about in the next room, and the radio began to blare loudly. Though I've always hated loud radios, somehow I liked it loud right then.

"Aren't you feeling well, Sam?" she asked, and I thought there was something special in her voice for me, something like concern, but then I told myself it was just my imagination.

I sat up on the edge of the bed. "I'm all right."

"You hardly ate anything tonight."

"I wasn't very hungry."

"Could I make something for you?"

"I'm all right. You needn't bother."

"I'd like to fix you something."

To change the subject I said: "How about the carbine? Did you try it today? It would be just right for you, a light gun like that."

She shuddered. "I tried. I tried real hard, Sam. I actually picked it up once, but that's all. I put it down right away. Guns make my skin crawl. They always have. I don't think I could ever force myself to shoot one."

"There's really nothing to it," I said. "I don't know why you should be so afraid."

"But I *am*," she said, shuddered again, and hugged herself with her arms. Her eyes widened and stared off into that secret, sad somewhere that only she could see. "Call it a phobia. Maybe something that happened when I was a child and which I can't remember." She uttered a small, nervous laugh, her lips twitching stiffly. "Maybe I should go see a psychiatrist. Are you sure you don't want me to fix you something?"

"I'm very sure. Thanks anyway."

"Well, good night, Sam."

"Good night, Missus Endicott."

There was something about those tracks that disturbed me from the moment I saw them, but I had no idea what it was. My mind was too full of other things, of hopelessness and frustration and disgust with myself, and that fear of the ugly evil I had not known I possessed. I had left Endicott in a clearing while I made a circle around through the woods to see if I could scare up something to drive past him, but there was no deer sign today. Only the wildness was there, green and somber and patient, full of awesome silence, full of lonesome brooding.

I doubled back finally and started up that hill, remembering yesterday and the dark impulse, and the rifle at my shoulder, and the sights staring at Endicott's back; and in the midst of all this frightening remembrance I noticed the tracks. They paralleled mine, except that they went up the hill, whereas mine had gone down. I noticed where, just before reaching the crest, they veered off to the left and seemed to have headed for the timber.

He was seated on the same stump below with his rifle across his knees, smoking a cigarette. I forced myself to continue without breaking stride or pausing. That could have been yesterday's mistake, the stopping, and the thinking, and then seeing her in my mind.

I made enough noise so that he heard me coming. He rose to wait for me. I could feel his eyes examining me. Did he suspect about yesterday?

He glanced at his wrist watch. "You've been gone a long time," he said, and the concern in his voice sounded genuine. "I'd begun to worry about you."

"What's there to worry about?"

He gave me that peering look again. "I don't know. You just don't seem to be yourself the last couple of days. If you don't feel so hot, we could knock off hunting for a day or two."

I began to breathe easier. It wasn't what I had thought it was. "I'm okay."

"So I don't get my buck. I can come back next year, can't I? Stay in tomorrow at least. I can hunt close to the cottage and along the roads. I won't get lost. Don't knock yourself out just because I hired you.

You'll get paid anyway."

I almost screamed at him: *Why do you have to be such a right guy?* Aloud I said: "I never felt better in all my life. Come on, let's get back and have a drink."

She sat between us, slouched a little with her thighs together and her hands clasped in her lap. Her face looked pale in the glow from the dashboard light, paler than I remembered. The shadows caressed her features, and I envied him for I dared not touch her.

"Turn left up ahead," I said. These were the first words I had spoken since we had left the cottage.

Endicott braked the car and turned off the road. There were several cars parked in front of the tavern, and, as I got out, I could hear the juke box going and the sound of voices. I hung back, letting her and Endicott enter first. There was a small vestibule just inside the entrance, and we hung our jackets there. I still remember what the juke box was playing because it fitted in with the way I felt inside:

**Got you on my mind,
Feeling kind of sad and low . . .**

It was a hunter's crowd, loud and jovial. The talk was almost all of hunting, of the deer they'd killed, the ones they'd wounded, the big ones they'd missed, good-natured ribbing and joking, everyone roughly dressed in heavy woolen shirts and red trousers, even the women; the men were unshaven and smelling of the woods, of spruce and pine needles and resin, and all of them talking loudly so as to be heard above each other, and in the background the juke box blaring.

No matter how I try
My heart keeps telling me that I
Can't forget you . . .

It was not long before Endicott became one of them, engaged with two other hunters in a discussion of the best rifle for deer. I'd had three more whiskeys, quick ones, and the liquor was working in me, mellowing me. Some of the gloom lifted from my mind, and I would have been glad, except that I knew it would return once the effect wore off.

A couple of times I caught her eyes in the bar mirror, and it was always me who broke the glance. Finally I turned and looked directly at her. At the moment she was toying with her shot glass, drawing moist circles with it on the bar and studying the pattern with a withdrawn preoccupation. After a while she looked up and around at me, and our eyes locked, and I thought I read a message for me in hers.

"Would you like to dance?" I asked.

She fitted nicely into my arms, and I realized that this, too, had been a mistake.

"What's the matter, Sam?" she asked as we circled the floor. "I thought going out might cheer you up. In fact, I was the one who suggested it to Elroy. What's the matter? Won't you tell me?"

The record ended, and we came to a stop. When the next one began, she seemed to have read my mind, for she made no move to resume dancing.

"It's stuffy in here," she said. "I think I'll get some air."

The cars were all frosted over from the cool, damp air coming off the lake. She stood there with her back to me like she was lost in those deep thoughts of hers again. At first I fought it; then I thought: *What the hell, this might be all the chance I'll ever have* — and it was a mixture of desire and frustration. I turned her around by the shoulders and took her in my arms.

I guess she struggled at first. Anyway it felt like that, but she was so slim and frail to begin with, and I was so angry and bitter that I didn't think about maybe being too rough. Her lips were cool and indifferent at first, and then they moistened and warmed, and I knew I had not been mistaken, after all.

It was the sudden blast of sound as someone opened the door that brought us out of it. She noticed it even before I did and pushed away. I spun around, thinking it was Endicott, but it was just another couple. They passed us by and got into a car.

We went back inside.

The day was gray, as gray as my thoughts. The clouds hung low in dark swells and billows. The air had a damp, bitter feel, the smell of an impending snowfall lay over the wilderness. I stood outside, waiting for Endicott to take his leave of her. They were always reluctant partings for him. He'd stand on the steps with her in the open doorway, hesitating like a high-school kid saying good night to his first crush. It made me grit my teeth this time, because I was remembering the night before with her in my arms.

"Didn't you hear her, Ludlow?"

That brought me out of it. I turned away from my study of the lake and looked at them.

"She asked you if you think it'll snow today?"

I caught her eyes but read nothing in them. She was

too far away for that anyway. "I'm pretty sure it will."

"Very much?" he asked.

"Could be," I said.

He kissed her then, long and hard. "So long, hon," he said.

"Be careful, dear."

I started up the road.

"Good bye, Sam."

For the briefest moment my step faltered, but I didn't stop or even look around. "Be seeing you," I called to her.

He made no attempt to talk as we walked along, and neither did I. The only sound was the soft scuffing of our boots in the snow. Where the road divided, I came to a halt, and he stopped beside me.

"Let's do it different today," I said. "Let's both strike out on our own. You know the country fairly well now, and you won't get lost as long as you follow this railroad bed. It eventually crosses the fire lane again, and you can come back that way or double back on this. I'll scout the timber. Maybe I can knock something over. Okay?"

He looked at me without answering. *Does he know?* I thought. *Does he understand the real reason behind this? Does he guess that I'm scared of myself, scared of what I might do?*

A couple of vagrant snowflakes fell, drifting slowly between us, and then he said: "Okay, Ludlow."

"You needn't wait for me," I told him. "Just return to the cottage when you're tired of hunting. Only don't go off into the woods. This is a big country, and you might never find your way out if the snow covers your tracks."

He nodded and started off.

I took the spur that wound and twisted its way up and

over the hills. In the old days it had been the geared Shay engines that had clattered and squealed their slow, tortuous way up and down these steep grades. Now they were only memories, eventually to be forgotten like I wished all my memories could be forgotten.

I picked up the deer tracks, heading south. They looked fresh, and so I turned off the logging spur into the timber. The snow was building up; the flakes were thicker. It would not be long before it was snowing full force.

It was not long before the deer tracks crossed the old main line. I could see the trail made by Endicott where he had passed earlier. When I saw the second pair of tracks following his, I pulled up sharply. They were the same tracks I had noticed the day before, and, as I stared at them, I realized with a sick feeling what it was about them that had disturbed me. They were small — tracks made by a boy, or a woman. I followed them. . . .

She was crouched behind a large stump, the remnant of what had been once a giant Norway pine, and she was so intent on aiming that she was not aware of my coming up quietly behind her. He had stopped some distance up the road to light a cigarette, and his back made a nice red target.

In the vast stillness of the forest the click as she cocked the carbine was a distinct sound. She had taken the mitten off her trigger hand. I still wore mine. I clamped down on the action just in time. Startlement made her pull the trigger, but my thumb was there, and the hammer snapped down and caught some of my glove between it and the firing pin, and that was what kept the carbine from going off. Surprise so unsettled her that I easily tore the carbine out of her grasp.

She huddled there in the snow, pressed up hard against the stump, her balled right fist against her mouth. She had uttered a sharp, short gasp. That had been her only sound.

He never knew what happened behind him. When I glanced his way, he was moving on, rifle cradled in the crook of his arm. He never once looked back. Soon he was out of sight.

I had known pain of mind and heart before, but it was nothing compared to what I experienced now. Now it was the deep anguish of final disillusionment.

I looked down at her. There was hurt in me, lots of hurt, the kind of hurt that fades but never dies, yet there was no hate, and I was surprised at that. Even now, when I finally knew her for what she really was, I still couldn't hate her. What I had felt for her had been too real, too deep to be replaced by hate.

"So you don't know how to shoot," I said, "and guns scare you, and you'd get lost if you wandered more than ten feet from the cottage." It was snowing steadily now, and a wind had begun to blow. The tracks we'd made were filling in. "You wanted to make sure you'd never be suspected, didn't you? That's why you didn't try it yesterday, why you waited until today. Today the snow would cover your tracks. And in case you were suspected, you prepared for that, too. My carbine. If they dug the bullet out of him and had a ballistics done on it, it would be me, wouldn't it, since you don't know how to shoot?"

Two tears welled up in her eyes, trembled a moment on the lashes, then trickled down her cheeks. She shook her head mutely from side to side. Another time this might have touched me and moved me, but I was old now and wise.

"Even last night," I went on, "when you let me kiss you and be seen kissing you . . . it was all to set me up, wasn't it? A motive for killing him. What could be a better one than his wife?"

She spoke now, her lips moving stiffly. They had lost their rose color; they were almost as pale as the snow that passed in front of her face. "I love you, Sam. I love you."

"Do you? Or is it someone back home? Is that why you tried it? Or is he too old for you, and you want to be free of him, but you want his money, too?"

"I love you, Sam. Please believe me." She saw it was no use. "What're you going to do?"

"I won't tell anyone. Who would believe me against you, anyway? Let's go."

"Go? Where?"

"Back to camp."

It would be my word against hers. Remembering how Endicott doted on her, I realized it would be useless to tell him anything. She would twist it around in her favor somehow. She would turn those big, sad, lost eyes on him and look frail and weak and persecuted, and he would believe her rather than me.

And she would try again. Not any more this way, perhaps, but some other way, some other time. I couldn't tell him — he loved her too much.

I turned off the fire lane into the timber. She stopped and hesitated. "That isn't the way back," she said.

"Short cut," I said.

Still she hesitated.

"Can't you see how it's storming? I want to get back as soon as I can. You coming?"

She followed. The timber closed about us. The wind

groaned in the tree tops, but down on the ground we hardly felt it. This was another world down here, a primeval world, a baffling world of trees and more trees, all of them alike, every direction alike, not even the sun to tell which way was which, nor the sky, for the snow swirled so thick and fast you could not see above the tree tops. I quickened my pace.

"Sam," she called, "please slow down, Sam. I can't keep up with you." Each word was a gasp.

I moved still faster.

"Sam!" she screamed finally, and began to run after me.

I broke into a run. "Sam, Sam!" and then she tripped and went sprawling, and I kept on running, running.

"Sam!"

Running, running, tripping, swiping my face against a low limb and behind me the shrill, terrified shrieking.

"Sam, Sam, Sam . . . !"

Fainter and fainter until I knew it was only in my mind.

I was with the search party that found her, and so was he. The storm had let up after two days, and we found her huddled behind a windfall, all curled up on her side with one cheek pillowed on her folded hands. The sheriff brushed the snow gently from her face, and she seemed to be asleep with her eyes closed and her lips a thin, sad line and that melancholy look on her features. I turned away and almost wept, but no one thought anything of it because they all felt the same way.

"Why?" Endicott cried, tears streaming down his cheeks. "Why did she wander away? *Why*, when she was so scared of the woods? Will somebody tell me why?"

The Mesteños

"Try to understand, Feliz," Eastland said. "We don't like to harm the *mesteños*, but we have no choice. Can't you understand?"

Feliz looked at the men in front of him, sitting in their saddles. *Cobardes*, he thought. *I understand. I understand so well I could kill you, Eastland, and you were once my friend.*

"You've known me a long time, Feliz," Eastland went on. Wind off the flank of the Coronados stirred his hat brim gently. "You know I wouldn't kill a horse, any horse, unless I really had to. You know that, don't you?"

"No one's going to hurt my *mesteños*," Feliz said.

"Your mesteños?" Crawford cried. He glared at the rifle in Feliz's hands. "Where the devil do you get that stuff? Mustangs are any man's property who rounds them up. They're no more your *mesteños* than the man in the moon's."

"Try to look at it our way, Feliz," Eastland said. "It hasn't rained for a long time. The *mesteños* come down from the Coronados and eat our graze and drink our water. The stallions run off with our mares. Things are going hard for us, Feliz. We don't like it, but the *mesteños* have all got to die."

"The *mesteños* were here before you came," Feliz said. "If things are going hard for you, why don't you go away? Why blame the *mesteños?*"

"Feliz," Eastland said, spreading his hands in a pleading gesture. "We're old friends, aren't we? You have always been welcome at my ranch. My wife has fed you. My son has learned all he knows about horses from you. You and I have talked together about the ways of horses many times. Do you doubt me when I say I wish it could be different, but there is no other choice?"

"I will not let you or anyone kill the *mesteños*."

"He's loco," Crawford said. His face was full of angry color. "He's always been loco. Look how he used to hunt mustangs, tracking them on foot, living with them until they took him as one of their own. Now that he's old, he's more loco than ever. Are we going to let a crazy man tell us what to do?"

"He might be loco," Ainsworth said, "but he's got a rifle."

"There's five of us," Crawford cried. "Are we going to let a crazy half-breed buffalo us?"

"You want to start it?" Bailey asked. "You want the first slug?"

"Stop that kind of talk," Eastland said. "We're not going to have any trouble. Let's give him a couple of days to think it over."

"You always had a soft spot for the crazy coot," Crawford told Eastland. "You think a couple of days will make him change?"

"It won't hurt to try."

"I'm tired of waiting. Dammit, I'm almost out of graze. If it don't rain pretty soon. . . ."

"A couple more days won't hurt you," Eastland said.

"You trying a stall, Eastland?"

Eastland turned on Crawford. Eastland's mouth was tight, his eyes hard. "I'm in the same fix you are, Crawford. In fact, I've got more to lose than you. I'm not

223

going to sit on my rump and let myself be wiped out. But we are giving Feliz a couple of days." Eastland's eyes moved back to Feliz. "Listen to me, Feliz. Listen to me as a friend. The old days are over. They are gone for good. The mustangs are through here in the Coronados."

They are not through, Feliz thought, *as long as I have breath to breathe, and bullets to shoot, and a knife to cut.*

"But there are other places, Feliz," Eastland went on. "There's plenty of open country to the south. Why don't you take your best *mesteños* and lead them there?"

"This is my home," Feliz said.

"I know," Eastland said, "and no one is trying to chase you away. But the *mesteños* have got to go, one way or another."

"This is their home, too. We will never leave the Coronados."

"Two days, Feliz," Eastland said. His eyes softened. "Will you try to understand? Will you take your best horses and leave? If you are not gone in two days. . . ." His mouth drew tight and thin. "I swear to it, Feliz. Two days. No more. . . ."

Feliz picked up the tracks of the *manada* heading north, and he turned his dun in pursuit. In the distance Carrizo Peak loomed high, ragged, and awesome. The wind blew hard down from the Coronados, filling the tracks in fast, but not too fast for Feliz.

Roano, he thought happily, *my beautiful Roano. I would know your hoof marks on solid stone. You will be mine yet. You are wild and wary, but you will be mine.*

He topped a rise and there below he saw the mustang band, drinking at the water hole. Some of the mares were rolling on the ground. Several colts frolicked. The roan stallion stood to one side, head high as he spied Feliz in the distance.

Feliz reined in the dun. He dismounted and tied the horse to a juniper. Then he started down the slope on foot. The stallion snorted and pranced, watching Feliz come on.

Oh, you are a great and wise stallion, Feliz thought. *From out of nowhere you came and took the manada away from the Grullo. You will make a great sire, and you will be mine. Some day soon you will be mine.*

The wind took his scent and carried it down to the *manada.* The stallion snorted, shied, and pawed at the ground with a front hoof. Several of the mares watched Feliz docilely.

Ho, you know my smell already, he thought. *That is good. You would already accept me because you know I mean you no harm. But you, Roano, you big red devil, you do not trust me yet, do you?*

He moved steadily on, without hurry. The whole band was watching him now, even the colts. The stallion nickered angrily and tossed his head. The long mane fluttered in the wind.

It is good that you are so careful, Roanito, Feliz thought. *You must be more careful than ever now. Those cobardes will kill you if they get the chance, and you must not give them the chance. You must be very careful, Roano.*

The stallion blew loudly and pranced nervously. One of the mares started toward Feliz, and the stallion jumped in front of her and nipped her in the neck. The mare turned back.

You are a good stallion, Roano, Feliz thought. *You still do not trust me, even though I am not like the other* men-animals who would like to kill you. Leave the Coronados, they said to me. Leave? When the Coronados are our home?

He moved on. The stallion trumpeted a cry of alarm and anger. He wheeled and started nipping the flanks of the mares. They were reluctant to go, but he started them. They left in a cloud of dust with the stallion trailing them, biting and kicking to urge more speed out of them. Feliz watched until even their dust was gone. Then he started back up the slope to get his dun.

Your day will come, Roanito, he thought. The day will come, and soon, when you will accept me. Every time you let me come a little closer. But it is good for you to be so careful. Be very careful. If anyone ever harms you or any more of my mesteños. . . .

Feliz awoke three days later with a strong feeling of apprehension. He came to his feet, and for a while he stood stock still, head flung up, sniffing the air. He could discern nothing out of the ordinary, but still the uneasiness would not leave him.

Roano, he thought, are you in trouble, Roano? I have not seen you in two days. The other manadas I have seen but not yours. Where have you gone?

He saddled the dun and rode off, chewing on a piece of dried jerky. Once he thought he heard shots, and he reined the dun in, rose up in the stirrups, and listened with his head cocked to one side. The sounds had been so faint, however, that he could not be sure he had heard anything. Nevertheless, his heart quickened. Dread made him ill.

Roano. Have they hurt you, Roanito?

When he saw the vultures gathering in the sky, a hand

of ice closed about his heart. He lifted the dun into a hard run. The vultures kept gathering, floating and wheeling high in the sky on wide-spread, motionless wings.

Is that for you, Roanito? If it is, I'll. . . .

His hand closed about the handle of the knife in his belt. A burst of rage made him tremble, but it was quickly gone. Only the dread remained now, the sick, cold dread.

He found them, what was left of them, at the foot of a mesa. Several vultures rose and left with a foul flapping of great black wings. Feliz stared at the rim of the mesa over which the *manada* had plunged and then down at the smashed, bloody carcasses. He began to weep when he saw the stallion.

"I will make them pay, Roanito," he said aloud. "I swear to you, you will not go unavenged. With my gun and knife and even my bare hands I will make them pay. If I could, I would bury you, my beautiful Roanito. Little horse, I will never forget you. . . ."

In the cold, gray dawn Feliz waited. He lay in a small depression on a knoll, and there below him he could see the ranch buildings and the corrals. His rifle lay on the ground beside him.

Five, he thought, *five cabrones. I remember you. The two Ainsworths, and Bailey, and that hijo de puta, Crawford, and you, Eastland. I will kill you, but it will be the Ainsworths first, father and son. When they come out. . . .*

Smoke curled from the chimney of the house. The elder Ainsworth came out, went to the corral, and pitched some hay to the horses penned there. Feliz picked up the rifle, but he did not shoot.

I will wait until I have them both, he thought. *I want them both.*

The elder Ainsworth was through now, and he went back in the house. Feliz watched the smoke curling out of the chimney. His fingers grew numb from holding the cold rifle, and he put it down and shoved his hands underneath his buckskin jacket to warm them.

The boy came out after a while. He went to the corral and saddled two horses. He led them out and stood there, waiting. The elder Ainsworth came out then. He was carrying two rifles and a pack. He walked toward his son and the horses.

Feliz picked up the rifle. He put the stock against his shoulder and looked down the sights.

So, you are ready for another day, are you, cabrones? he thought. *Well, you will kill no more mesteños. I will make sure of that. Now, and now, and now, and now.*

The first shot dropped the elder Ainsworth suddenly and limply. The boy turned to run for the house. The second shot missed him, but the horses were squealing and wheeling in panic. One of them struck the boy, and he went sprawling. As he started to rise, the third bullet hit him, knocking him flat. He stirred and kicked feebly, and the fourth bullet stilled him.

A woman was screaming as Feliz rose to his feet and started for his dun. . . .

Feliz knew they were after him. They had learned about the Ainsworths, and so they would be after him. He had not seen anyone yet, but he could feel it in the air, ominous and deadly.

Let them come, he thought. Cabrones. *Go ahead and*

come. I am ready for you. Kill my mesteños, will you?

Once he heard a flurry of shots, and he came up erect in the saddle. He began to tremble with rage. With each shot he flinched. It was as though every bullet was tearing into his own body. He started to weep.

You have not stopped, have you, cobardes? Even with the Ainsworths dead you have not stopped the killing. But I will kill, too. Not innocent mesteños but every one of you. I will not stop until the last one is dead.

He knew it was folly, but he had to see. Which *manada* was it this time? The *bayo coyote*'s, or the Grullo's, or the *negro*'s, or the *tostado*'s? He had to see no matter what the consequences.

He found them scattered over a small plain. He counted fourteen mares and colts and the white-stockinged black. They had all been shot to death. The smell of blood and dying still lingered in the air. Tears welled up in his eyes, but they were as much of rage as of sorrow and pain. He rose up in the stirrups and brandished a fist.

"*¡Cabrones!*" he cried aloud. "Tonight. I will get you tonight. All of you without exception. You will kill no more horses. After tonight you will kill no more."

He was taking one last look at the black when the bullet hit him. It took him in the back and smashed him forward. The saddle horn dug into his belly, and he felt himself begin to slide off on the side, and so he made a desperate grab for the horn and caught it. He had already touched the dun with his heels, and the horse was off at a gallop. He pulled himself back up the saddle and then flattened himself along the dun's neck. He heard the roar of several other shots, but none of these seemed to hit him.

Faint behind him came shots, a rumble of hoofs, and finally a shot now and then. He did not look back. He urged the dun into a great burst of speed down a slope and then veered him sharply into the mouth of a cañon. He knew of a hidden pocket far up the cañon, a pocket whose mouth was concealed by a growth of junipers and scrub cedars.

Feliz made this pocket. He sat in the saddle with the dun blowing hard under him. At first there had not been much pain from his wound, but he began really to feel it now. It sent searing streaks across his eyes and frightening intervals of blackness. He reeled once in the saddle and almost fell off, but he caught himself in time.

His pursuers passed him and swept up the cañon. He could have shot them as they went by, but he was too weak and unsteady. His whole back was a mass of hurt. Some of the blood was running down a trouser leg. He waited until the riders passed from sight around a bend, and then he sent the dun out and back the way he had come.

By late afternoon he knew he had eluded them, but he kept going until nightfall, even though he could hardly stay in the saddle. He had torn strips from his shirt and fashioned a crude bandage for his wound, but it still bled. He realized he could not lose much more blood. Already at times he grew light-headed and drowsy. So, when he came to the water hole at nightfall, he reined in the dun.

He could not step down from the saddle. All he could do was work his right leg over the cantle and then slide down. Even so, his legs refused to support him, and he sprawled on the ground. He lay there, gathering his strength. When he had a little of it back, he crawled on his belly to the edge of the water and drank. The dun drank beside him.

After a while he tried to rise to get his blanket off the saddle, but the best he could do was get up on his elbows. A few attempts at this and his strength was so far gone that he couldn't even do that. So he rolled on his back, lay on the cold ground, and stared up at the stars.

I can't die, he told himself. *Not as long as one of those* cobardes *is alive. I must protect my* mesteños. *I must live long enough to kill every one of those* cabrones. *So I will not die. I will not let myself die. I will sleep and rest tonight. In the morning I shall be all right. All I need is a little sleep and rest.*

He closed his eyes and lay there a while, listening to the sounds of the dun stirring about and to the night noises. Gradually they grew fainter and soon he slept. . . .

Something woke Feliz. He had no idea what it was, and he opened his eyes and saw that it was dawn. The world looked gray and unreal. Tendrils of mist hung over the land. The sound that had waked him came again. He was sure it was the dun, but, when he looked, the dun was nowhere to be seen. Instead another horse was standing there. Feliz came up on an elbow, heart quickening.

"Roano," he whispered. "Roanito *mio*. Is that you, Roano?"

The roan's ears pricked forward. He was standing there at the water's edge with arched neck, all wary and suspicious and alert. He nickered softly when Feliz spoke.

Feliz sat up. He was surprised at the ease with which he moved. It was like in his younger days when each movement was effortless and flowing. He thought he'd try to stand, and he gained his feet without trouble. He seemed a little weak, but his wound no longer pained. The blood was crusted dry and black on his clothing. He could hardly feel the earth under his feet.

"Roano," he said, taking a step forward. "Then you are not dead, Roano? Every one was so smashed and broken, I was sure it was you, but I was wrong. You fooled them, didn't you, wise little horse? I always knew you were too smart for them."

He took another step ahead. The roan snorted softly and shied a little.

"Little horse, I will not hurt you," Feliz said. "I am the only friend you have. I am not like the other men-animals who want to kill you. I want to be your friend. Don't you know that?"

The roan nickered again, a plaintive, lonely sound. He watched Feliz take another step ahead.

"You are in trouble, and so you've come to me," Feliz said, "because at last you know you can trust me. Roanito, you can always trust me. You and I together. Little horse, don't shy."

He reached out a hand, and for a moment it looked as though the roan would flee. He snorted nervously, shrank back slightly, then paused there while Feliz moved his hand ahead a little more and touched the stallion's muzzle. The roan shuddered, but he did not flee.

"There. You see?" Feliz said. "I have not hurt you. Don't tremble, Roanito *mio*. We are going to be great friends. We are going to have many wonderful times together. Don't be afraid, little horse." He moved in close to the roan. He reached up and grabbed a fistful of mane. "I am going to ride you. Without a saddle. You want me to ride you, don't you? We have a long way to go, and you are going to take me, aren't you?"

The roan nickered gently. Not a muscle flickered in his body.

Feliz did not know if he had the strength to climb on the roan. He felt weak yet somehow buoyant. His hands grabbed the mane, and, when he threw himself up, something seemed to lift him and carry him gently up on the roan's back. For a moment the roan hesitated. Then he wheeled, gently however, and started off. In Feliz there was hardly any sensation. The smoothness of the ride made him marvel.

The roan's speed increased. Soon he was running at the fastest pace Feliz had ever known. They seemed to float over the ground with the roan's hoofs not even touching the earth. *Like a bird,* Feliz thought. *We are soaring along like the birds. Oh, I always knew you were a wonderful horse, Roano.*

Somehow they seemed to be rising even higher. Ahead of them Carrizo Peak loomed, high and lofty and jagged in the first bright light of the sun. *To the top, to the very top, Roanito,* Feliz thought. *We must reach the very top.* As if in response the earth seemed to fall away beneath them. Feliz looked down and saw nothing. So he lifted his eyes and looked straight ahead, and all he saw was the ultimate crest of Carrizo Peak, and in this moment Feliz at last knew where he was going. . . .

The three riders reined in beside the water hole and stared down at Feliz, who lay on his stomach with one hand reaching out pointing at Carrizo Peak. The dun stood to one side with trailing reins.

"He's dead all right," Eastland said.

"Nothing like making sure," Crawford said. He drew his six-shooter and aimed it at Feliz.

Eastland jumped his bay in front of Crawford and batted Crawford's gun up.

"I say he's dead!" Eastland shouted.

"What you so worked up about?" Crawford shouted back at him, face heavy with anger. "He killed the Ainsworths, didn't he? And he'd have killed every one of us if he'd got the chance. Fill him full of lead, trample him, and leave him for the buzzards, I say."

"The buzzards will never touch him," Eastland said. "I'll see to that."

"Well, I'm not going to waste any time burying him," Crawford growled, reining his horse away and riding off.

"I'll help," Bailey said.

"Thanks, John," Eastland said. "But I'd rather do it alone."

When Bailey also had gone, Eastland dismounted. He stared down at Feliz. "Old friend," he said, then words failed him. He stood there, looking down at Feliz.

After a while Eastland went and started gathering stones. . . .

Those Bloody Bells of Hell!

I

"THE CALL OF THE BELLS"

Red Merriam came into the Palace and stopped inside the swing doors, blue eyes searching the room. The fetid warmth of the place swam about him as he let his glance go over the line of tables up against the wall, probing the sitters at each table. His eyes moved to the left, to the crowded bar. One of the two sweating bartenders, catching Merriam's glance, nodded toward the rear.

Merriam started across the barroom with long, lithe strides, the big rowels of his fancy Mexican spurs jingling. Tobacco smoke eddied about him, and the air was filled with the soft murmur of voices, an occasional laugh, and the stench of sweating bodies.

At the rear of the Palace were three rooms. The door of one was ajar. Merriam aimed for that and paused on the threshold, one hand resting on the jamb.

The room was bare. There was a lone, scratched, pine-board table and six chairs. Two horse drawings, almost obliterated by dust, were nailed on the wall. Flakes of whitewash littered the floor like snowdrops. A man sat at the table, a half-filled whiskey bottle before him. He sat slumped in the chair, his long legs thrust under the table, and he lifted his eyes only long enough to recognize Merriam, then dropped them to the table top again.

"I thought I'd find you here," Merriam said.

Barroom sounds kept swimming in, and Merriam, frowning, turned his head that way a moment.

"About time for the wedding, ain't it?" The voice was that of a man out in the bar.

"Hell, no! Got another hour yet," another man said.

"Shut the damned door," said the man at the table.

Merriam stepped ahead and kicked the door shut with his heel. Flakes of whitewash floated down on the table. Merriam swung one of the chairs around opposite the man at the table and sat down, straddling it, his chest against the back. Reaching out, he grabbed the bourbon bottle and took two deep swallows. He sighed with pleasure and put the bottle back.

"Well, anyway," said Merriam, "you're drinking good stuff."

The man at the table lifted bloodshot eyes that seemed sunk deep into his gaunt, narrow face. Black beard lined his cheeks and chin and ran down his neck. He combed long, rope-burned fingers through his thick black hair. A thin frown clouded his brow as he studied Merriam, noting for the first time the thin alkali dust that hung on the man's clothing.

"Well," Merriam said, "what you gonna do, Lin?"

"I'm killing the dirty son of a bitch," Lin Carmody said.

Merriam sighed. He made a small abortive gesture with his right hand and sighed again. "Now what you want to do that for, Lin? What's it gonna get you? You'll have to hit the hooty owl road. Let her marry Wiley Barrow and leave it like that."

Carmody stirred in his chair, eyes darkening. "I didn't say I was killing him right away."

"Oh," Merriam said, breathing the word. Then, as the significance of it struck him, he said it again, even more softly. "Oh. I didn't know that you could hate that way, Lin."

It was there, strong in Carmody now, bringing a raging tension in him. He threw up his head, eyes glittering. "He took my girl from me . . . while my back was turned. Why shouldn't I hate him? He took Louise from me. I'll kill him for that."

"Well, he's your clay pigeon," said Merriam.

Carmody studied the other again. The dust lay thick on the flat crown of Merriam's hat, some of the powder trickling over the rim as the man inclined his head. Carmody's eyes ran swiftly down Merriam's body, taking in the gray flannel shirt and black vest and resting on the big, black-handled Dragoon Colt at the man's right hip. On the opposite hip, in a buckskin sheath, he wore a bone-handled Bowie knife. Merriam had always been partial to knives, and it was this about him that had never appealed to Carmody.

"What do you want with me?" Carmody asked suddenly.

Merriam came up at that. His blue eyes glittered evasively, then his breath came out in a wheezing sigh. He said: "I've got something big, Lin, down in *Viejo Méjico*." His fingers tightened around the back of the chair until the knuckles were white. "Big enough for the two of us. Forget about Wiley Barrow and Louise. This is big enough to make you forget everything."

It was still stirring deeply inside Carmody. It had been like this for a month now, boiling inside him, filling him with hate. He didn't like hearing it talked about all the time.

"Will you stop talking about Wiley and Louise, Red, or get the hell out of here?"

"Two bells, Lin," Merriam said, ignoring Carmody's statement. "Solid gold, both of them. A quarter ton of gold. That's what I got down in Old Mexico."

Carmody's eyes narrowed. He took a long look at Merriam's flushed face and the big, freckled hands gripping the chair so tightly. Some of the man's fever came to Carmody. He could feel it begin tingling the back of his neck.

"So that's where you've been the past two weeks," said Carmody. "How did you find these bells?"

"I got hold of a map," Merriam said. "The Mex was drunk and an easy mark. It was one of these old Mexican *derroteros*, and, I thought, what the hell, I had nothing to lose. So I bought it off him. It looked real enough."

A derisive smile twisted Carmody's lips. "So that's how it is. A map to buried treasure. They're floating over the whole Southwest. Maps to the Lost Breyfogle and Jean LaFitte's booty and Steinheimer's millions. I never thought you'd fall for that line."

"But I've seen the bells, Lin! I've used the map, and I've seen the bells. I've touched them with my hands!"

There was no doubting the man's sincerity. It showed in his glowing eyes, in the hot, excited flush heating his face, in the hoarseness of his voice.

"You've seen them and touched them," Carmody said slowly. "No one but you knows where they are. Yet, you're telling me about it, offering to cut me in. That's not like you, Red."

Merriam laughed, a short, embarrassed bark. "All

right, it isn't like me. But those bells are so damn' heavy. I can't handle them alone. I need another man. One I can trust. You, Lin. They're solid gold. Enough to put both of us on easy street for the rest of our lives. I don't mind splitting with you. There's enough of it for that."

"Where are these bells?" Carmody asked.

"In the Sierra Pintada range. There's an old story about them. Seems they were made by some *padres* two, maybe three hundred years ago. They're beautiful, Lin. Solid gold with elaborate etchings all over the outside. All gold, even the clappers. Seems like the *padres* had made them for a present to the big auger riding the throne in Spain in those days. But I guess they didn't treat the Indians any too good, and they was laying for the Spaniards. They ran into an ambush and buried the bells when they saw there wasn't a chance of getting out of it alive. They made a map, and it got lost, and I finally found it. Convinced yet, Lin?"

"Yeah," Carmody said slowly, getting to his feet. "I'm convinced, even though you may have garbled the details a little."

"Then you'll come? We can leave right away."

"Not right away," said Carmody, a dead look coming into his eyes. "I've got a little chore first."

The chair rasped harshly as Merriam lurched to his feet. He moved in close to Carmody, clutching at the man's sleeve.

"No, Lin. Don't be a fool! Those bells. . . ."

Carmody pushed out with his hands, caught Merriam in the chest, sent him teetering back until he brought up against the table.

"You keep your damn' hands off me, Red!" Carmody shouted, the chords swelling in his neck.

Merriam's lips twitched back from his teeth. He crouched there, half sitting on the table, left hand clenched about the bone handle of his Bowie. His blazing eyes took in the man, standing straight and tall before him. Carmody towered two inches over six feet. The big wooden-handled Remington .44 dangled at his hip, and the palm of his hand kept brushing against the butt. Merriam took his fingers off his Bowie.

"All right, Lin," Merriam said hoarsely. "All right. . . ."

Carmody took the alley to the rear of the St. Joe Hotel. A flight of steps ran up the side and into the back of the second floor. Carmody went up these, listening to their creaking and the shrill, mournful jingle of his spurs, thinking that all these sad, lonely sounds fitted in with the way he felt.

He walked down the hall, and it struck him strange that his throat should be so suddenly dry and that sweat should have popped out on the back of his neck. At one of the front rooms he raised his hand and knocked on the door.

Someone inside said petulantly: "Who is it?"

Carmody knocked again, louder. He heard the sharp click of a woman's heels approaching the door, then it squeaked open, and a thin-faced, severe woman faced him. Her face paled, and she put a hand to her throat.

"Lin Carmody!" she gasped. Then the color rushed back in her features, and her voice rose sharply. "You can't come in here."

"Step aside, Helen."

"You go right back down those stairs, Lin Carmody."

He gripped the edge of the door with his right hand, holding it open like that, and he said again, through his

240

teeth: "Step aside."

"Yes, Helen, step aside and let him in," said a weary voice inside the room.

Helen threw a frightened look over her shoulder, then dropped back a step, and Carmody pushed past her into the room. The weary voice spoke again. "You may go outside, Helen. I won't need you for a while."

Carmody heard the door closing behind him, but he did not look that way. He was staring at the woman who stood in the far corner of the room. She was tall, slim, and full-bosomed. The white satin wedding dress clung to the soft curves of her body. The small, dimpled chin was high, and the red lips were tight and firm. There seemed to be a shadow in the blue depths of her eyes. Her blonde hair was a golden aureole about her head.

Carmody felt his breath catch in his throat. The hurt began anew. This was the day he'd always longed for since he'd known Louise Durant. The day that he'd see her in a wedding gown. He had always dreamed of that day as the brightest and happiest in his life, but instead it brought a searing hate, for in a matter of minutes Louise Durant would be leaving this room to become the bride of Wiley Barrow.

"I dropped by to offer my congratulations," Carmody said.

She did not move. "Thank you, Lin," she said quietly.

"I came by to let you know I'm letting Wiley be."

Louise gave a long, relieved sigh. "Oh, I'm so glad to hear that, Lin. Thank you!"

"Don't thank me. I only said I'm letting him be . . . for a little while."

Her hand flew to her mouth, and he saw her teeth biting into her knuckle. Shrinking back, she brought up against the wall.

"Sure. That's how it is," he said, biting off the words. "Marry him. Live with him for a while. Know some of the happiness I'll never have. And, when you're the happiest, just stop and think that at that moment I may be on my way to kill Wiley. I want you to live with that knowledge a while. I want you to know some of the hurt I've known. Because, as sure as I'm standing here, Lou, I'm killing Barrow. When, I don't know. Maybe a week, a month. When I feel the time is right. I promise you that, Lou."

She was beating her knuckles against her forehead, head bowed, mouth contorted. Sobs racked her shoulders. "Lin. It wasn't that serious between you and me. . . ."

The pain was in his throat, tempering the bitterness of his words. "Maybe with you it never was that serious. With me, it was. You were my girl since we were kids. I never looked at anyone else. I expected some day to marry you, and I thought you looked at it like that. You knew how it was with me, and you never discouraged me."

She was crying steadily now. "I was very fond of you. I still am fond of you. But I love Wiley. That's why I'm marrying him."

Some of his fury had died, leaving him full of empty bitterness. "Do you really love him, Lou? Or is it his ranch, his big cattle herds, his money in the bank that you love? I'm a nobody. Would you have married me, if I owned a fortune?"

Someone was knocking on the door, an insistent impatience in the rapping. "Are you ready, Louise?" came Helen's voice. "It's almost time."

"Well, I've had my say," Carmody said. He took one more look at the weeping girl, wondering that her tears did not move him. "I'm going now. I wouldn't want you to keep Wiley . . . waiting."

II

"SEÑOR BLANCO"

The barren peaks of the Sierra Pintada seemed to hang sullenly beneath the burnished sky. Down here in the cañon all the glaring heat of the sun seemed concentrated, bouncing off the high, jagged walls, gathering into a sultry, suffocating mass that was almost tangible close to the cañon floor. The mesquite clumps were gnarled, twisted, as though cringing from the constant beat of the sun. Even the scent of the sage held a dry, irritating tang.

The two men had picketed their horses and two pack mules under the meager, warm shade of twin mesquite trees. The animals stood with drooping heads, half-heartedly flicking their tails at the flies and insects buzzing about them. The men had dug a hole directly between the two trees. Sand lay piled where they'd thrown it beside the hole, bits of quartz in it flashing dazzlingly in the sun's rays.

Red Merriam crouched down in the hole, laughing up at Carmody. There was an insane tone to Merriam's laughter, the sound of it cracking now and then.

"Now do you believe it, Lin?" he cried. "Now do you believe that they're real? Look at them, Lin, and then say this is all a crazy dream."

The hoarse labor of his breathing grated in Carmody's ears as he peered into the hole. The two bells lay side by side in the hole. The sun, where it struck them, glanced off with eye-searing brightness. They were the cold yellow color of gold. Looking closer, Carmody could see the exquisite etchings on their surface, the tiny perfect crosses and figures. Carmody felt the frenzy sweeping him, the desire to laugh, to shout. With an effort he kept himself in check, hearing the fast, hot thumping of his heart, feeling the sweat coursing down his face.

Merriam lay with his arms about the bells, hugging them. The fingers of his big, freckled hands moved lightly, caressingly over the etched surfaces, and he made small crooning sounds in his throat.

A sudden wave of disgust hit Carmody, and then the fever was gone, and, remembering, the old, cold thoughts came back. For a moment in the excitement of uncovering the bells he'd forgotten the raw, gnawing hate in his heart, the cold, driving purpose clawing at him.

"Aren't they pretty, Lin? Aren't they the prettiest things you've ever seen? And they're ours! I tell you I almost went crazy mad with worry over them. I was half loco most of the time for fear somebody would come riding up this cañon and notice where I'd been digging. I covered the spot so it couldn't be noticed, but always there was the crazy thought I'd slipped up somewhere, and someone would come along and steal them from me."

Carmody straightened slowly to his feet. He stood there, casting a long shadow in the sun, an empty look in his eyes. His fingers were clenched into fists.

"Well, let's get those things out of the hole and on the mules," he said. "I want to get the hell out of here. This place is like an oven. . . ."

With their lariats they snaked the bells out of their cache. Then came the back-breaking labor of lifting each bell on a mule's back and lashing it in place. Sweat streamed down the men's faces, running off their chins, and their shirts were plastered to their backs. When the last lashing had been made secure, Merriam dropped to the ground under one of the mesquite trees, groaning and puffing, wiping the perspiration off his face.

"Well, that's that," he said, glancing up at Carmody. "Now you know why I needed help with them." He gazed off at the high, ragged rim of the cañon and shuddered. "Will I be glad when we're out of here. And it ain't just because of that damn' sun. I won't breathe easy until we're back in Marietta with those bells. Ain't a man south of the border, or north of it, wouldn't hold us up if they knew what was under them tarps on the mules' backs."

"How right you are, *señor!*"

It was said behind them, from a clump of dried greasewood about fifty feet beyond the twin trees. Carmody turned, hand stabbing for his Remington, but, when he saw them, his hand froze with the big .44 half out of its holster. His fingers came away from the butt, the weapon sliding back.

Merriam rolled over, crouching on all fours, and froze like that with his head thrust up, looking off past the trees. His breathing was a shallow, whining moan, and then suddenly he began to curse. He grabbed fistfuls of sand and scattered it around him. He thrust his head down between his shoulders and kicked with his toes at the ground. Suddenly he looked up again and foam was flicking at the edges of his mouth. His cursing rose to a piercing scream.

There were two of them, and they came down toward the twin trees, walking rapidly though cautiously. Both were armed, one carrying an old Tyler Henry rifle while the other, the smaller one, held a .38 Colt Lightning revolver.

They stopped in the shade of the trees. The one with the rifle poked it at Merriam and said: "Get to your feet, *cabeza roja!*"

Carmody stared narrowly at the two. Both were Mexicans, wearing wide-brimmed, peak-tipped sombreros. The one with the rifle was quite old. He had a mustache and a small goatee white as alkali. His seamed face could have served as a relief map of some rough terrain. His black eyes, watching Merriam struggle to his feet, burned with a terrible light.

The other was small as a boy. He wore a *charro* jacket with the gold lacing badly faded and torn in spots. The cotton shirt revealed the curvature of breast, and Carmody, suddenly startled, raised his eyes, staring again at the smooth, round face. The little one was a woman.

Merriam had stopped his cursing. He, too, was staring at the girl. She colored under the hot stares of the two men, and the .38 in her hand wavered slightly.

"Raquel!" barked the old man, and she stiffened, chin lifting, lips thinning.

The old man wore tight *chivarras* and above them only an old, tattered, and patched gray vest. His bare arms and chest were almost black from the sun. There was not much flesh on him, but the muscles writhed and rippled under the leathery skin.

"Get their weapons, little one," he said.

The girl slipped quickly behind Carmody. He felt the lifting of the weight of the Remington at his hip and, looking sidewise, saw her relieving Merriam of his Dragoon pistol and Bowie.

The old man said: "Let me see that knife, little one."

She passed the Bowie over to the old man, then turned, her gun covering Merriam and Carmody. The old man held the Bowie so that the sun flashed off its keen surface.

"A *cuchillo* is a Mexican weapon," he said musingly. "Not many *Yanquis* fancy *cuchillos*."

"I always pack one," Merriam said evenly. "It comes in handy sometimes."

"Like for instance?"

Merriam said nothing.

The flames flared in the old man's eyes. "Like for instance?" he shouted. "Should I answer that, *cabeza roja*? Like for instance the procuring of a valuable *derrotero!*"

Carmody turned his head and stared at Merriam.

The redhead's lips twitched. "I don't know what you're talking about," he said harshly.

The old man brandished the knife. It made a glittering, flashing arc in the sun, and Merriam shrank back a step. The old man stepped forward, pressing the sharp point of the Bowie against Merriam's stomach.

"He was like a son to me," the old man growled, face contorted. "Is this what you used on him, *cabeza roja*? Is this the *cuchillo* that was used on Pio Vasquez?"

247

Sweat streaked down Merriam's face. He tried another backward step, but the old man moved with him, the keen Bowie never losing contact with Merriam's belly.

A frantic cry tore out of Merriam's throat. "I used no knife. He was drunk, and I stole the *derrotero* from him. I stole the chart. Does that satisfy you? You have the bells. What difference does it make?"

"We have the *campanas*, but Pio Vasquez is dead. All cut up by a *cuchillo*. He was last seen alive in the company of a *Yanqui, una cabeza roja,* a redhead. I loved him like a son."

"Lin," Merriam cried, face twisting. "Stop him, Lin! He'll cut me open!"

The taste of gall was in Carmody's mouth. A cold, rancid anger gnawed at him. "This is your party, Red. You do the talking."

Carmody looked at the girl, catching her eyes on him, but she glanced away quickly, then back to him, and those brown eyes were again cool and impersonal.

"You, *señorita. Digame.* Listen to me," begged Merriam, almost babbling now. "Talk to the *viejo.* Tell him how it was. I stole the *derrotero* from Vasquez. I used no *cuchillo.* I swear to the *Madre de Dios* I didn't. There must have been others who knew he had the chart. They must have reached him after I'd stolen it. They used the knife on Vasquez. Not me."

"Lies!" the old man snarled, pressing on the knife. "Do you think I am that great a fool? How do you like the taste of a *cuchillo, cabeza roja?*"

"¡Blanco!"

It came from the girl, startling Carmody. His glance whipped back to her. She stood with chin firm and shoulders squared. There was the stamp of authority

248

about her that seemed out of place with one so small and young.

Blanco stiffened, easing up on the knife.

"¡Blanco!" snapped the girl again, and the old man took the knife away a little.

"I loved him like a son, Raquel."

"And he was like a brother to me, Blanco. Perhaps the *cabeza roja* speaks the truth."

"He lies!" Blanco snarled. "I can see it in his eyes."

The girl's voice was forceful. "Perhaps he lies. Perhaps he tells the truth. Put away the *cuchillo*, Blanco, and then bind them."

Blanco whipped back his arm and threw the Bowie. Merriam screamed, jumped violently aside as the knife flashed past him to thunk into the trunk of a mesquite tree.

"You squeal like a pig, *cabeza roja*," Blanco laughed. "Have no doubt. Had I thrown the *cuchillo* at you, you would not have leaped aside."

"Bind them," Raquel ordered.

Carmody felt her eyes on him again and turned his head that way. This time she did not look away. As Blanco removed the lariat from Merriam's saddle and began tying the man, the girl directed her words at Carmody.

"Perhaps, because I am a woman, my heart is not as cold as your *compadre*'s, señor . . . or my Blanco's. We should shoot the two of you and leave you here. But it is not in my heart to kill you. We shall bind you and leave you here. In time you will be able to free yourselves. We shall leave your horses here and also your pistols, though not your carbines."

Blanco had finished with Merriam, who now lay flat

on the ground, bound hand and foot. Blanco took Carmody's lariat, slipped behind him, began swiftly tying his hands.

"When you are free, *señor*," Raquel continued, "do not attempt to follow us. We shall have your carbines. You shall have only your pistols. I shall not stop Blanco again from killing you. Take heed, *señor*."

It was as the girl had said. She and Blanco rode off, driving the two mules with their heavy loads, leaving Carmody and Merriam bound on the sand. They quickly rolled toward each other, back to back, and began working at their bonds, but the old man had knotted them well. It was two hours later that they had finally freed themselves and rose, aching and cramped, to their feet. They found their six-shooters and shell belts on a rock. They strapped on the belts.

Merriam walked over to the mesquite tree to retrieve his Bowie. The knife had penetrated the wood deeply, and Merriam had to tug hard to remove it. Holding the weapon in his hands, he ran a callused thumb along the keen edge of the blade, his eyes hot and brooding.

Carmody had walked over to his mare. He swung up into the kack. The sun had gone down behind the cañon walls, and long, jagged shadows were crawling across the floor. Already coolness prevailed in the air.

Merriam was still fingering the Bowie. Carmody watched. Distaste filled him again, and his hand began to itch for the butt of his Remington .44. Finally Merriam put the Bowie back in its sheath and mounted his bay.

Carmody spoke. The thing he felt inside, the cold, biting contempt, edged his voice. "So you stole the *derrotero*. So that's how it was. I hate your yellow, crawling belly, Red!"

Merriam reined his bay around, facing Carmody. Color flooded the redhead's face. His voice held a tight, warning ring. "Watch your talk, Lin!"

"I'll watch nothing, Red," Carmody said through his teeth. "You yellow, pig-sticking son of a bitch! You used that knife on Vasquez. That's the only way you could have got the *derrotero*."

Merriam's hand twitched back toward the handle of the Dragoon Colt, but the furious readiness about Carmody deterred him. With an effort he closed his fingers about the pommel of his saddle.

"I take it we're through, then," said Merriam.

"My heart never was in it," said Carmody. "Now that I've seen how it is, I want no part of it. You're welcome to the bells, Red, both of them, if you can get them back. Me, I'm going back across the line to Marietta."

"Yeah," said Merriam, sneering the word. "Go back to Marietta and kill Wiley Barrow. Wind up with your neck in a noose while I live the life of Riley." He rose in his stirrups, leaning forward toward Carmody. "Because I'm finding those bells again, and no one's taking them from me next time. No one!"

"You'll make sure of it with your Bowie?" said Carmody, contempt curving his lips. "Is that how you'll make sure?"

"With my Bowie, my *cuchillo*. I'll cut up that Blanco son of a bitch like I cut up Vasquez. And I've half a mind to cut you up, too."

"Try it!"

"Do you think I don't dare?"

Carmody laughed. "I've seen the color of your guts, Red. Like Blanco said, you squeal like a pig. . . ."

III

"CAPTURE"

The town was tucked away at the end of a cañon. Here the land fell away to gentle slopes and rugged hills, with the Sierra Pintada looming big and purple and forbidding behind them. Mesquite and sage dotted the hillsides, and down on the flats the alkali stretched out like a gray, phantom cloud.

The town lay up and over both sides of the crest of a hill. It wasn't much of a town. It was comprised of sorry, mean little *jacales* and adobe walls pitted and marked like the aftermath of some dread disease. Candelaria was its name.

Carmody came upon it an hour after nightfall. He came upon it alone, for he had parted with Red Merriam back in the cañon. Merriam had ridden away, cursing bitterly. Remembrance of it brought a chill to Carmody, for he did not underestimate Merriam's treachery.

It was Carmody's plan to stay in Candelaria overnight. The mare was tired and blowing. Weariness lay heavily on Carmody, too, so he rode slowly down the narrow, winding streets of Candelaria, looking for some presentable *cantina*. He passed many people on the streets, individuals in brightly colored serapes. Many of them paused to stare up at the tall, grim *Yanqui* horseman, a tangible curiosity in their glances. It was the one who did not look up that interested Carmody.

There was something familiar about the tall, peaked sombrero, the hunch of the shoulders, the litheness and grace of the walk. It came to Carmody in the instant that the other had passed him by, and Carmody reined the mare around.

They were in an open field. The dark, solid blankness of brush loomed ahead, the running figure making for it. Carmody's horse, for all its weariness, fairly flew along the ground. Carmody had almost caught up with the running figure. He cried out, leaping from the running horse's saddle, striking the ground with knees bent, but even so the mare's speed almost upset him. He went staggering forward, colliding with the figure.

It had turned, and Carmody saw the bulge of a gun in one hand. He clutched for the weapon, tearing it out of the other's grasp. A toe kicked Carmody in the shins. He muffled an oath and tried to grab his assailant. Hands clawed at his face, scratching painfully. Then his fingers closed about the other's arms, whirling the figure around, holding it like that with hands clasped behind its back. A shrill, whining moan reached Carmody's ears.

"If I let loose, will you be good?" he asked, breathing heavily. "If you won't, I'll just twist your arms some more."

The cry was burdened with hurt. *"Sí, señor, sí."*

"All right," Carmody said, releasing the other. A tight grin touched Carmody's lips. "You're a regular hell-cat. *Una tigra,* Raquel. A tigress."

She had whirled to face him. During the scuffle her sombrero had been knocked off, and now her long black hair spilled down on either side of her face.

Perhaps it was the shadows, her face looming pale and strangely piquant in their midst. Her eyes were dark hollows and the line of her lips a dark mark, but the delicate roundness of her face was there for him to see and admire.

Raquel's voice came, a high, thin growl, turning Carmody cold with the primal quality of it. "If you were the *cabeza roja*, I would not have run, *señor*. I would have killed you!"

"That's strange," Carmody said. "If you hate the redhead so much, why didn't you let Blanco finish him off this afternoon? Blanco sure had his heart set on that."

Raquel said: "If I had let Blanco kill the *cabeza roja*, I could not have prevented him from killing you. You cannot imagine the rages Blanco is capable of. And he loved Pio Vasquez as if he were his own son."

"Why should you have kept him from killing me?" asked Carmody sardonically. "What was there about me, a stranger and a *Yanqui*, to make you do a thing like that?"

"That is a fair question, *señor*," Raquel said. She paused for a moment, looked away from Carmody, as if considering something. Then her face lifted again toward his and she spoke earnestly. "We had been watching, Blanco and I, while you and the *cabeza roja* were digging for the bells. We had trailed you into the cañon, and it was Blanco's idea to remain concealed while the two of you did all the work, then step in and possess ourselves of the *campanas*. We saw and heard all that occurred. He acted naturally, *señor*, at the discovery of the bells. He went loco. You remained passive, *señor*. You looked at the bells, and no sign came from you. That is not natural. Even I was moved at the sight of the bells. If it had not been for Blanco, I would have cried aloud. Blanco, too, was moved deeply. But not you, *señor*. That is what puzzles me. What is there about you to make you so disdainful of so much wealth?"

It came out of Carmody inadvertently. "I have a man to kill."

"Oh?" the girl whispered. Wonder was in her voice. "You must want to kill him very badly. Is that why you are not with the *cabeza roja*? Is that why you were so indifferent when Blanco and I possessed ourselves of the bells?"

The anger was building inside Carmody, the anger that always came when this thing was discussed. It was so much a part of him, yet he hated fiercely its obsessive grip on him. The fury broke out into his voice, putting a raw edge to it.

"So you think I am indifferent concerning the bells? Why do you think I pursued you just now, Raquel? I want to know what you and Blanco have done with the bells. True, I am no longer *compadre* with the *cabeza roja*. Now, if I recover the bells, they are both mine. Understand, *señorita?*"

He could feel the weight of her eyes on him. Her voice was disdainful. "Do you expect me to inform you as easily as that?"

The anger was roiling inside Carmody. Roughly he reached out, grasping her arms. "Tell me, Raquel."

"You can twist my arms again, *señor*. You can beat me. You can torture me. You can kill me. But I will not tell about the bells."

Frustration swept Carmody. All was confusion for a moment in his mind. He did not know what to do. He did not even know what he wanted to do. The bells did not matter so much. Memory of them was vague in his mind, as if it had all happened long, long ago. It was that other thing plaguing him.

There was nothing more for him here. He raised his

eyes to look for his mare and saw the gray shadow of the horse, off a little way. Then there was the sudden blur of sound and movement behind him, and Raquel cried out sharply, and then they were all over him, overwhelming him.

Carmody had whirled, stepping back, to face their swooping rush. His hand flashed to his Remington, yanked it out, but, before he could fire, they were on him. Stinking, sweating bodies crashed against him. Warm, fetid, hissing breaths exploded in his face.

Carmody heard Raquel scream again. Then the cry choked off to a strangling gurgle. The Remington was torn from his grasp. He had gone down on his knees beneath their weight. There were two of them, Carmody knew now. Their arms were rapidly closing about him, imprisoning him.

Carmody kicked out with a spurred boot. A hoarse, agonized scream blasted Carmody's ears, and the hold of one of his assailants loosened, then slid off.

The other attacker had caught hold of Carmody's arms behind his back. They were both on the ground, threshing about on the sand. Grit got into Carmody's nose and mouth and eyes, choking and blinding him. He tried kicking out with his boots again. He lunged around on the sand, but the other held on like a leech.

"*Ahora*, Manuel. Give it to him! Now!"

Carmody sensed it coming. He seemed to feel the weight of it descending on his head even before it touched. He gave one last desperate lunge, breath strangling in his throat. Then lights flashed across his eyes, and the dim sense of searing, pressing pain, and then only the cloying blankness. . . .

IV

"THE MAN CALLED MARTINEZ"

The hut was small, a one-room affair. The lone, tiny window opened out on the misty grayness of approaching dawn. Carmody stood at the window, watching the tendrils of mist litter the ground, moving around on the slight breeze like writhing, creeping things. The breeze felt good to Carmody's aching head. He had recovered consciousness scant minutes ago, finding himself lying on the dirt floor of the *jacal*, his head pillowed on something soft and warm. He had looked up into the wan, drawn face of Raquel. Her cool fingers had been caressing his brow and that was her lap on which his head had been resting.

The pain lay like a solid mass, throbbing a threnody in the back of his head. The coolness eased the ache a little, though it still hurt his eyes to stare out of them. He could see the primeval thrust of the Sierra Pintada off in the gray-enshrouded distance. Sage, mesquite, and cactus began taking on definite shapes as the darkness lessened, standing like silent sentinels about the *jacal*.

There were two men fifteen feet from the *jacal*. One was lying on a blanket on the ground. The other stood, a straight, silent figure, the cigarette in his mouth a red, glowing dot in the shadows. Carmody took in the uniform and the rifle cradled in the man's arms and swore under his breath.

Someone was standing beside him. It was Raquel. She, too, was staring out the window, and, as Carmody bent his head toward her, her face lifted.

"*Soldados*," she said briefly, answering the question in his eyes.

Carmody moved away from the window. His head began to ache harder as he thought, running over everything in his mind. "Raquel," he said sharply. "What is the meaning of the *soldados?* What is behind those bells?"

She crossed over beside him. For a moment she was close to him, her cool fingers soothing his forehead, then as suddenly she had dropped back a step.

"You have a right to ask, *señor*," she said quietly. "This is more than just a matter of an old *derrotero*, buried treasure, and an old man and a girl seeking it. The heart of my people is in it." She paused, as if seeking the right words. "Have you ever seen a peon, *señor?* Have you seen how they live? But that means nothing. You must be a peon to understand the inhumanity of it. We are beaten. We are starved. We are no better than slaves. The whip is our reward, torture and death our punishment."

Carmody could feel her eyes on him, as if studying him, weighing him. It made him slightly uneasy. There was a sincerity about this quiet girl that was beginning to work into him.

"As you've probably guessed, Blanco and I are *revolucionarios*. We are many in number but short in wealth. With the money realized from those *campanas*, we could purchase many guns and much ammunition."

Carmody again went over to the window, leaning his elbow on the sill, cupping his forehead in the palm of one hand, letting the air sweep some of the shadows from his brain.

"But you, a girl, and Blanco . . . ," he began, then

stopped as the thread of thought tangled. A growing irritation at the lethargy of his mind began to stir in him.

"Why not? *¿Porque no?*" Raquel said, spreading her hands. "We were sent to help Pio Vasquez when he informed our group of his possession of the *derrotero*. Who would suspect an old man and a helpless girl? But the government has many spies, and even Blanco and I were detected." She nodded at the two soldiers. "That is why you and I are here."

The sound was a faint rumble, barely audible, and Carmody stiffened, ears straining. One of the soldiers spoke, and his companion rose quickly from the blanket. They were both peering down the slope.

The rumble grew louder, broadening into the staccato pounding of galloping hoofbeats. One soldier said something and dropped the butt of his rifle to the ground.

The dawn had come, and the land lay vernally quiet in the light. The pungent scent of sage drifted in to Carmody. Already a perceptible heat was in the air.

The rider pulled up in a spray of flying sand beside the two soldiers and leaped from the saddle. There was a rapid exchange of questions and answers. Then the rider's face turned toward the *jacal*, and his loud, satisfied exclamation was clearly audible to Carmody.

"*¡Bueno!*"

Raquel shuddered. "That is the leader. He is the one who held me up while the two *soldados* subdued you. He had us taken here and rode off almost immediately."

All three men were striding toward the *jacal*. Carmody faced the door, Raquel moving closer to him.

There came the sounds of a bar being removed from the door. Then the *portal* swung outward, yellow light lancing into the dim room, and the three men entered. The two soldiers remained in the doorway. The third man, the horseman, took two steps ahead of them and halted, stiff and straight.

"Ah?" he said, swift eyes taking in Carmody and the girl. "Ah? What a touching tableau. Would you really protect her, *Yanqui*?"

He was tall for a Mexican, almost as tall as Carmody. Black, darting eyes were set deeply in a long, narrow face. There was a predatory look in his prominent nose and unsated cruelty in the narrow slash of his mouth. He was wearing a huge, straw sombrero. From the neck down he was enshrouded in a bright-colored serape. His black polished boots glistened in the light from the doorway.

"Who the hell are you?"

The tall Mexican's lips curled. "Truculent already, *Yanqui*? Why, I've hardly begun." He straightened even more, throwing back his slim shoulders. "Pardon this apparel," he said, indicating his clothes with a deprecatory hand. "Expediency prompts me to wear these in place of my rightful clothing." His chin tilted, and his heels clicked loudly, sharply. "Permit me to introduce myself. I am of the Federal Army. *Teniente* Higinio Martínez!"

"Spy," the girl hissed. "Filthy spy!"

Martínez's lips tightened until they were white. "So?" he said softly. "You don't like my apparel, *señorita*? I do not blame you. I have many beautiful uniforms. Ah, yes, I, *Teniente* Higinio Martínez, cut quite a dashing figure in my dress uniforms. Picture, if you please, *señorita*, silver epaulets, gold braid, a row of flashing medals here" — indicating his chest — "a saber of finest Toledo steel. . . ." He broke off abruptly. "But, alas, *señorita,* you shall never see me dressed thus. Isn't it a pity?"

Anger was throbbing in Carmody's brain. "Look here, you tin soldier," he growled, "stop strutting and tell us what you want with us."

Martínez deigned a quiet, vain smirk. "How good of you to remind me, *Yanqui.* We really must be getting on with our business. I am concerned first with the *señorita.*"

Martínez waved a hand languidly toward the door. "If you please, *señorita.*"

"No," Carmody said.

"No?" purred Martínez. "Perhaps you would want me to deal with you first, *Yanqui?* I shall attend to you in good time. But the *señorita* comes first. The matter of her is much more pressing. Please, *señorita.*"

"No," said Carmody again.

Martínez stepped aside, beckoning one of the soldiers. The man advanced, rifle butt held high, aimed for Carmody's face.

"No," Raquel screamed. "They will beat you. They will kill you. Let me go."

She broke loose just as the soldier drove in with the rifle. Carmody whirled, feeling the brush of the butt pass his face. The force of his drive carried the soldier on past, and Carmody made a grab for the man, getting both hands on his rifle. Then he froze, a silent groan in his throat, feeling the gun barrel in the small of his back.

"I would as soon shoot you, *Yanqui,*" came the cold, emotionless voice of Martínez. "Release the rifle."

Carmody let go his grip, stepping up against the wall as the soldier threw him a vicious look and started for the door. Martínez put the revolver back beneath his serape. Raquel was at the door, covered by the

261

other soldier's rifle.

Carmody's voice was tense. "There's nothing you want with her, Martínez. Why don't you let her go?"

Martínez uttered a short laugh. He motioned to the soldiers, and they led Raquel away. Martínez slammed the door and barred it in front of Carmody's face. Carmody shouted through the heavy *portal:* "What are you going to do with her, Martínez?"

Martínez had come around to the outside of the window. His smug, vain face looked inside. "You have a window, *Yanqui*," he said. "Why don't you look out and see?"

Carmody crossed swiftly to the window. Outside there was a post driven into the ground that could have been used for hitching horses. The soldiers were binding Raquel to the post. Martínez walked over to his buckskin. He took a quirt off the saddle and stood fingering the whip, watching the soldiers tie the girl.

The soldiers stepped back. Without a word Martínez moved forward, quirt held high, bringing it down viciously on the girl's back. Carmody saw Raquel stiffen, and it seemed to him that he, too, could feel the sting of the whip on his own back.

"Just to give you a taste of it," said Martínez to the girl. "But you peons have such thick hides. I imagine you've all grown accustomed to the whip by now. Still, I'll wager you felt that one, did you not? You know what I want. The location of the *campanas.* I have been on your trail and the *viejo's* these several days, but you managed to evade me until last night. I know that you and the *viejo* had possession of the bells. You must have them again. I want to know where. Consider this blow of the quirt and know that I have countless more in my arm. I do not tire easily. Consider it, please, *señorita*. When you are ready, speak. I shall not ask again."

Martínez waved one of the soldiers over to Carmody's window. Martínez himself walked over there, a cruel smile on his thin lips.

"So the *señorita* has nothing for me?" he said to Carmody. "On the contrary, she has enough to allow me to exchange the pips of a lieutenant for those of a captain." His eyes closed dreamily. "*Capitán* Higinio Martínez."

Sweat was beading Carmody's brow. He felt the harsh laboring of the breath in his throat. "Leave her alone!"

Martínez shrugged. "I have sent word to headquarters in Chihuahua that I shall soon have a complete dossier on rebel activities in the entire north of Mexico. I have sent for enough troops to clean out every rebel in the northern provinces. Would I not lose prestige if all this turned out to be a fiasco? How would you make the girl talk, *Yanqui*? Just by asking her? I, *Teniente* Higinio Martínez, will show you how to make her talk!"

Carmody watched with dull, aching eyes as Martínez walked back to the girl. They had removed the *charro* jacket and only the cotton shirt covered the flesh of her back. With deliberate slowness Martínez removed his serape and hung it over his saddle. Then he took his stance beside the girl. The right arm of Martínez rose high, hung a moment in the air, then descended swiftly, powerfully.

The lash of the whip was a vicious, flat hiss. Carmody's eyes closed with the blow, the hurt of it seeming to sear his mind, but no outcry came from Raquel. Again Martínez raised his arm, brought it down.

Carmody glanced wildly about the barren room, but

263

there was nothing to lay his hands on. The sound of the whip came again, and a frustrated sob wrenched out of Carmody. He rushed to the window, wild eyes seeking. The soldier on guard threw a leering grin at him. Again the whip cracked, and Carmody's teeth clenched.

He felt it tearing at his brain, the unreasoning madness. His helplessness doubled the fury in him. The crack of the whip came again — loud, sibilant.

"No," Carmody shouted hoarsely, leaping at the window. "No, Martinez! Stop it, you son of a pig! You obscenity, Martinez. Your father has no name. Your sister. . . ."

A sharp, stinging slash across his face broke Carmody's frenzy, opening his eyes. He had his head thrust out the window, and Martinez had drawn his arm back for another swipe with the quirt. Carmody leaped back, the quirt cracking about the sill.

The cruel face of Martinez was at the window. The black eyes were distended; the slash of a mouth peeled back from the man's teeth. His nostrils flared.

"So?" Martinez shouted. "You would insult me, *Yanqui*? I shall attend to you, have no fear. With the girl it is only a matter of making her talk. With you it shall be the matter of making you scream."

With that, Martinez whirled on his heel and strode back to the girl. Raquel hung limply in her bonds, head lolling to one side, but not a whimper had come from her. Martinez's arm rose and fell, and the whip whined again. This time a faint, hollow moan tore out of the girl.

"Tell him, Raquel!" Carmody cried. "Tell him what he wants to know!"

"Yes, Raquel, tell me." Martinez's face was diffused with blood, the veins standing out thick on his brow, the cords of his neck like cables. His arm rose and fell methodically now, the girl whimpering and crying with each blow.

"Tell me, Raquel!" Martínez screamed. "Where are the bells? I shall beat you until you tell. Where have you hidden the *campanas?* Who is behind the rebellion? How many are you? Where are you concentrated? How many rifles have you? How much ammunition? What are your plans? When do you strike? Where do you strike? *¡Digame! ¡Digame!* Tell me!" His scream beat cadence with the whip strokes.

Blood streaked the girl's shirt. Carmody gripped the window sill until his nails hurt. "I'll kill you, Martínez," he shouted. "I'll break your arms. I'll kick your ribs in, Martínez. Then I'll kill you!"

He was trying to crawl through the window. The soldier came at him. This time there was no dodging that driving rifle butt. It took Carmody in the forehead, rocking him with searing pain, and he felt himself hurtling back into the room. The soldier grinned mockingly at him through the window.

Carmody scrambled to his feet. His raving shouts filled the small room with furious sound as he rushed at the window again. "I'll stop you, Martínez! I'll tear your tongue with my hands! I'll gouge your eyes out! I'll cut your belly open and drag your guts all over hell!"

The sound of the shot was a flat, snarling noise. Carmody froze, his face in the window. The guard threw a frantic, startled look over his shoulder, rifle still held high.

Martínez had pitched to his knees, his quirt arm hanging limply at his side. As if a gust of wind had touched and moved him, he fell over slowly on his face.

The gun snarled again. The guard at the window gave a choked, muffled cry and went slamming back against the wall of the *jacal*. Carmody made a frantic grab for the rifle, but the soldier had taken it with him, still grasped tightly, to the ground.

The other soldier, who had been standing beside the girl watching Martínez, was racing madly for the shelter of some mesquite. The gun roared a third time, and the soldier went sprawling on his face in the sand.

A man came down from a rise. Carmody saw the white hair and white goatee, the brown leathery skin, and the name came out of him in a loud cry.

"¡Blanco!"

Blanco walked over to Martínez. With the toe of his boot the old man turned Martínez over.

"So?" said Blanco, still trembling with rage. "You would flog my little one, would you?"

His heel made a sickening crunch as he ground it into the dead face of *Teniente* Higinio Martínez.

V

"THE RETURN OF RED MERRIAM"

The land lay desolate under the beat of the sun. Saguaro cactus reached supplicating arms toward the burnished sky. Mesquite and greasewood were lonely solitary dots, scattered here and there on the sand. There was no patch of shade big enough for a jackrabbit to stretch in.

Carmody had sweated over the loading of the bells for the second time. On this occasion it was Blanco who helped him. The man was old, in his sixties, Carmody thought, but those muscles rippling under his skin were like steel cables and just as strong. Blanco's breathing was only slightly ragged by the time they were through.

Raquel lay to one side on a blanket, watching them. Her face was pale. Her eyes clearly indicated the agony she had endured, and the hurt she still experienced. But no word of complaint had come from her lips.

She had explained to Carmody. After she and Blanco had taken the bells, they had had the feeling of being followed. Knowing that spies would be watching, and not wanting to risk moving the bells by themselves, they had reburied them here. Then Raquel had gone to Candelaria to summon help while Blanco remained to guard the bells. When Raquel did not return, Blanco set out to seek her.

Raquel glanced at the lowering sun, then at Carmody who sat beside her. "Our escort should be here at sundown. Then you shall be free to go, *señor*. Blanco would have released you back at the *jacal*, but he needed someone to help with the bells. We want to be prepared

267

so that we can leave instantly when the escort arrives. Martinez has alerted the *federalistas,* and we must hurry." She began tracing aimless patterns in the sand. "Where will you go, *señor?* Back to your country? Back to your home?"

"Back to my home, Raquel," said Carmody, that bleakness coming over him again.

Blanco was sitting off by himself to one side. The Henry rifle was held across his knees and at his feet were Carmody's shell belt and holstered Remington .44. At his back lay the rim of a wash that wriggled crookedly out into the desert like the trail of a snake in the sand. Beyond that there was only a glaring emptiness.

Carmody stared at Blanco, watched the nodding of the huge sombrero. Then he looked beyond the old man, and suddenly his blood froze. The man had come up out of the wash, crawling on his belly, as silent as a cat stalking its prey. He was directly behind Blanco.

Carmody opened his mouth to cry out, but it was too late. The man leaped to his feet, the huge, long-barreled Dragoon Colt in his right hand. Blanco sensed the peril. His head lifted, his fingers gripping his rifle. But, before he could move, the long barrel of the Colt flashed down.

A retching groan clawed out of Blanco. Again the long barrel of the Dragoon fell, smashing against Blanco's skull. He toppled forward, a slight, limp figure on the sand.

Carmody had lurched to his feet, started to rush forward. The Dragoon Colt barked harshly, the slug plowing a furrow in the sand in front of him. He pulled up short, curses choking in his throat.

"Damn you, Red!" Carmody raged, the whole of him shaking with fury. "Damn you for the sneaking, bushwhacking killer you are!"

Merriam was planted with legs spread wide, the Dragoon centered on Carmody's belly. Merriam was hatless, his red hair wild confusion.

"Serves him right," Merriam said. "He should have killed me when he had the chance." His glittering eyes flicked briefly, covetously, to the heavy packs on the two mules. "Turnabout is fair play, I always say. Blanco let us load the mules for him once before he stepped in. I've been down in that wash for an hour, waiting for him and you to load 'em again. Now they're mine again."

Raquel was sobbing brokenly behind Carmody. He looked about him. There was nothing hopeful to see. His mare and the mounts of Raquel and Blanco were off to the left with the mules. Merriam's spread legs straddled the Henry rifle and Carmody's carbine and .44 that Blanco had been guarding.

"What's the matter, Red?" Carmody derided. "Lose faith in your Bowie? Then all the while it's just been bragging about how good you were with it. You and your *cuchillo*. What does it have to be before you use it on a man? Does he have to be tied and helpless? Didn't I hear you say once you had half a mind to use it on me?"

The redhead snarled: "You pushed me around in Marietta, and I took it. You pushed me around in the cañon, and I took it. You think you can keep pushing me around all the time?"

He fished in his pocket with his left hand and took out a pigging string. Tossing it at Carmody's feet, Merriam beckoned with his head at the girl.

"Tie her up," he ordered. "Tie her good. I don't want her running around loose while I'm cutting you up."

Carmody obeyed. Raquel whispered over her shoulder,

269

"Don't do it, *señor*. You haven't a chance. Your bare hands against his *cuchillo*. Please, *señor*."

"He'll kill me anyhow," Carmody said, drawing the knot, feeling the hurt himself as the girl winced. "Have no fear. He's yellow clear through."

He raised his voice at the last, and Merriam heard. Anger flushed his face. "Step away, Lin," he said, his voice quivering. "Let me check the knot, and then we'll see if you'll take me."

Merriam tested the knot with his left hand, then with the Dragoon he motioned Carmody away from the girl. "Keep walking, Lin," Merriam said. "I'll tell you when to stop."

A hundred yards from the guns Merriam said: "All right, Lin."

Carmody halted, facing Merriam. The man took his Dragoon by the barrel and cast it as far as he could. Then the Bowie glittered in his hand.

"How do you like the look of it?" he said, crouching. "It's sharp. I can split a hair with it. I always keep it that way."

Merriam came in at a crouch, shining Bowie held against his thigh, the keen point slanted upward. Carmody's eyes seemed mesmerized by the point of the knife. With an effort he tore his glance away, fastened it on the lithe, cat-like approach of Merriam.

Carmody took a step aside. Merriam swerved with him. They were close now, Merriam five feet away. Suddenly Carmody leaped, foot kicking out for Merriam's knife hand. The man shouted, voice hoarse and startled, dropping to the ground and rolling away. He came swiftly to his feet, sand dripping from his clothes. His breath panted wheezingly. He came in cat-like, feinting to the left with his knife. When Carmody moved with him, Merriam straightened swiftly, leaping in with the Bowie held high. Carmody's hand lashed up, hitting Merriam's wrist, deflecting the Bowie. Even so, Carmody felt his sleeve rip, then the sharp sting of the cut on his arm, and the warm flow of the blood.

Carmody had wheeled in close to Merriam, chopping a short blow hard against Merriam's nose. The redhead jumped back, holding his bloody nose.

"That's the first cut, Lin," Merriam said, his voice thick through his smashed nose. Blood dripped down over his lips. "How did the Bowie feel? How was the taste of it?"

He began circling slowly in that crouch again, blade against his thigh. Carmody pivoted with him. Blood soaked Carmody's sleeve. The breath kept laboring out of him.

Suddenly Carmody kicked his boot deep into the sand, spraying the grit over Merriam. The man sputtered, choked, the knife slanting aside a moment, and Carmody rushed in. With his left hand he clutched for Merriam's knife wrist, gripped it. Carmody got both hands around the wrist, hanging on tightly. Merriam whirled, trying to shake Carmody loose. The Bowie lifted high, both men straining. The waning sun flashed off the blade. Sweat drenched the two men. They were close together, faces an inch apart.

"What are you going to do when I've taken the Bowie from you, Red?" Carmody panted.

Merriam spat in Carmody's face, mouthing an obscenity. "You'll never see the time you can take my Bowie," he snarled. Carmody sensed it, but it came so swiftly he could do nothing about it. The knee ground into his groin.

With a groaning effort he submerged the sickness. His grip on Merriam's wrist became a hold of steel. Carmody swung Merriam spinning in a circle, a shout roaring out of him. Then he stepped in swiftly, bearing down hard on the wrist, snapping Merriam's arm behind his back.

Merriam's breath was spasmodic, filled with retching agony. Carmody summoned the rest of his strength. He swung Merriam's arm back, hearing the man's tortured scream blast his ears. Then Carmody swung the man's arm in toward him, the Bowie aimed straight. Merriam's shriek was a wailing, anguished howl that ended as the Bowie sank up to its hilt in his back.

Raquel knelt beside Blanco, her face buried against his chest. She heard the approaching footsteps behind her, and the sobs froze in her throat and a tenseness came over her.

"It's me, Raquel," Carmody said quietly.

She jumped to her feet, trying to turn around, but Carmody held her away until he'd untied her hands. She was laughing and crying, all mixed together. "Oh, *señor, señor!*" she cried. "I was so afraid. I could not bear to watch. Oh, *señor,* it is you, and you're alive!"

After she had bandaged the cut on his arm, Carmody took hold of her. He looked down into the round delicateness of her features, feeling a strange regret. "The bells mean much to you, don't they, Raquel? The cause of your people means so much."

"It is my life itself, señor. I live for nothing else but the day that we shall be free."

Bleakness entered Carmody's eyes. The old bitterness came back to his voice. "There is just one thing I live for, too."

A sadness tinged the girl's voice. "To kill your man?" Carmody nodded. "To kill my man."

The escort arrived at nightfall. There were five of them. Carmody and Raquel had buried Blanco. Raquel made a few hurried explanations to the five, then she swung up on her horse. The five were already leading the laden mules away.

Raquel held out her hand, and Carmody took it in both of his. She leaned there a moment in the saddle, and he thought he glimpsed a sadness in her eyes. There were words in him to say, words that came from deep down inside, but it all choked up in his throat. Gently Raquel withdrew her hand and without a word rode away.

Carmody watched her go. The night swiftly swallowed her. He swung aboard his mare. His carbine was in its boot beneath his left leg, and the Remington hung heavy at his right hip. The border was thirty miles away, Marietta about forty.

Well, Carmody, what are you waiting for? he thought. *She's gone. You'll never see her again. Start for the line, now that it's night and cool. You can be in Marietta tomorrow. Then you can square accounts with Barrow. It's what you wanted, isn't it?*

Suddenly the shots rang out, dim with distance. Scattered, ragged volleys, echoing across the sands. Carmody grew tense in the saddle. The firing continued, the steady, monotonous shooting of a pitched battle. Carmody touched spurs to the mare, heading south.

From the top of a rise he saw the scene of battle. It was laid out below him like a giant wheel. The hub of it was where Raquel and her escort must be forted up.

The rim was the ring of federals surrounding them. Lances of gunflame were spokes. He pulled the carbine from its boot, stepped off the mare to the ground. He patted the critter's neck and struck out afoot.

Go back, Carmody, go back, his mind kept telling him. *Marietta is where you belong. Go back, Carmody. . . .*

The firing was closer now. He could smell the acrid odor of black gunpowder. A sense of urgency possessed him. It was Raquel in his mind. Raquel of the soft features and softer voice. Raquel, the uncomplaining. Raquel, the gentle and firm and purposeful.

I've got to know was the thought running urgently through his mind. *I've got to know how it comes out. I can't ride off with you in a fight like this, Raquel. I want to be with you. I want to fight beside you.*

The roar of the battle was loud in his ears. He could see the shadow of a soldier ahead. A strange contentment filled Carmody as he dropped on his belly and began crawling forward on the sand. . . .

THE END

ABOUT THE AUTHOR

H(enry) A(ndrew) DeRosso was born on July 15, 1917 in Carey, Wisconsin. In the decades between 1940 and 1960 he published approximately two hundred Western short stories and short novels in various pulp magazines, known for their dark and compelling visions of the night side of life and their austere realism. He was also the author of six Western novels, perhaps the most notable of which are *.44* (1953) and *End of the Gun* (1955). He died on October 14, 1960.

All stories, with the exception of "The Hired Man," were edited by Bill Pronzini for publication in this collection.

The Dark Brand

H. A. DeRosso

Driscoll made a mistake and he's paying for it. They stuck him in a cell—with a man condemned to hang the next morning. Driscoll learns how his cellmate robbed a bank and killed a man...and how the money was never recovered. But he never learns where the money is. After Driscoll serves his time and drifts back into town, he learns that the loot is still hidden, and that just about everyone thinks the condemned man told Driscoll where it is buried before he died. Suddenly it seems everybody wants that money— enough to kill for it.

___4412-9 $4.50 US/$5.50 CAN

WAYNE D. OVERHOLSER
RIDERS OF THE SUNDOWNS

Once Mack Jarvis goes to work for the Tomahawk brand in Pioneer Valley, it doesn't take him long to fall in love with the owner's daughter, Rosella Wade. He knows it will take money to support her, so he works hard and buys himself a little feed store. Then he hears local banker Lou Kyle announce his engagement to the fair Rosella. And to make matters worse, Kyle plans to open up a feed store to compete with Mack. When three hundred head of Tomahawk cattle disappear, Mack's suspicions of the truth earn him threats on his life and a price on his head. Mack has never felt so alone in his life, but if he wants to get out of this alive, he'll need all the friends he can get.

___4530-3 $4.50 US/$5.50 CAN

WAYNE D. OVERHOLSER

NUGGET CITY

Nugget City is a Colorado mining town that made the transition to a ranching community. But the transition wasn't easy and it left a lot of bad blood. A range war has been brewing for a while, and greed, gossip and rage are threatening to blow the town apart. The last thing the town needs is a spark to set off the tinderbox. Everyone is afraid that is just what they got when a mysterious stranger steps off the stage—a stranger who wears two guns. Is he the latest recruit brought in to fight the escalating range war? There is only one thing everyone seems sure of: He is a killer.

___4454-4 $4.50 US/$5.50 CAN

DARK EMBERS AT DAWN
STEPHEN OVERHOLSER

Like many a veteran of the Civil War, Cap McKenna went west to the Rockies to build a new life. But that new life changes forever the day he comes across an abandoned infant, whom he takes in and cares for until the baby's Cheyenne mother appears at his door. Alone and terrified, all the woman wants is to find the baby's father. Cap helps her locate him at the U.S. Cavalry encampment, but Colonel Tom Sully stands defiantly between the father and his family. When the desperate man deserts to be with his wife and child, Sully sends a detail after him and suddenly Cap finds himself caught in a deadly pursuit—ready to risk all for what he knows is right.

___4657-1 $4.50 US/$5.50 CAN

JASON EVERS:
HIS OWN STORY
FRANK RODERUS

Jason Evers wants to set the record straight about himself and his exploits. He has a reason for his first murder, his second . . . and the rest. The first, when Jason was only a boy, had not been deliberate, but the man had it coming to him anyway. The rest were unfortunate, but Jason did what he had to do to survive. Whether it was in the wilderness or in a town, Jason learned how to stay alive any way he could. But now Jason wants folks to know his side of the story, a story of how a boy becomes a man, and how a man becomes a killer—a killer who can take a life without blinking an eye.

___4573-7 $3.99 US/$4.99 CAN

Dorchester Publishing Co., Inc.
P.O. Box 6640
Wayne, PA 19087-8640

Hayseed

FRANK RODERUS

Arnie Rasmussen is a big guy, with the general build of a young ox, and he might not know much, but he knows one thing: He loves Katherine Mulraney. Sure, she's too good for him; she is beautiful and fine, and he is, well, just Arnie. Just as he is steeling his nerve to talk to her, she disappears. Folks say she up and ran off with a fancy travelling man, but Arnie can't believe that. So he sets off after her. But the Wyoming Territory is a mighty tough place, and Arnie has never been off of his father's ranch. He has a lot to learn, and he'll learn all right . . . the hard way.

___4432-1 $4.50 US/$5.50 CAN

Old Marsden

FRANK RODERUS

When he was born his parents named him Alvin, but that was a good long time ago. These days pretty much everybody just calls him Cap. Maybe he isn't quite as spry as he was back in his trapping days, but he can still sit a horse and his aim is almost as fine as ever. Most of the time, though, he is perfectly content to regale his granddaughter with tales of his exploits. But when someone kidnaps that lovely little girl, Cap isn't about to leave her rescue up to somebody else. He won't rest until she is home safe and sound—and until whoever took her learns just how much grit Cap still has in him.

___4506-0 $4.50 US/$5.50 CAN

KIT CARSON
BLOOD RENDEZVOUS
DOUG HAWKINS

The high point of any trapper's year is the summer rendezvous, the annual gathering where mountain men from all over the frontier meet to trade the pelts they risked their lives for. But for Kit Carson, the real danger lies in getting to the rendezvous. He is leading a party of trappers, all of them weighed down with a year's worth of furs. That is enough to make them a tempting target for any killer on the trail—especially when the trail leads through Blackfoot territory.

__4499-4 $3.99 US/$4.99 CAN

Dorchester Publishing Co., Inc.
P.O. Box 6640
Wayne, PA 19087-8640

Please add $1.75 for shipping and handling for the first book and $.50 for each book thereafter. NY, NYC, and PA residents, please add appropriate sales tax. No cash, stamps, or C.O.D.s. All orders shipped within 6 weeks via postal service book rate. Canadian orders require $2.00 extra postage and must be paid in U.S. dollars through a U.S. banking facility.

Name_____
Address_____
City_____State_____Zip_____
I have enclosed $_____ in payment for the checked book(s).
Payment <u>must</u> accompany all orders. ❏ Please send a free catalog.
      CHECK OUT OUR WEBSITE! www.dorchesterpub.com

HIGHPOCKETS

DOUGLAS SAVAGE

In the autumn of his days, Highpockets stumbles upon a half-frozen immigrant boy, nearly dead and terrified after being separated from his family's wagon train. For one long, brutal winter Highpockets tries to teach the boy all he needs to know to survive in a land as dangerous as it is beautiful. But will it be enough to see both man and boy through the deadly trial that is still to come?

___4400-5 $3.99 US/$4.99 CAN

Dorchester Publishing Co., Inc.
P.O. Box 6640
Wayne, PA 19087-8640

THE GALLOWSMAN

WILL CADE

Ben Woolard is a man ready to start over. The life he's leaving behind is filled with ghosts and pain. He lost his wife and children, and his career as a Union spy during the war still doesn't sit quite right with him, even if the man sent to the gallows by his testimony was a murderer. But now Ben's finally sobered up, moved west to Colorado, and put the past behind him. But sometimes the past just won't stay buried. And, as Ben learns when folks start telling him that the man he saw hanged is alive and in town—sometimes those ghosts come back.

___4452-8 $4.50 US/$5.50 CAN

Dorchester Publishing Co., Inc.
P.O. Box 6640
Wayne, PA 19087-8640

Please add $1.75 for shipping and handling for the first book and $.50 for each book thereafter. NY, NYC, and PA residents, please add appropriate sales tax. No cash, stamps, or C.O.D.s. All orders shipped within 6 weeks via postal service book rate. Canadian orders require $2.00 extra postage and must be paid in U.S. dollars through a U.S. banking facility.

Name_____
Address_____
City_____ State_____ Zip_____
I have enclosed $_____ in payment for the checked book(s).
Payment <u>must</u> accompany all orders. ❑ Please send a free catalog.